Plus Size

By

Alex 'Hood' Fuller

Dedicated to the BBW Queens

Latoria, Lashawn, Natalie and Sherry

Front cover image artist credit: Malcolm Croswell

Purple Eye Productions

Sign up for the latest news about the A-men Universe. Find out about new releases, give-aways, and the never-ending adventures of the A-men in their fight against the kingdom of darkness.

https://www.facebook.com/TheAmenGenesis/

The struggle -- against the kingdom of darkness -- is real

Contents

Uncertain Path

Before you begin, know this

The world is not what we have been led to believe...

What we see every day -- the people, the places and the things — are only half the story. The world is split into two. The physical, which most of us live our whole lives in and the spiritual, which only a few of us see. There is a war going on all around us, creatures we have been told were fantasies, struggles we were told did not exist. Brave men and women fight this unseen war. Individuals who have been endowed with fantastical abilities. We call them "Miracles". You can tell a Miracle by their eyes. The purple eyes. Some use their power to fight the invisible war, some never discover it. But if you are seeking this world, or the individuals who harness power beyond compare, follow the eyes…

Chapter 1

Trisha Morgan

"Looks aren't everything", a message that most people heard numerous times growing up. A message that in theory was most likely meant to inspire everyone to do their best to become their best self. In actuality, or at least how Trisha Morgan had come to understand it, it was just a saying to make the unattractive people feel better about themselves. It was fine to look like a dish rag if they could compensate with some kind of talent. That was the first rule that she had learned while growing up. Perhaps a person did possess what could be considered a deformity; statistically, it had to be some of the population. That was alright if the person could sing, dance, play an instrument, paint, or do anything that was remotely impressive. That was the compromise that carried Trisha through her childhood. Even while other children mocked her relentlessly, for reasons that her now mature brain couldn't understand, her talent drained quite a bit of their power. Her singing voice was angelic, her writing was superb, and her acting was always the second best a person had ever seen. No, she didn't like the game. She didn't like that she had to make up for how she looked, but it was an imperfect world, and this is how she got by. But, then the rules changed.

Childhood turned into early adulthood, and she learned a hard lesson about the outside world. Looks were not everything, but neither was talent. It was true that she was a prodigy, but as she grew up, she realized that she was surrounded by a great many prodigies. As time went on, it became harder and harder for her to distinguish herself from the masses. She watched other people who were less talented than she, have their names and faces plastered on billboards. She watched others who were far more skilled be denied what should have been as natural as breathing. It came to her in the middle of working the stage during a musical at her college. Talent opened doors for many people, but for the physically challenged, it opened a lot of back doors. The headliners, the main stars, the people in the spotlight, all had one thing in common. They had found that special place, that critical place that sat between looks and talent. Some had worked for their looks, others were gifted with them, but Trisha found that she was neither one. The angel of beauty had passed over her...or so she had always been told.

It was another standard morning. Trisha stood in front of her mirror which had been coated with fog from her volcanic shower. As she wiped away the steam so that she could remind herself of what she looked like, memories of yet another misconception took center stage in her mind. Her face was nearly flawless, with one or two misplaced pimples. Nothing about it screamed hideous, in fact it cried out stunning in every language. Her eyes were perfectly shaped, brilliantly spaced, and boasted a rare representation of royalty, purple, without the aid of colored contacts. She looked at her hair, and although it resembled a jungle now, such a thing was remedied with the aid of a comb and self-taught patience. Apart from that, she had an advantage that couldn't be taught, learned, or faked. It was frustrating to know that it was only viewed as some sort of fetish to most of the white driven country, but on the small stages where she sought to shine, that was one rule of the game that she had on lock-down. Her smooth ebony skin placed her on a pedestal; everyone loved a good-looking sister. The African American community praised women like her, at least most of them did. The white community followed suit, but whether it was because they secretly wished they could have it or were genuinely enticed by the display was not for Trisha to say. It was never her face that she was teased about.

See, the game had switched up on her again. In her childhood, Trisha had believed that if someone found another to be unattractive, it was safe to assume that all parts of that person suffered from the unfair criticism. It was another misconception that only experience would straighten out. As she got older, she understood that it wasn't her face that was holding her back. The masses loved her black skin. They were fascinated by her purple eyes. And who didn't have a weird desire to touch a sister's consummate afro? If all of this was orderly, and by all indications it was, then what jarring kryptonite continued to stab her in the back? What Achilles heel was she overlooking? It never made sense for years. All the billboards, all the labels, all the everything that mankind could put something on always paraded the face. That was the selling point, the golden ticket, the keys to the kingdom of streets paved with gold. Her confidence wasn't always high, but at a point Trisha decided that she had a face fit for a label. She played by the rules of the game. She honed her skills to make up for her physical weaknesses, she kept her face in its most endearing state for others to see. Clearly more research was needed.

When she did in fact figure it out, it drove her to tears. The face was the ticket into the door, but there was an entire world behind that door. Eventually, people would have to see, and would want to see everything else. Those who made it big were "beautiful", as the world put it. Trisha had solved the puzzle. By "beautiful" they meant one thing: thin. She gave herself another stare down in the mirror. There were no two ways about it. She didn't meet that one specific guideline. The world had decided that beautiful meant one thing, and she was something else. She was plus size, or big boned, as sensitive and politically correct people would have put it. But, the children always had a different word for her: fat. On the day she discovered it, everything fell into place. There were no fat superstars. She studied tv, movies, and comic books. The superheroes, the protagonists, the hot chick, the main person to root for was not fat. And on the few occasions that he or she was fat, it was the joke. Those who were heavy were a novelty, a sick twisted game to be played with until the masses tired. The fat one was used to enhance the thin one. The fat one was used as a desperate ploy to be inclusive. And if the fat person saved the day, it wasn't because they were smart enough to solve the riddle, or strong enough to stop the violence. Fat was a punchline, and that's why Trisha had not made the cut. She refused to be a punchline.

She finished up her morning routine, and exited the bathroom, taking care to ensure that she did not forget her earrings. They were a recent purchase from the AFRAM festival that she had attended in the downtown area. Now she wore them as often as she could. In addition, she had a small nose ring that she preferred to wear whenever she left the house. She brushed her teeth, applied lotion to her skin, and Vaseline to her lips: perfection. The next step would require her to travel to her bedroom where a mountain of clothes, the size of which had grown out of control, awaited her. There was always a challenge when it came to picking out clothes for the day, and it wasn't because she was indecisive; there were just too many. This ironically caused her to rotate the same general six outfits, leaving the rest of her abundant treasure trove abandoned in a dark closet with only the dust bunnies, and occasional misplaced flies, as comrades.

Usually, she would have already settled for which outfit was next in her revolving collection, but today was a special day. She needed the perfect combination to accomplish a few paradoxical objectives. Trisha needed to dress her absolute best, but she also needed to dress like no extraordinary effort was being made. She needed an outfit that portrayed confidence, but not arrogance. She needed clothing that said she wanted to be seen, but didn't say she wanted to steal the show. It was a daunting task finding appropriate clothing for a woman. After standing around far longer than she thought she should have, Trisha finally decided on her perfect outfit for the day.

She picked out a pink halter top, and a blue skirt that she pulled all the way up to where her top ended. It was moments like this when she sometimes wished that she lived the semi-easy life of a man, or a less heavy girl. They had the luxury of allowing their stomachs to show without being judged. And somewhere very deep down, Trisha didn't care if people judged her. However, even if she could find the strength to access that place right now, it was not the time for her to throw caution to the wind. Important eyes were going to be watching her, and she needed to ensure that those eyes approved of what they saw. The time to show off would come later, once she was in position. With her top and bottom picked out, there was nothing left to do except select an appropriate shoe. A brown pair of gladiator sandals had been tossed in the corner by her bed, and she needed to wade through a messy room to get to them. After promising herself for the thousandth time to clean the room eventually, she made the journey to the shoes, and laced them up. She looked over at her collection of hair scarfs, debating if she wanted to endure the hot September day for the sake of her favorite hair accessory. Not today. Today needed to be perfect, and sweating could prove disastrous. She grabbed her glasses to ensure that she could see, threw her phone into her purse, threw her purse over her shoulder and exited her room. She could write an entire script for a movie based on an exaggerated version of her morning routine.

Making her way through the clutter between her bedroom and the kitchen was yet another adventure. Right before she got there however, her attention was caught by a DVD that sat on top of one of the boxes. It was the Broadway production of a musical called 'Phantasm'. She found it in the basement the previous night and told herself that she would watch it this afternoon. She picked it up to look at the cover, more specifically the leading lady. There was so much to admire about the character, and the actress who portrayed her, but it was her flawless beauty that Trisha was drawn to. She had watched this musical more times than she would ever admit, and yet she never found any etch in the canvas of the woman that she saw in her mind. She put the DVD back down. The time for shameless admiration would come. Right now, she had bigger things to concern herself with.

She walked into the kitchen. There was a small table fit for a collection of toddlers and not a grown woman that rested in the middle. This is where Trisha took her seat. Her mother was busy washing dishes with her back turned to her. There was a game that Trisha liked to play as often as possible. Her mother was good at focusing on any task that she was engaged in, almost too good. The running water from the sink served as an aid, but Trisha could have walked in without it and still have gone unnoticed. Trisha checked her phone, noting that she still had a few minutes before she had to leave, and so she could wait and see how long it took for her mother to realize she was there. She also started composing a message to someone in her phone named Nita. A few short seconds later, the mother screamed at the top of her lungs, calling for her daughter to come downstairs.

"I'm right here, momma." Trisha said between giggles. Her mother jumped like a startled cat, which in turn only made Trisha laugh harder and harder until a snort escaped her.

"You're gonna give me a heart attack one of these days. Then who is going to help you navigate this maze?" Her mother asked gesturing to the boxes stacked on boxes that littered the surrounding rooms, the contents of which Trisha had long forgotten. Clutter seemed to caress every corner of her home except the kitchen, the only room in the entire house that had escaped the carnage.Thinking back on all the years that she had lived in this house, she found it impossible to determine when she had allowed it to get this bad. Part of it, she could take the blame for. She didn't like throwing things away for fear that she might one day need them for some unforeseen purpose. The other part could be attributed to her mother. Her mother had the same habits, plus the authority to decide things weren't going to be thrown out even on the rare occasions that Trisha found the strength to finally take that step. As more things accumulated, the need for the boxes arose. Now, it was to the point that it looked like they had just moved in, rather than amassed an assemblage of almost useless trinkets that had grown beyond their control. Trisha made another promise to herself that the day would come when she would clean the house from top to bottom. A hysterical chuckle echoed from her as she recognized the lunacy of what she had just thought. The worst part about the mess was that it covered up the finer things of her home. The paintings on the walls, family heirlooms, and the expensive furniture, were obscured in this sea of disorganization.

"That's nonsense, and ya know it. You're gonna outlive all of us. You might even live forever." Trisha answered.

"You go on and keep saying that. But one day you may walk through that door and see me sprawled out on the floor."

"If you can even find enough room." Trisha mocked. She went to the refrigerator to pick out a plum, but her mother interjected.

"I thought you liked bananas. I just bought a bunch of them yesterday, even though we still had a few from the last time."

Trisha's hand stopped, and she drew back. She grabbed a banana from the lower shelf instead. When she bit into the yellow mushy substance, she was reminded that she did in fact like them, but lamented that she had not continued her original path. There was always a next time. She prepared to leave.

"Where are you off to looking all dolled up?" asked her mother.

"I'm heading to Dreyfus. They're having the beginning of the semester picnic, and everyone is going to be there. This is the last chance before classes really get started to be lazy and just have fun. Today is also the day for Phantasm. I know we've talked about this a bunch." Trisha said excitedly.

"I'm sure we have. You know my nights get a little crazy sometimes and my memory isn't exactly what it used to be. Well, you go right ahead and enjoy yourself." Then her mother noticed the earrings dangling from her ears. "Oh, you're wearing those again? They look nice."

"You hate them." Trisha stated.

"I didn't say that."

"You didn't have to." Trisha said as she took the earrings off.

Her mother's eyes rolled. "Ya know if you used that more often, you could have a little side hustle of your own. Everyone is into that voodoo stuff these days. Easy money is all I'm saying."

"It's not voodoo, momma. It's a gift, and I don't want to abuse it."

"I'm just saying, if I could do that, I would have been found myself a husband." There was a pause as Trisha's mother indulged in a daydream. Quickly, she returned to reality. "At least, put it to good use then. Start cleaning up some of the trash around your school. I can't remember the last time you came home without a horror story about the stuff you hear. You could do a lot of good if you let yourself."

"You know I want to. But I'm not a superhero. I would love to take down some of the slime balls, especially Isabelle, but she's the dean. You need proof that she's up to no good. Plus, ya need a reason to talk to her. I can't just walk in there, and I don't have a reason to. That's the part I really don't know how to do, ya dig?"

"Well, you could certainly do something. She pocketed a student's financial aid, so he couldn't attend Dreyfus, right? And she did it just to make herself richer. You got access to all of her darkest secrets."

"All the stuff I tell you, and that's what you hang onto? She's done worse than that. But like I said, she's got the position, and I can't exactly go up to everyone and say, *I read her mind.* The only people who know how corrupt she is are in this room…and Nita."

"Use that brain of yours. You're smart Trish; I know it because I pushed that big head of yours out personally."

A look of disgust zipped across Trisha's face. "Okay. I'm leaving now."

The arrangement of the house made it difficult to rush out without running the risk of slipping and falling into an abyss of long forgotten mementoes, and yet Trisha did her best. The image that had just run through her mind was unpleasant, and it was time to put some distance between her and her mother. She loved her mother more than anyone else on the planet, but there was no denying the fact that the woman had to work on saying the right things.

Trisha departed from her home, double checking to make sure she had locked the door. Then, she made her way out of the neighborhood. Dreyfus Community College was quite a distance from her home, but the subway station wasn't, and it was a nice walk from the stop to the college. On warm days like this she liked to walk. However, if someone came by with an offer, she often did not refuse the ride. Such was the case this time. She had just arrived at the stop sign at the end of her block, which led to the straight path to her school, when a navy-blue car pulled up next to her. The music was loud, filling the neighborhood with the sound of hip hop. Trisha wasn't sure how to feel, as she liked the idea of jamming out to good music, but also hated the fact that this new arrival had no qualms with being a nuisance so near her house. The window rolled down to reveal a young woman wearing sunglasses.

"You're usually further along than this Trish. What's going on?" The woman asked.

"Just had a slow start this morning; it happens sometimes." Trisha eyed the back of the car, which she could not see through because of the tinted windows. "Is Dom in the back?"

"Of course. I had to drag him out of his house myself. There's no way I'm letting him miss today."

Trisha walked to the passenger side, opened the door, and got in. The second she sat down, she turned the music all the way up. No time was wasted pulling off once she was in the car, so all her previous concerns were about to be irrelevant. Before she could even consider it, her friend took off down the street.

"Did you look both ways, Nita!?" Trisha yelled.

Nita looked dead ahead, as if she didn't want to dignify the question with a response. "I hate to be the one to have to tell you this, but the joke isn't funny anymore."

"Well if you had done it the first time, there wouldn't be a joke at all." Trisha responded. Then she turned the music down and looked in the rearview mirror. "Where you been stranger? We missed you last week. And, while I'm on it, where is Amaya?"

"She caught the bus. Guess she wasn't feeling the group vibe right now. She just hasn't been the same." Nita said.

"I mean, I get all of that, but it's been like four months; she has to let it go eventually." Trisha said.

"Good luck with that." Dominick said. "You'd be pissed too if Justin cheated on you."

"First off, I would never date Justin. Secondly, I would be for a while, but I would've at least started trying to bounce back by now." Trisha said.

"Whatever." Dominick said. He was staring out of the window, and Trisha had to address him again before he gave his attention. Even then, he didn't give more than a grunt as a response. Trisha chose to leave it alone. Instead, she turned her attention back to the music.

"I haven't heard you bumping this before. Is it new?" She asked.

"Oh yeah. It's the new 'Rockstar Productions' album. I bought it last night, and this one has Ill-G headlining on every track." Nita turned the music down ever so slightly. "Still can't believe he managed to get signed by them."

"I'm digging it. Remind me to get it before the day is over." Trisha demanded.

"You making money now? I know you didn't get a job yet." Nita gasped. "You a stripper now?"

"Girl bye. That's not happening any time soon." Trisha dismissed.

"But it is happening?" A snicker came from Nita.

As the ride continued, Nita and Trisha talked about everything under the sun. Dominick occasionally commented, but it was a short one-word answer. Trisha complimented Nita on her new hairstyle which Dominick referred to as braids but was instantly corrected as they both insisted that the correct term was 'singles'. Then he went back to being quiet, and they continued to talk. Nita asked a myriad of questions about the imminent audition ranging from what section she was going to audition with, to how she was going to walk onto the stage. Trisha answered each question as it came, finding that she was becoming more and more excited. "Girl, you know I'll be in the audience," Nita said. "I wouldn't miss it for—"

"OMG!" Trisha interrupted.

Nita slowed suddenly as they stared at a major car accident on the side of the rode. The vehicles were not positioned in a way that they could impede traffic, but everyone drove slowly so that they could get a glimpse of the vehicular pandemonium. One car in particular stood out: a black and yellow camaro. There was no telling what had transpired, but based solely on the image, it was likely that someone had put both cars into a room, shook them around for a while, and then drove whatever was left of them into each other a couple of times. Police cars lined the side of the road on both sides, and a firetruck could be seen approaching from the distance. If there were any survivors, the ambulance had already arrived and carried them away. If they hadn't, there wouldn't be any survivors to save by the time they arrived. Trisha wasn't the type to become desensitized. She saw displays like this all of the time, but it never got any easier. The idea that something like this could happen to two people made her sad, and the fact that it was early in the morning led her to believe that it must have been a split-second mistake that made all the difference. They had passed through a couple of lights, and an intersection. Maybe a driver had run the light, or perhaps didn't see a stop sign. It was possible that the person was texting and being completely irresponsible. Whatever the case, it was over, and now all that was left to do was deal with the consequences. Times like this made Trisha reflect on her gift even more.

"Can't remember the last time I saw an accident that bad." Nita said.

"Really?" Trisha asked in a shocked tone. "You don't remember that truck incident on eighty-three last year?"

"Oh right. How did I forget that?" Nita murmured.

"These are the types of things I wish I could stop." Trisha said somberly.

"I mean, what would you really do in a situation like this?" Nita tried to console. "You can help in a lot of ways, but a car accident?"

"I'm sure I could absorb enough of the impact, act as a bumper."

"So you want to be a human shield? Gotta be a better solution than that somewhere. Besides, you gotta be there at the right time."

"That's another problem, Nita. How do I make sure that I'm there to stop it? The way the news is, you would think it would be impossible not to be around when this sort of stuff happens, but I never am. I'm always either reading about it, hearing about it, or stumbling upon it after the fact. That kinda sucks, ya dig?"

"I mean, you could always dedicate your life to preventing trouble. Sit up all night prowling on gargoyles, jumping from rooftop to rooftop obsessively, spend your life in the shadows, only coming out to save the day while the rest of your friends and loved ones continue life without you. Do we even have gargoyles around here? Or, ya could just like, steal a police scanner."

"I think I'll pass on both of those, thank you." Trisha said.

Nita wiped her brow. "Glad to hear that. Cause I wasn't looking forward to having to give up my life to follow you."

"What?" Trisha asked.

"Come on. You're telling me that you wouldn't let me be your sidekick? Every superhero needs a sidekick if they aren't going to join a team." Nita said excitedly.

"So, you get a little good at your kung-fu, and suddenly you think you're ready to take on all the bad guys? Does that stuff even work?" Dominick asked.

Nita resisted the urge to look at him. "Krav Maga can be deadly, sweetheart. I'd like to see someone try to mess with us."

"I don't think the kind of hero life I want to live requires picking fights with muscular strangers. I was thinking more about saving kittens out of distress and stuff or stopping bystanders from getting run over by cars." Trisha said.

"And stopping evil deans with terrible wigs who blackmail students."

"That too." Trisha responded.

"Seriously, ya never know when you might get yourself into some trouble. And I've seen you try to fight. It makes me cry." Nita retorted.

Trisha and Nita continued this way until they reached their destination. From the moment the front tire crossed the line into Dreyfus territory, Trisha could feel the energy of her school surging through her. Even without looking up, the atmosphere changed in an instant, and she had journeyed into another world. Once her eyes could take in what her body was already experiencing, it elevated to an even higher level. Trees were painted, buildings were vividly decorated. Students walked their campus with smiles, face paint, food, and everything else that would be expected. Music could be heard in the background, and Trisha could only imagine how animated the quad must be at this very moment. She would get to study it in greater detail later, once her priorities had been tended to.

Of course, there was nowhere to park. There was never anywhere to park. All the free spaces available for students were always taken, and the restricted spaces that required a pass carried too much of a risk. Trisha kept insisting that it was worth the investment, but her friend was convinced that the universe was out to get her. Once she purchased the pass, everyone else would purchase the pass and there would be nowhere for her to park anyway. Trisha believed that to be complete absurdity, but there was no way that she was going to be able to convince Nita of that. The worse part was that since all the close student spaces were taken, the only ones left were the ones that were nowhere near where they were trying to go. With Trisha's nerve's already on edge, this parking delay was the apocalypse in her eyes.

After circling the relatively small campus a couple of times, both Trisha and Nita accepted the fact that they were not going to find any prime parking space. They had to drive down a hill, which neither of them were looking forward to having to walk up, but they had already lost a lot of time trying to avoid what was inevitable. However, it seemed that on this day, even these undesirable parking spots were popular. They almost had one a couple of times, but they were either victim to someone stealing the spot, it being marked by a handicapped sign, or the classic 'big car conceals small car' situation. They finally found themselves a place they could call their own, in a tight corner. Fortunately, the car was small enough to fit, and now that they had found a place, the day could begin.

"Gotta tell you, I'm not so much a fan of having to squeeze out of this small space. You know I'm the size of a doggone minivan." Dominick said.

"We gotta talk about these self-attacks you always indulge in." Trisha said. "But I guess we can do that later."

"So, are you going to be a famous actress by day and superhero by night? Because that would be a freaking awesome combination. You could write scripts based off your life and get money just by living. That's gonna be so dope once we're out in the world." Nita said. Trisha allowed her friend to have the fantasy for the moment. Her mind was on other things.

Trisha stepped out of the car, and found that Nita had quickly rushed to her side to embrace her. Sometimes she forgot how encouraging such a simple gesture could be. Nita promised that she was going to get Dominick to his destination and then she would quickly rush over to the theatre. Then, Trisha leaned against the car, waiting for the others to leave. Once they walked away, she took a moment for herself.

This had been her home away from home for the last four years, and so many things had happened to her. She met great people, tried new things, and gathered memories that she wouldn't trade for anything. But of everything that she had gone through, none of it compared to what was going to happen today. Today, everyone in her theater department was going to see exactly what she could do. The tragic car accident that she had seen fell away; her concern about being a hero fell away. Even her excitement for the school's festivities fell away. All her aspirations outside of school would come to her in time, but there was a personal victory she needed to claim, and more than just stardom hung in the balance.

Chapter 2

Aesthetically Displeasing

Trisha examined the building that she had spent so much of her life in since she started at the school. Ever since she had gotten there, she had participated in every production they had put on, but none excited her more than the selection they had made for this year. Growing up she watched more times than she could count, the musical 'Phantasm'. It told the story of a disfigured man who performed amazing feats of magic and fancy, who also sought after the love of a beautiful woman named Crystal. Ever since Trisha had seen it the first time, her dream was to portray the role of Crystal on stage. Ideally, she wanted to one day play the character on Broadway but doing so on the small stage of her modest school would be a good start. In her wildest fantasies, she got the part, and performed her absolute best on the day that a critic with connections just so happened to walk in. This would lead to the critic being blown away by her performance and pulling any and every string that he could to make sure that Trisha was able to take her talent on the road. From there, Trisha's name would become synonymous with the character Crystal, and she would be the new metric by which all other women would be compared. It wouldn't be long after that, that Trisha would get the opportunity to become the most famous actress who ever lived. However, due to her other goal in life, she would turn down this opportunity, content that she had made a name for herself in the performing arts. That was just one of the things that she thought about when she allowed her mind to soar. She caught herself and shut it down; this was the time to focus.

Today was the last day for auditions. Rehearsal was set to begin on the first official day of classes, and the performance was scheduled for the end of the semester. She had been practicing for months to prepare for the role, perfecting every issue. Coupled with the fact that she had practiced for years just by simply committing the show to memory, she was sure that she was going to be the favored choice. There was no one else who had dedicated as much time as she had to truly bringing Phantasm to life, save for the professionals who got paid to do it. She would never dare disrespect them by comparing herself to them while in her humble beginnings.

She walked into the building confidently, imagining all the ways she was going to wow the director. She already had a preexisting relationship with the man, and if she delivered an unblemished performance, there wasn't going to be any excuse that could be used to keep her from the part. She had just thought about the best audition that she had heard, but there were others too. She had seen quite a few auditions over the last week. In a business class that she took during one of her earlier semesters, she was taught to either be one of the first or one of the last. Falling somewhere in the middle increased the chances of her being forgotten. When it came to the other choices, many of them were poor, a few were good, and there were a couple that she would consider exemplary. But most of the other students had never seen this musical, and the few that had were either auditioning for other parts or working back stage. So, she strolled into the auditorium, and to her surprise, there weren't many people in there. The director, and his assistant were at their post, presumably discussing business about the show, and there were a few pockets of students conversing with one another. Before she approached the director, she scanned the small crowd to see if she saw her friend. She didn't see her, but it was only because in the time that it took for her to look, Nita had snuck up behind her. Getting Dominick to his spot must have taken no time at all, or so Trisha concluded. Though, she knew that it was certainly possible that she had not been moving as fast as she thought she was. Now that Nita was standing in front of her, and the moment of truth was upon her, a feeling that she had not anticipated began to seep in. She noticed a 'caution' black and yellow traffic sign that had been used in a previous production.

"Uh, Nita, I have to pee...like really bad." Trisha said.

"Okay, wasn't expecting that." Nita said. "Just take a deep breath, count to ten. You know it's not real, and you've worked too hard for you to let nerves stop you now. There's barely anyone in here so it should be easy for you to imagine that you're alone. If it's anything like it is when we're in the car, you got this part yesterday. Okay, girl?"

"To be honest, that makes me feel a lot better." Trisha said. "What if I don't get it? Any chance I have will be ruined." Trisha said.

"Not even true." Nita contradicted. "If this doesn't work out, we'll find another way."

In truth, there were ulterior motives behind this audition. As much as Trisha truly wanted to encompass the role of Crystal, there was a far more important agenda behind it. The year before Trisha had arrived, the school had gotten into some trouble because Professor Henry put on an incredibly offensive production. Knowing that it would never get approved, he announced an entirely different play to the public, and then spent his entire rehearsal time putting together the real goal. Because of this, it was decided that every show now had to be heavily monitored from beginning to end, to avoid a situation like that again.

After reading the script, Trisha didn't think there was anything wrong with it, as it simply explored the idea of a society that gradually transformed into savages as it got more and more relaxed with moral ambiguity. She felt like it was something that the world was going through currently. But, that wasn't the point. The point was that the dean took it upon herself to personally observe all rehearsals, meetings, promotional events, and the sort. And while being in the production in any capacity meant that she would experience time around the dean, being a part of the principle cast ensured that she would receive the optimum opportunities. She would meet her personally, and almost always be around her. Trisha figured that if she was going to find a way to prove that the dean was up to no good, then she would need to get to know her. She could think of only two ways, and this was the easier one by far. It pained her that she had to lie to her mother about having absolutely no method of acting out against the dean, but she feared that her mother would not approve of her approach. In the end, this audition was still about her, and a point she needed to make.

Then, just as suddenly as her bladder had flared up, it went away, and she had transformed into her confident diva-like self again. Once again, memories overtook her. The message of the musical spoke to her on a personal level, and even if she slacked and couldn't fully capture Crystal through her acting chops, she would only need to funnel her own likeness into her performance. She saw her director, Professor Henry, who also taught history, and broke protocol entirely by marching up to his desk.

"Ah Trisha, I was beginning to think you weren't going to come." Henry said as he brushed a pile of papers to the side.

"Come on, Professor. No one has been looking forward to this more than me." Trisha answered.

She harked back to when she first met Theodore Henry. There were flamboyant characteristics about him that led her to make assumptions. All those assumptions were put to rest when he ushered in his wife and kids the opening night of their first play. It was that night that she first suggested the idea of one day adapting Phantasm. The first time, Henry completely laughed it off, saying that he wasn't interested in musicals for the school. Then time went on, and they got to know each other better, and Trisha kept suggesting the idea, explaining its timeless message and what it could do for students if they were ever to do it. Henry told her that these were arguments he would've made himself, hearing it come from a student directly finally swayed his decision. Trisha always felt a certain amount of pride for being the one student who had convinced the director to break his rule about musicals, which would make landing the part even more impressive. At this point, it was almost as if Phantasm was her baby.

"Well I'm glad we have you on board." Mr. Henry stated. "In fact, I've been thinking about who you should play since I selected this production. You're quite easily the best singer we have in our little entourage. Add that to your natural beauty, and I think you would be perfect for the role of the Prima Donna of the show."

It was something Trisha didn't want to hear, but it was expected. She would prove that she was worthy of the top bill, and not the supporting cast.

"I was actually coming to audition for the part of Crystal."

Professor Henry had no difficulty watching his mouth, but his face reacted faster than his mind could tell him not to, and Trisha saw it immediately. The doubt, the disappointment, and the uneasiness were all there on his face, and even without her powers, Trisha had been around the man long enough to know how he rationalized things. That's why she was ready to jump on the defensive, to make sure he understood her position.

"Look, I know it isn't conventional, but I can do this. My acting chops are well developed, and you said it yourself; I'm the best singer here. I know this musical inside and out, better than everyone except you.... maybe even you. At least let me show you the audition. I'm not asking for a handout. I'm going to earn the part."

Trisha watched as Professor Henry turned through pages of the script. Most of them had markings of some kind on them, and rehearsals had not even started yet. It was one of the ways she knew that it was going to be a hard road for anyone who was involved with the project. He finally settled on a page close to the end. She didn't have to look at the words to guess what was about to be asked of her.

"I just think that you would make an impeccable Prima Donna." Professor Henry said.

Trisha's spirit was about to be broken. She knew that she was going to have to make a hard decision if the professor didn't let her audition for the part of Crystal, but she had asked and pleaded her case, and he seemed unmoved. Just then, Nita ran to her side.

"With all due respect, you're not going to find a better Crystal." Nita said.

Trisha didn't know if she should feel flattered that someone was fighting for her, or embarrassed. But she knew that there was no way she was going to be able to stop Nita from doing something she wanted to do. She listened to Nita explain the many nights she stayed up listening to her sing, all the times she was forced to watch the musical, and how there were times she literally confused Trisha with the actress who portrays Crystal on Broadway. Trisha certainly wasn't on board with Nita having the gall to say such a thing, but she wasn't going to argue as it was being used to help her out. And it looked as though it was working. Soon after she said all that she needed to say, Professor Henry reconsidered.

"I have a particular vision for this show, but I've been wrong before. Perform the last monologue Crystal has, and I'll see if you fit the part."

Sometimes, even when Professor Henry was already convinced that someone could handle a role, he would pretend that he wasn't just to see if they carried the same confidence. In a case of a role like Crystal, confidence was essential. However, this wasn't the professor's usual antics. This was real skepticism; which Trisha would have to dismantle brick by brick. Even if she landed the part, Professor Henry wasn't a one-time sell. You had to work hard to prove you deserved to be given a part, and even harder during the entire process to prove that you deserved to keep the part. It was the reason he offered most of his aid to understudies and little to none for the main player. If you didn't earn the right to keep the part, he had a well-prepared replacement.

"You don't want me to sing a few bars first?" Trisha asked.

"Don't waste my time."

No one knew how to give an insulting compliment like Theodore Henry. On that note, Trisha took the stage. Mr. Henry announced to everyone that Trisha was going to audition for the part of Crystal, and instantly the entire room went silent. Trisha locked eyes with the girl who she believed had the best chance of getting the part if she failed, and she could now say that she had never seen such scorn in her life. All the other students were waiting with baited breath, wondering if her performance was going to be as good or better than the current leading lady. It was at this moment that the pressure really started to set in again.

Trisha possessed all the confidence in the world, until she was put on the spot to prove herself. Her bladder felt as though it was about to burst. Before, she knew every line for every character, every song lyric, every dance move, every stage direction. Now it seemed to come and go in fragments. She struggled to hang onto the few words she needed to speak. She started and then stopped, choosing to start over. However, this time she took a deep breath and closed her eyes. The scene was being set in her head, she saw herself before a large audience, in costume and in the presence of greatness. This wasn't just an audition for her school, this was an audition for her future. One day she would make it on Broadway, but she needed to know that she could make it here first. There was no room for mistakes, or shyness. To make it with the best, she had to presume that she was being judged by the best.

And then it flowed as naturally as blinking. Every word poured from her mouth, faultlessly enunciated, expertly crafted. It was just like reciting the speech at home. She never opened her eyes as she worked to recall every single detail from memory, while adding subtle nuances of her own to separate herself from the others who gave this very same performance. She was even beginning to impress herself as she realized how much of a mastery she had of the character. She was making Crystal truly her own. When she opened her eyes after she had reached the conclusion of her noble attempt, she examined the crowd before her. Every eyebrow was raised as no one had expected such a thing to come from her. They were aware of her singing talent, and her acting talent. But the fact that she had completely redefined a character that had existed for decades in a matter of moments: no one would have guessed that it would be her to do it, or that they would be around to witness such a historical moment. Now that Trisha had done her job, she awaited judgement.

Trisha saw the professor flipping through pages, her eyes fixated on him, waiting to hear what he would say. It was almost as if he wanted to strain the tension as much as possible. He finally stood up and closed the script. Following that, he offered a loud applause that was joined by everyone else who had just experienced the magic. Then when he felt that enough praise had been given, he silenced the auditorium.

"I have never slept on your talent Trisha, but even I did not anticipate such an awe-inspiring performance from you. You aren't just the most talented singer among our student body, you are simply the most talented period. How someone with talent like that avoided all the Ivy League schools and ended up in our humble presence, I will never know, but I thank the universe that you did."

"That's an honor to hear, Professor Henry." Trisha said.

"You'll be an even better Prima Donna than the original actress."

"Excuse me?" Trisha said in utter shock. She didn't mean for anything vocal to escape her, but in a moment of complete befuddlement, she couldn't help it.

A deep sigh escaped the seasoned director. He stroked his gray chin hairs. "Listen. You are an astonishing actor. I've meant everything I've said to you from the moment we met, even what I just said. But the part of Crystal requires a certain look, and you just don't have that look. The whole point of Phantasm is the most beautiful woman in the world finding something to love in the most hideous man in the world. If we want this production to carry the kind of power that I am hoping it will, then the lead actress must appeal to the masses. Now, don't get me wrong, there's nothing ugly about you. However, people have their own definition, and I need this to land."

Trisha blinked the tears away from her eyes, as a startling realization came to her. "You knew that before you let me up here. You weren't going to give me the part no matter what I did, were you?"

"You are entitled to know how great of a performance you gave. I owe you the praise that you earned. But some things can't be controlled. Please Trisha, try to understand. The other part is of course yours if you want it."

"Oh, I understand completely. If I was thin like anyone else, you would've given me the part before I even finished the monologue. You would've thrown it at me, begged me to do it. I know how the game is played, but I thought maybe you were above that...I guess not." Trisha said angrily.

"That is enough Trisha!" Professor Henry declared. "I will not have you speak to me like this in front of the others. You would do well to remember the position here. I am the professor, and you are the student."

"And that's all the justification you need." Trisha remarked before leaving as calmly as possible. It was in this moment, and similar moments in the past that made her question whether trying to be noble was worth it. Her gift would have allowed her to see the trap she was walking into, saving her the embarrassment of being declined in front of everyone. But she was honor bound to only use it for the right reasons. Still, the easy road was hard to resist when this was the reward for taking the hard one.

Before she could get far from the theater, she was on her knees with tears streaming down her face. She tried with all her might to stop them, shake it off, and keep moving, but she needed at least a moment. Now the musical that she loved, and fought so hard to even get approved, was going to be performed by someone else, only because they were thinner. Nothing was worse than being the victim of something that couldn't be controlled, and she couldn't control this, though she should not have had to. Being the better actor should've gotten her the part, even if she wasn't considered the better model. It wasn't long before she felt the comforting arms of her friend Nita wrapped around her. This was love, a real and specific kind of love that she had only ever experienced with one person. And even though it didn't rid her of sadness, it did well to make her feel a lot better.

"I would've given it to you even if you sucked. You bleed Phantasm, Trish." Nita said.

Trisha wiped her face. "It's good to know that somebody thinks so. Thanks, Nita." She hugged her friend back. "But what are we gonna do about Isabelle?"

"Plan B. You can still get a school event approved, it's just gonna be a lot harder."

The dean was obligated to be a part of all the school functions, but while the theatre department was a requirement, extracurriculars were strictly up to the people in charge, and Isabelle was an extremely difficult sell.

"Now, I only gotta ask this because I know that your love for Phantasm would've gotten you to accept even stage crew if that was the only thing you could get. You really want to be a part of this production, so why didn't you take the part of uh…Prima Donna?" Nita asked.

"You want the honest answer?" Trisha asked.

"Do you even know how to lie?"

Trisha rolled her eyes, but then answered the question as well as she could. "You know how she is in the show. She's the big, loud, histrionic, and unlikable one. She's the butt end of all the jokes. Yeah, she has some talent, but the way she's written, it plays into certain stereotypes. Sure, I'm loud, and I'm a little dramatic, but there are plenty of girls my size who aren't like that. There are certain stigmas that come with looking like me, and that

27

character hits all of them. It's the only thing I never enjoyed about it. I can't let him reduce me to that part, because it will only prove that all of those assumptions about people that look like me are true. Plus, she's a background character. For once, I want to be in the spotlight. I'm tired of always being behind the scenes, ya dig?"

"Girl, you are my hero. Why didn't you say that to him when he offered you the part?" Nita said.

"I wanted to." Trisha said. "I've practiced that speech plenty of times in my head whenever I thought about the possibility of him pulling something like this. And I mean…actually…I don't know why. I guess I lost my nerve."

Upon leaving the theater building with her friend, Trisha discovered an undesirable sight. Her friends Dominick and Amaya seemed to be surrounded by a few girls, specifically one that she and most of her friends knew well. The lead girl went by the name of Casandra Tyler, but everyone called her Sandra. She was a gorgeous tall girl, dark brown eyes, perfect cheek bones, and a body that was crafted in the warehouse of angels. Her skin was honey and smooth, with perfectly glossed lips. The nails were done, the toes were done, the makeup was exquisite. She was always dressed in designer clothes, rocking her trademark black leather jacket. Her arms were always decorated with jewelry, and today's feature was a silver bracelet with a name engraved in it that Trisha had never seen.

The other girls were her cohorts who neither Trisha nor anyone else around campus seemed to know personally or care to learn about. As a group, they were notorious for causing trouble, something that frustrated Trisha from the moment she met Sandra. She had gotten to college thinking that all the childish practices of high school would be put behind her, that everyone had grown up at least enough to focus on semi-important things. For the most part she was right. But then again, there would always be cases like Sandra. Four years attending community college, and Sandra was still a regular bully, still did whatever she could to seek attention, and still refused to be wrong. It was probably why she was still here four years later, while in cases like Trisha and Nita, it was more about financial situations that dragged the process on.

Everything Sandra said she expected people to take as gospel, as if God had given her the gift of omniscience. And whenever someone tried to call her on it, she put them on the top of her list. The only thing worse than that, was her textbook style of attack. Now that Trisha was watching it happen, there was no way she was going to avoid getting involved. Trisha had not made a habit of being confrontational, and personally hated the idea of it. However, someone was hurting her friends. And if she wasn't going to explain herself to pompous directors for her own sake, then the least she could do was stand up to a bully for someone else's. In addition, if she didn't do anything then Nita was going to, and that could go wrong.

She aggressively walked to make sure that when they saw her, then they would know that she meant business. She didn't even think about what she was going to do or say, but she knew how to think on her feet when she needed to. By the time she had gotten up to the situation, they were just now noticing her presence. She pulled Dominic and Amaya away from the pack and stood in their place. Her priority was to size everyone up. She had dealings with Sandra before, but never with the entire crew at the same time. So, she quickly did her research through their minds, taking care to only focus on violent tendencies. She didn't want to be invasive, but she did need to know if she was in any danger.

This was the first time that she had ever used her powers as a means of defense. In fact, it was one of the first times she had used her powers since she learned how to control them. When they first manifested, she heard thoughts from everyone she walked past, just trying to get everything to quiet down. This led to her learning deep secrets about complete strangers, and she had not felt as disrespectful at any other point in her life. Once she mastered it, she barely used it. Last year, during a difficult emotional time, she lost control of her powers at a campus vigil. This led to her receiving a lot of thoughts, including the dean. That was the day she learned about some of Isabelle's corruption.

But all things considered, Trisha felt as though using one of the powers here was perfectly acceptable. She wouldn't dare think about using the other one, or she could seriously hurt someone. After her search, she found that only Sandra was involved in fights, which she always won. The rest of them were afraid of the prospect. Now, Trisha knew that there was a very low chance of this devolving into a violent encounter. With the added frustration of what she just went through, no one was happier than her that she was dealing with cowards.

"It's a little hot for the leather jacket; don't you think?" Trisha asked.

"What's it to you?" Sandra retorted.

"Aye watch your mouth." Amaya demanded. "I'll snatch that wig right off your head, if you don't check your tone. And pink ain't a natural color."

"Relax, Amaya." Trisha said, as she tried to calm her. She knew well that her friend had a quick temper, and there was enough tension between the two already. So, she addressed Sandra herself. "We got a whole picnic going on today and you gotta mess with my friends? Is it even worth asking what it was about?" Trisha asked.

Sandra didn't move physically, but the vibe from her changed dramatically, almost as if she thought she was staring death in the face. She shot a glance at each of her other friends, just to reassure herself that they were still there and weren't going to abandon her in this time of need. This was the first time they had met while Trisha had a real purpose, and she knew that Sandra knew it.

"It's nothing really. We were just joking with 'em that's all." Sandra said.

"Always lying." Amaya snapped.

"I got this." Trisha said. Trisha turned to Dominic, his tear stained cheek being all the evidence she needed. "He must've been laughing pretty hard to get a reaction like that. I'll give you the benefit of the doubt. Maybe it was only a joke to you, and not to him, and maybe you knew that, and you were just being a scoundrel. So, if you admit that you were intentionally trying to demean my friend, and promise never to do it again, then I'll act like I never saw this. On the other hand, if you lie to me, then we're gonna have a whole new set of problems. By the way, trust me when I say, I will know if you're lying to me." In truth, she figured that she had already been lied to.

"It was nothing. They were just playing." Dominick would say whatever was necessary to defuse the situation. "I mean, it's not like she said anything that wasn't true."

"Bull. Stick up for yourself, Dom. I'll smack her for you if you want me to." Amaya offered.

Trisha had enough and signaled for Nita to take Amaya away. She didn't go willingly, but she couldn't overpower Nita. Sandra looked at Dominic, then her friends, and then back to Trisha. Trisha knew that Sandra believed her to be more bark than bite, but she also knew that Sandra knew how to put on a brave front. As an alternative to relying on her easily corruptible abilities, Trisha studied body language and psychology so that she could essentially do the exact same thing, only legally. Everyone was hoping that Trisha would take Dominick at his word. After all, she hadn't heard anything. There was no way she could prove any of it, and she was too good of a student to do anything reckless.

"That's all." Sandra answered.

Trisha removed her glasses to scratch her eye for a moment, and then promptly put them back on. Then she took a breath, trying to figure out the best way to go about the situation. She had already probed her right after she made the threat. She knew what Sandra had said that hurt Dominick. Beyond that, she didn't care for the specifics, or anything that came before what was said to Dominick. She would've been true to her word to let them go if Sandra had been honest, but she wasn't, and now she had to be true to the other side of her word.

"I want you to look at me, Sandra. Study my face as best you can, because this is what a whole new set of problems looks like. I'll be honest; I don't know you that well. I wouldn't even know your last name if I hadn't seen your student ID on a table once. I just know your reputation, and the few times we've talked. The things you've said to me haven't been pleasant, but I've let it go because it was me. I won't do that when it's someone I care about. So, I'm giving you a warning now, I don't know you...but I will. I will find out every dark secret about you, every insecurity that haunts you at night, every facet of life that makes you hesitate. And I won't say a word to anyone, but you'll know that I know. And you'll find out that the only thing scarier than someone who bullies, is someone who can, but chooses not to."

Trisha signaled Dominic and the two of them walked away together. Nita bucked at the girls before turning to leave as well. Watching all of them jump back was all the satisfaction that any of them needed, save for Amaya. And these cowards stood frozen at the sound of Trisha's declaration of purpose and watched her walk off until she was out of sight.

"That was pretty terrifying." Nita said. "Kinda makes me wonder why you never talked to me like that back in high school."

"Come on. You weren't that bad." Trisha said.

"You're right. I was worse." Nita insisted.

"Guess I was a little too biased, but you found your way." Then she approached Dominick. "I wish you would accept that there's nothing wrong with you. I know how you feel, Dom. It's not always easy living day to day, but there are plenty of people who are going to say mean things about you. There's no sense in saying those things about yourself."

Dominic nervously looked down. "Still never been laid. No one likes me, and they call me emotional."

31

"Some people are okay with it; some people internalize it. People like you express it. I know you're self-conscious about your appearance, trust me I know what it's like; there's a five-pound difference between us. You don't have to feel bad because their comments upset you, you got a right to feel. They should never have said any of it; no one should ever say that about someone period, but especially not to their face. Feel bad right now; cry if you want. I'll make sure they stay off you, but you win by fighting as hard as you can to accept yourself. Your friends have your back. Now, how about we skip this picnic. I'll call up Ace, and the whole squad if you want. We can go somewhere and have our own outing. And we won't stop until you can't remember this happened." Trisha said.

"I have to tell you something." Dominick said nervously.

"What's up?" Trisha asked. She saw Dominick look at Amaya who gave him a threatening look.

"It can wait." Dominick replied.

Trisha knew there was something there but chose not to pursue it. If there was a problem, now was not the time to deal with it. She hugged Dominick and suddenly her own problems didn't seem that bad. However, it wasn't easy hiding her pain. She had to for the sake of Dominick. Other people needed a chance to be weak, and for that reason, it was a luxury that Trisha had to sacrifice. She didn't know it at that moment, but she had just started down a path, and this confrontation would be as easy as it got. She knew who she wanted to be now. What was coming next, she could never have predicted.

Chapter 3

Complicated

Just a few hours later, the disappointing audition experience was receding into Trisha's subconscious as her mood was buoyed by her friends. Nita and Dominick did well to have her back when things didn't go her way, but there was a completely different dynamic to be observed when everyone got together. After resolving to skip out on the college event to instead have a good time in the student lounge, they all rode the bus home together. Trisha would have taken a ride home with Nita, but Nita had somewhere to be that evening, and this was Trisha's night for bible study. It wasn't a big deal to her as she reveled in the time with her comrades. She had been fortunate to be blessed with such a loyal group of friends, and times like this were why. She listened to the jokes being told, the appropriate and inappropriate conversations being had, and everything else that gave the ride it's entertainment factor. As she sat and listened, she thought about each one of them and how their relationships had transpired.

There was Ace sitting in front of her, the first person that she met at the college, back when she was sticking especially close to Nita to avoid awkward encounters with strangers.

"Welcome to Dreyfus. I'm Ace and I run this joint. If you're ever looking for friends, you can run with my crew." He so proudly introduced himself.

He was the one in the group she was least close to. Not that Trisha didn't like him, but he seemed to think he knew everything. It was a pity that he had this unfortunate character flaw about him because he was a deep thinker, compassionate and fun to be around. It was just his ostentatious demeanor that made him the kind of person that was best handled in small doses.Whatever Ace's legal name was, she didn't know. Trisha at one point had made it her personal mission to figure it out, but after a while she let it go, content with the never-ending mystery. It certainly gave her something to always speculate about. All she knew about the name Ace was that it was given to him because he was obsessed with playing cards, 'Spades' being his favorite; if there was a deck involved, then he was involved.

One seat in front of him was the power couple Zoey and Brent. She had met them while searching for a music room to practice in. When she found one she thought was empty, she entered. That's when she discovered them sucking face.

"Uh...am I interrupting?" she asked shyly as she covered her eyes to save herself the intimate details.

"No." Zoey lied, her face revealing her embarrassment."

"Yes." Brent said annoyed.

There was no living that moment down and it gave the three of them a launch pad to build their friendship on. Trisha liked what they represented. In her mind, this was exactly what everyone should be striving for, and it gave her hope that she would one day be able to find true love of her own. Outside of that, they told the best jokes, and the occasional peek into the drama of their lives offered light amusement, if no boundaries were breached. They were the perfect yin yang. One was tall, muscular, and possessed a wild amount of hair, while the other was short, scrawny, and had a buzz cut. Zoey used to have long hair just like Brent, but it was all cut off when she lost a bet during her second year.

The seat behind Trisha was claimed by a girl named Katie. This was the only person that Trisha initiated a meeting with. She saw Katie sitting alone one day and had a rare stroke of social courage.

"Is this seat taken?" Trisha asked.

"Nah. I usually sit with Veronica, but she's not here. Feel free. You play Uno?"

She used to get involved in all the drama of the others, always having a slick comment, or trying to control things. Or at least, that's what everyone thought. A former friend of hers had possessed an uncomfortable amount of control over her, before Katie finally decided to call it quits. Now that she had matured and grown into her own, she decided that she was going to be the quiet and reserved type. She was best known for her blue lipstick that she wore no matter what outfit or accessories graced the rest of her. Sometimes it matched, and other times it didn't, but she was a creature of habit. She had tried to get her product off the ground, the lipstick being a concoction of her own making, but she didn't find much success at her college. Most of the other students were more interested in offering words of support, rather than financial support. She had begun to find a modicum of success elsewhere. Trisha made it her business to buy some whenever she could, even when it meant that she was giving up the little bit of disposable income she had.

As much joy as her peers brought her, it was still a shade of its former glory. This time last year, Trisha could've counted on another face to be present, most likely either sitting next to herself or Katie. His name was Edward, and he was easily the most understanding, forgiving, compassionate, and lively person any of them had ever met. He had been kicked out of the university he had previously attended and was using Dreyfus to get back on his feet, but this turned out to be a blessing to Trisha and others. Trisha remembered the beginning of last year when he came.

"This spot is pretty dope. I know y'all ain't gonna be able to help yourselves, but don't get used to this face. I'm gonna be out of here in no time."

It sounded harsh, but he meant no harm. He was determined to always move forward. He said that he was going to be transferring soon, and he even came into the new year with a fiancé. None of them had ever met the woman of his dreams, but Trisha thought that she had seen a picture once. If there was a model that everyone could get behind, it was Edward. Trisha took it the hardest when the news of his suicide hit the campus. It was as if the entire college came to a complete stop. This was the first time Trisha had ever known a person who took their own life. It wasn't the first time someone she knew had died, but it was the first time it could have been prevented. There were times since the tragedy when she wondered if she could have made a difference if she had used her gift, but Edward had done a great job in covering his feelings. Even if Trisha would've been willing to use it, she would not have known.

The thought of Edward began to alter Trisha's mood, and her next sight only worsened it. At the front of the bus was Sandra. Such a thing was odd to her, because she had never seen Sandra travel any way except by car. She remembered the first time she saw Sandra pull up in a red and white convertible, carrying all her crew with her. It was the first impression she made on the school, and it did well to jump start her career as the empress of the social world. Trisha knew that she took good care of the car, and had even heard that Sandra turned an entire extracurricular club against one boy who had accidently scratched it. That was the kind of power that Trisha couldn't believe people still possessed in college. Trisha must have been staring too long because the two of them locked eyes and Trisha quickly looked away. She comfortably assumed that the earlier encounter assured her that future confrontations were unlikely, but people change under different circumstances.

Trisha stopped thinking about everything for a second. She was in a place where she could be happy with her life, even considering what happened with Professor Henry, or what could happen with Sandra. Trisha felt good, the way a young woman should daily. That of course went away when the bus reached her stop. The bus took her almost directly to her church, which was another reason it was convenient to travel this way on Wednesdays, since Nita lived in the opposite direction. When Trisha got up to exit the vehicle, she noticed that Sandra was getting up, too.

Now, the luxury of not having to think was gone. Had she walked herself into a trap? Were there three other girls ready to jump her? The church was visible from the stop where Trisha got off, but that was more than enough distance for Sandra's friends to cover quickly, if it came to that. Trisha took a deep breath before getting off the bus, because her imagination proved to be a dangerous thing when it was left to run wild. What if Sandra wanted to kill her? What if Trisha had ticked her off more than she thought regarding the Dominick situation, and now Sandra was ready to retaliate? What if Sandra was here to destroy Trisha's church and take away one of the great things in her life? Even Trisha knew that the last one was complete nonsensical blabber, but that didn't stop her from thinking it.

The anxiety coursing through Trisha's body was almost unbearable. She felt like she was about to regurgitate everything that she had ever consumed since the day she started eating, and the tattoo of a plum on the left side of her chest started to throb, as if she had just gotten it the previous day and not years before. She was off the bus, and so was Sandra, and Trisha found herself in a particularly undesirable position. There were no rules out here, at least, not the kind that would do anything for her before incident. If something ridiculous happened, Trisha could be sure of one thing. There would be plenty of angles for her to view it from later after someone inevitably recorded it, and first responders or concerned citizens would arrive long after the damage was done. People around here were more interested in seeing something dramatic happen than they were in helping those in need; after all, this was Baltimore.

Trisha again took a quick peek at her church, taking care not to turn her back on Sandra for too long, although Sandra didn't even seem to notice her presence. It was a trap, and Trisha knew it. The second she stopped paying attention, the wrath of a queen, dethroned in front of her kingdom, would shower down on Trisha and flood her soul with misery. The church was a quick sprint, and then she would be safe. What if she was attacked while her back was turned? It wasn't impossible that Trisha could be faster than Sandra, but it wasn't a stretch of the imagination to think that she wasn't. When Trisha had completed her glance at her church and looked back in Sandra's direction, their eyes again met. Their spirits were connected through the unique intimacy of predator and prey. The confrontation was coming, and the only control Trisha had over it were the terms of the chase. She could initiate as she had done earlier that day, grab hold of the reigns and force Sandra onto the defensive side. Regrettably, the bravery that existed in Trisha earlier that day had fled to a distant corner of the universe. She was going to have to run.

And then just like that, her body was in autopilot mode. Her legs were carrying her to the sanctuary of her church faster than she could even realize what was going on. In fact, with the ferocity that she possessed, anyone or anything that got in Trisha's way was going to lose. There was nothing that she was afraid of facing more than what was behind her, not wild animals, armed robbers, spawns of Satan, or anything in between. She would wage war against the entire world, confident that she could win, before she would turn around and challenge the empress. Although running from the bus stop to the church took only a handful of seconds, the journey seemed to take hours, with each second creeping by.

When Trisha finally reached the church, she flung open the door so hard it crashed against the brick wall. In her panic, Trisha forgot to keep a handle on her strength, and now she was just praying that the door was structurally intact. She was still working overtime for her pastor to make up for the last time it happened. If there was any positive to this, it was that Trisha had spent years trying to master her abilities, and keeping them in check had become second nature. Even in this moment of weakness, her subconscious was still trained to maintain some level of control. When she pulled the door to close it, it shut without incident. Trisha was pleased, but it was short lived as she turned around and saw her pastor.

"You're right on time." Pastor Pauline said. She was dressed in jeans, pink tennis shoes, and her college sweatshirt. Despite her casual apparel, she was still capable of putting the fear of God in Trisha. Her armor bearer, a man named Lionel Fonz, stood next to her.

It wasn't a stretch to think that Trisha was going to be hearing about this later, although knowing her pastor, it would probably be a simple joke and nothing more. So, Trisha entered the sanctuary and got settled. On any given Sunday, the sanctuary was hot, small, and filled to the brim with eager minds both young and old, ready to hear the word of God. They were known for their marathon praise breaks, and despite the modest size of their worship house, they praised as if they had an entire field to run through. Usually it was loud, the keyboard booming, the cymbals crashing, hands clapping, and feet stomping so hard it was amazing that the integrity of the floor had not been compromised. People would be on their knees, tears would be flowing from the faces of nearly everyone inside, and time would exist everywhere else except within their walls. Three hours became mere moments on Sunday. Today was not Sunday. Today, they were here to be taught. The headcount was drastically lower, with only the faithful few consistently attending. Without all the generated heat from their worship, the sanctuary was quite cold. Once everything got started, Trisha's mind wasn't on the temperature or who was present, it was on the word of God.

She was feeling the sadness of not being cast in "Phantasm" but focusing on the words of her pastor helped to keep the feeling in check. The lesson wasn't directly related to what Trisha was currently going through, something that a part of her regretted, but she knew that it was something that someone else needed to hear. And there was no part of the bible's teachings that she couldn't find some worth in. So, she took what she was hearing and made the most of it. Fragments were lost as her mind tended to stroll into other matters. Sometimes it was about the musical. At a point, Sandra was in her head. It was only when she became aware of what was happening that she appreciated how hard it was to focus on one thing. It was a workout that Trisha was still practicing. Before she knew it, Trisha saw the offering plate being passed around. Without a job, she wasn't making too much money. She relied on financial aid to get her through school, and the odd jobs she did for her mother and pastor kept some play money in her pocket. Still, the little she possessed needed to be prioritized. She fished through her pockets until her hands grabbed a bill. She pulled it out and looked at a crumpled up five. After straightening it out as best she could, she dropped it in the plate and waited for the final prayer of dismissal.

When it was done, everyone got up and began to greet each other and engage in other conversation. People were talking about their day, their jobs, their plans for when they left this place and many other things. It always amazed Trisha because some of them were people who never saw each other outside of the two days spent at the church, and yet, they interacted as if they were the best of friends. She would have been talking to someone too, but she wasn't great with initiating conversation, and the few people she was most comfortable with in her congregation were not there. Someone had to tap her on the shoulder to let her know that the pastor was signaling for her to meet in the back. Now, she would have to answer for the door.

The hallway led to the rear of their building which had several rooms. Two bathrooms, a food pantry, two separate offices for the pastor, and her husband, resting quarters for any visiting ministers, a room with all the decorations, and a room that Trisha had never seen opened before, were all a part of the building. The pastor escorted her into her office which was painted pink from top to bottom, complete with a white couch, a desk, a clothing hanger, huge flowers, and a motivational quote painted in black directly in front of whoever was walking through the door. The pastor sat in her chair, and Trisha plopped down on the couch, a casual move that she would have never attempted when they first met. The pastor's husband, an average height brawny man, checked in to make sure everything was alright, and the pastor ensured him that it was.

"He's such a gentleman. Sometimes, I think he works even harder than I do to look out for this church." Pastor Pauline said. She was never shy about talking about Mr. Pauline. "So, tell me what's on your mind Trisha. I haven't seen you slip up at all in a few months, and it's been at least two years since it has been as egregious as that one." Pastor Pauline was sincere, but the way she spoke sometimes sounded accusing, even when she did not mean it. It took Trisha quite a while before she grasped how to tell the difference.

"There are a couple of things to be honest. I didn't get the role in Phantasm. Guess I should put down the fork every now and again."

"Now, I've told you about debasing yourself. There are far more constructive things you could be saying." Pastor Pauline said. "I'm sorry things didn't go your way, but that just means there is something better. Still, the way you came in made it seem like there was a more immediate concern."

"Sandra was on the bus, and then she got off at the same stop I did. It freaked me out a little bit." Trisha said weakly.

"Still letting her torment you, huh? I'm not sure if that speaks to your strength or your cowardice. Guess we'll find out in a second. Do you pray for her at all?" Pastor Pauline asked.

"Nothing good." Trisha stated with authority.

"No, you can't do that, Trisha. You must bring a sincere and compassionate heart to God when praying for His children. It's not for you to ask Him for any harm to come to her."

"You don't understand, Sandra is an as-"

"Watch your mouth young lady. You know I don't tolerate that kind of language in here, or anywhere for that matter." Few things could make the pastor furious, but nothing did it quite like showing a disregard for the Lord's house. "I'm not telling you to be her best friend. You don't even have to like her, but you should pray for her. You never know the kind of life other people are living."

"I'm sorry, pastor. I'm a work in progress."

"We all are." There was silence. "Have you found a way to put those talents to good use yet?"

"No." Trisha lowered her eyes. "It's so hard trying to figure out what good I could do. It always seems like movies have the hero in the right place at the right time, but I keep coming across things after everything has already happened."

"Have you given any more consideration to transferring over to the spiritual realm?" Pastor Pauline asked.

"I still feel the same way." Trisha answered. "They do things on a global scale, and that's great for them, but I want to focus on the little guy whose problems are gonna be a bit too small for them to worry about. Plus, you told me about that new group up in Flint. I'm sure there's a bunch of heat right now, if we're hearing about it. I don't want that in my life. I'm no soldier."

"I know that's right." Pastor Pauline said. "I'm glad I met Robert after he served , because I just don't think I could handle that. No one knows who this group is, just a few unreliable details concerning what happened. Even Diana doesn't know much, and she was part of SOUL. Diana keeps me pretty well informed."

"You've got people everywhere don't you? Delaware, California, New York, even in France, is there any place you could go and not be recognized?"

"Nebraska." The pastor answered.

"How is Miss Diana?" Trisha asked.

"Oh, she's doing well. I'll let her know you asked about her. She's thinking about leaving and bringing the grandkid down here; says she's

40

getting too old for the noise up there, but she's got issues with this environment."

"Come on. Baltimore isn't that bad. She should come here; everyone loves her. Plus, we would finally be able to see her again. Unless you want to get us another bus and we go back to New York."

"Not anytime soon, Trisha. So, about this problem of yours."

"You know, my neighbor lost her job because she kept being late? She can't see too well at night, so she doesn't drive. I use my mom's car at night, so I could have been helping her, if I had known. And I could have known if I had used my gift, but I can't just go around invading people's privacy because I want to make a difference." Trisha lamented.

"I agree. I am cognizant of your dilemma. But also, I think you should give yourself more credit." Pastor Pauline said. "I've met a handful of people like you in my entire life, and I've seen a couple different gifts. Of the few I've met, I haven't been convinced that any of them would be able to show the level of restraint and respect that you have shown with your power. Truth be told, I don't know if I would be able to do it, maybe that's why God didn't give me any." Pastor Pauline stopped to laugh. "But back to the point, this could in fact be the sign that you need to use this gift in a way that allows you to find out what people are struggling with. You found out about them when you were young, and you've done nothing but use them responsibly ever since. If I remember correctly, you said you only used them intentionally a couple of times when you knew something was wrong, and it has happened a few times when you lost control. That's someone who can be trusted with such a privilege. You have one of the most dangerous things in the world, and you only devoted so much time to learning how to use it so that you wouldn't use it by accident. God gave the gift to you for a reason, so take the self-control that you've fought for, and use it. If you need any more encouragement, you can always talk to Minister Frankford. He's in a meeting right now, but he'll be finished shortly."

"Thank you, pastor. Would you like me to wait for you to leave?" Trisha asked.

"Oh no, you go on home. Lionel and hubby will see to me." Pastor Pauline answered.

Trisha left the office. She went back in to ensure that her leader did not need anything, and once she was confident in that knowledge, she exited the building to wait for Minister Frankford. She typically had an issue with waiting outside doing nothing, but she also hated the cold and her church was cold.

She didn't know how long the minister would be, so she walked to the parking lot and retrieved her phone from her pocket. However, she was reminded why it was always a good idea to plug it up whenever she got the chance. It was minutes away from dying, and she hated carrying a dead phone, so she put it away in case she ran into any unfortunate emergencies.

Trisha always felt better after talking to Pastor Pauline. Even when she would occasionally be scolded, the encounter was still constructive, and she believed Pastor Pauline was one of the few people who would always be genuine with her. If she was doing a good job, Trisha was told that, but if she was messing up, she was told that too. There were so many people afraid to speak the truth or give advice because they were afraid of what would be said to them, or about them. This was nothing that Trisha ever had to worry about from her pastor because the woman was just young enough to understand, and just old enough not to care. In the middle of this train of thought, Trisha saw something that she had not been expecting.

The sun had been setting when Trisha arrived at the church, and by now it was dark, the only light sources were the street lamps and the natural brightness of the moon. Anyone who wasn't part of the church or trying to get to the liquor store right next to it, were gone. Yet, Trisha saw Sandra standing in the same place that she had been standing before. Suddenly, all the fear came back, everything that Trisha had felt when she got off the bus and took off for her church was now in the forefront of her mind. Had Sandra intentionally waited all this time just to catch her after dark? It was certainly a possibility, but it wasn't one that made her feel safe, so she tried to ignore it. Trisha was going to have to take the bus home, but she still was waiting for the minister. These truths left her vulnerable for longer than she would like. However, she decided that she was going to try it the pastor's way. It was true that Trisha had no way of knowing what Sandra might be going through, without using her powers. So, since seeing her on the bus was odd, and seeing her still here was equally odd, Trisha entertained the idea that there could be more to this situation than a petty vendetta. She approached Sandra as delicately as possible. The girl wasn't wearing her trademark leather jacket, but the second she saw Trisha, she threw it back on.

"Are you okay, Sandra." Trisha asked.

"The hell do you care?" was the immediate response.

This was almost enough to make Trisha give up and go back to waiting alone. But, she recognized something in the voice, something that she was used to feeling, but didn't recall ever sensing from Sandra: pain.

"It's just that you're always driving, and today I saw you on the bus. And now it's almost ten at night and you're still here. I just want to make sure you're good."

"Get off it, alright?" Sandra said. "I'm not one of your little friends that you have to pity; I'm good."

"You don't think that came off as just a little unnecessary?" Trisha asked. "I'm just trying to help you. If you need a ride home or something, I can see if pastor can work something out."

It was at this point that Sandra got close to Trisha, in the most threatening manner that she had ever experienced. Trisha already knew that she wasn't about to be the same tower of confidence that had faced down this bully before. Earlier, it was easy, because the situation was someone who stood for justice up against a bully which really meant one thing: a coward. That's why it was so easy to win the first time, because Trisha's foundation was remarkably firmer than her enemy's. However, this time the foundation was shaky. Trisha had nothing to really fight for in this exchange, while Sandra possessed a desire to protect. The question was what Sandra was attempting to protect, and what was she willing to do to keep it safe? Trisha knew she wasn't going to win this one, so she didn't stand tall. She shifted into a defensive position to hopefully diffuse the situation.

"I got too much to worry about without you getting in my face. If I say I'm good, then I'm good." Sandra bumped into Trisha on purpose while storming off. Trisha took notice of a slip of paper that fell out of her trademark leather jacket. She thought about calling out to Sandra, but selfishness and a desire for revenge took over for a minute. If that's how Sandra was going to treat her, then there would be consequences.

The curiosity was too much for Trisha. Sure, she could keep herself from probing other people's minds, that was something she could always do, but often chose not to. This was an opportunity that was presenting itself in rare form. There was no telling when she would get another chance to peak into Sandra's life, so she had to take it.

The paper was folded, which explained how it could fit in the small pocket, because once it was unfolded, it was larger than it looked. When Trisha looked at it, she wasn't sure if it was something she should have expected, or if it was a complete and utter shock. It was a flyer for a modeling competition. It was a well-known fact that Sandra boasted modeling opportunities around the school, and people had seen some of her work. It's how most people assumed she got all her money. Judging from the information on the flyer, Trisha could believe that easily. It was a competition that was coming up in about a month, and the winner was promised ten thousand dollars, and a contract with someone that Trisha had never heard of and a name she couldn't pronounce. If this was the kind of thing that Sandra did on a regular basis, then Trisha couldn't imagine what would be bothering her so much. She had the looks she needed to win something like this, and all the money she needed if she didn't. With opportunities such as these, it explained the arrogance of the girl, but not everything else. Trisha didn't have any more time to think about it, because Minister Frankford was coming her way.

"I saw the last little bit of that." Minister Frankford said. This was a man who was truly the definition of tall. His posture and cane compromised his height ever so slightly, but he was growing older, so it was to be expected. His age was revealed by his head and face of white hair, and his old-fashioned way of thinking. He was another case of the difference of the church on Sunday and Wednesday. Tonight, he looked as though he struggled to walk, but on Sunday, he would be lapping the sanctuary just like everyone else. "I'm guessing that's a friend of yours."

"That's Sandra, the girl I told you about." Trisha said.

"Hmph. Pretty face, can't say much for her pissy little attitude though, just a ray of sunshine that one. Are you alright? The pastor said you had a problem that I could help with. Sandra looks like she loves drama, like the type of people we used to deal with who would chase down our engines, just to see the action." Minister Frankford declared. Those were words that Trisha would hold onto.

Trisha saw him as an interesting case. In her life, there were typically two groups of people. There were people like her mother, Nita, and pastor who knew about her gifts. And there were people like Sandra, and Amaya, who had no idea that there was anything special about her. However, Minister Frankford seemed to introduce a third group. People who Trisha couldn't tell if they were aware or not. There was no telling what Minister Frankford knew and didn't know. Much like the pastor, Minister Frankford had done a lot of living. He had seen a lot of places, and people, as well as done a plethora of things, many he knew he should have, and many he knew were wrong. He often said things that were just vague enough to keep Trisha guessing.

"She didn't give me any real details." He said. "She did tell me however, that you're having difficulty deciding whether you should use a talent to help someone. I'll let ya know, when I was young, I never thought I would end up being a part of the fire department for twenty years. If anything, I would be the delinquent starting the fires. But I was meant to do something positive with my life. We saved a lot of lives in my day and inspired many people. I can't even really tell you the path that led me to that career, because it seemed to come out of nowhere, but as it was happening, I struggled with things too. I didn't know if I should, or even if I could, but one thing I know for sure in looking back is, I'm glad that I did. One day, you'll be my age, Trisha. When that day comes, you'll experience this plenty of times, but never quite like the first time it happens. You'll experience mortality, and I mean truly experience it. No matter what you do in your youth, no matter how many risks you take, or dangers you avoid, you'll never understand mortality the way you will when you get older. Because that's when you'll start to realize that the time for thinking your way out of it, fighting your way out of it, and talking your way out of it, is all behind you. You'll be staring time in the face and realize that it never runs out, just the loan it gave you. When that epiphany hits you the first time, you'll examine everything you've done in your life, and everything you've accomplished. Use that gift now, however you think you need to, because when it hits, all you're gonna hope, is that you like what you see."

Chapter 4

The Moment It Should Have Ended

Chasing police vehicles, the perfect way to guarantee seeing action of any kind. Or perhaps it was the way to guarantee seeing a bunch of cars get pulled over for driving without a license plate. Trisha decided that she was going to focus on the first possibility. After the brief conversation that she had with Minister Frankford, she was almost upset that she had not thought about something like this sooner. Her only reservation was being perceived as the same type of people that the minister was criticizing when he was on the job, however they were only doing it because they wanted something to see. When Trisha did it, it would be because she wanted to make a difference. She read story after story online, as well as saw on the news all the time, the senseless violence that plagued her city. People killed each other over clothes, words exchanged, drugs, material possessions, relationships, and plenty more. There were things that she believed were genuinely worth dying for, but she had a difficult time accepting the idea that there were things worth killing for. If there were, it certainly wasn't any of the things she was reading about.

Perhaps, Trisha surmised, the dissonance came in the two parties being unable to get into each other's heads. Party one is ignorant to the fact that party two is about to start a fight, or try to kill, or walk away. There's no way of knowing, but with Trisha there was. She could be an expert negotiator as she would always know what to say, and if things were about to get out of control, she would know and be able to stop it. It wasn't a flawless plan, there were still variables involved. The most important of them all being that there was always the chance, the high chance, that any car she chased down would be responding to something that already happened, rather than answering to an altercation already in progress. That wouldn't do any good for her cause to save people. She had no desire to run around her city looking for revenge. She desired to encourage behavior that made revenge unnecessary.

Even if she was always led to a crime in progress, and there was time for her to make a difference, she would probably have to deal with the police at some point, especially if she became a regular presence. Every time she got involved, they would attempt to arrest her for taking matters into her own hands, and that wasn't a battle that she was convinced she was ready for. She didn't have the resources to disappear, and it wouldn't take much effort to figure out who she was if she was going to be so close to them. That little detail certainly did well to throw a major wrench into her plan. Beyond having a way to handle it, she wasn't sure it would be worth the trouble. After all, there were going to be times when they could manage whatever situation they were up against, better than she; it's what they were trained to do. Then she thought about the times when they were supposed to do something, and they did the exact opposite. She thought about the times someone who looked like her was arrested without cause or killed without a reason. She thought about how her heart rate increased whenever one of their cars passed by even when she wasn't doing anything wrong.

Her city was a mess in a lot of ways, and there were a lot of little people who needed help because of it. No, she didn't have the resources to wage a one-woman war against crime, but she had all she needed to help the would be small time offenders from committing the acts that would send them into the criminal justice system. No, she couldn't bring the dead back to life, but she knew that she would be able to stop some of these people from pulling the trigger. No, she couldn't take on the corrupt police department, but she could look out for her peers before they ever got involved. She couldn't carry the world on her shoulders, but perhaps she could carry her neighborhood.

Trisha had been waiting in anticipation ever since her conversation with Minister Frankford, and time seemed to be creeping and crawling by. The last hour felt like a day, the last minute an hour, and the last second a minute. Now, it was nearly one in the morning, and she still had to wait to be sure. Her mother usually fell asleep around midnight, but she did not fall into her deep sleep until about an hour later. She proved difficult to wake up, even when she was sleeping light, but once she entered the deep sleep, she might as well have been dead. Trisha knew that if she could just wait for that, she would be able to ride through the city all night without her mother ever suspecting a thing, if she was back by six. That was when her mother needed to wake up for work. Trisha had never kept anything from her mom, not even her powers. After she confirmed what was going on, she told her mother everything, and it was perhaps her biggest secret.

Not long after, a mysterious man, who only gave the name Samuel, visited the house in search of her. This is how Trisha first learned about the bigger universe surrounding her powers. Samuel explained the spiritual world that ran parallel to theirs, the angels, and the demons, and other people born with powers as well who aided one side or the other. She was told that she would make a great addition to the ranks. Her initial thought was that she should accept, but she chose to speak to her pastor first. Pastor Pauline was the one who helped her discover that she wanted to use her abilities to help the individual needs of the people of her own city, and it was clear that following Samuel's plan would not leave any room for her own. So, Trisha declined the offer and started looking for ways she could help on her own, and she told her mother this as well. A week before her graduation, she was approached by a different person with the same offer, and once again right before she started her third year of college. Her answer was always the same. She knew that in addition to her own satisfaction, Trisha was making her mother happy by turning them down. They were talking about wars, dangers the likes of which were beyond anything Trisha had ever experienced, and her mother would have hated sending her off to something like that. For this reason, Trisha created her first secret. It wasn't anything she planned on keeping from her mother forever, just long enough for her to start getting her alter ego synonymous with positive change. Once she could show her mother that the city was better off with her, then there wouldn't be much of an argument for her to stop.

Trisha got out of her bed and floated to her closet, the first time in years that she was looking forward to the prospect of digging through it. T-shirts, sweaters, crop tops, halter tops, skirts, dresses, and every other form of clothing was tossed callously to the side as she journeyed into this world of cloth that she had singlehandedly created. After what felt like twenty minutes, she came across her black sweatpants. They were covered in lint, but that wouldn't matter in the dark. She also found a black long sleeve shirt. Once she was finished with the closet, she threw all the other clothes back in, which barely fit, and then grabbed a large trash bag that was next to her closet. In this bag was all her many shoes. Again, she had to dig, but it wasn't as bad because the bag wasn't that large. She claimed her black knee-high boots. With her 'costume' assembled, all that was left was to put it on. All her jewelry came off, any accessory that was not useful to her, as she shed her bright colors for the color of darkness. Once it was on, she went into her bathroom, and looked at herself in the mirror. To her dismay, she didn't like what she saw.

She didn't read a lot of comic books, or watch those kinds of movies, she always felt more at home with the stage, fashion, and music. But even with her limited knowledge of the world, she knew that superheroes didn't look like what she was seeing in the mirror. Heroes were supposed to be towering statues of strength, bringing hope and security with them wherever they went. However, standing at only five feet, Trisha was more inclined to believe that she was looking at a girl trying to play dress up. The bad thoughts were taking over, the memories of what children used to say about her weight, the self-awareness of how she felt about her own body. If she was going to be a hero, then it would be her job to exude confidence. But how could she do that if she didn't even have enough confidence for herself? She took hold of her stomach and shook it a couple of times, nearly forcing herself to tears. This was supposed to be the start of something grand, and up until this moment, she believed it was going to be.

There was no way to precisely know how much her physical appearance *had* held her back, but she could name all of things people said it *would* hold her back from. She was told she would never be Crystal, because she didn't have the right look. She was told she was inferior because she was too dark. She was told that she would never find true love. It was all considered out of her league, and as much as she tried to fight against these awful thoughts, the evening brought with it isolation, and a harder battle. No one could make Trisha feel worse about herself than she could, and now she was mere moments away from running back into her room and forgetting the entire thing. If she were to be truly honest, it would probably save her a lot of trouble.

"My face." Trisha said out loud at a volume above what she intended. She realized that she had done nothing to conceal her face.

That was rule number one for this, always have a secret identity. If she got into trouble, and people came knocking, she needed to make sure that they wouldn't come knocking on her door. So, she went back to her room and started to look everywhere. She saw the pile of headscarves and knew that she had a black one. She could wrap it around her face, poke holes in it, and go out like that. But she would never really be able to wear it for fashion again, and it was her second favorite color. Until she got a second one, that idea was out. Truth be told, it would probably be too small anyway. She collapsed onto her bed, beginning to accept the fact that her plan was not going anywhere, and then it hit her. Her head was resting on a silk pillow case, more specifically a black pillow case. It was certainly more than big enough to go on her head. She took it off the pillow and stared at it.

"How badly do you want this?" Trisha asked herself. For now, a pillow case would have to do. She placed it on her head, tore holes where her eyes were, looked around the room to ensure visibility, and then promptly took it off.

"Hey, everyone has to start somewhere."

Soon after that, perhaps a half an hour, Trisha heard the booming sound of what could be described as a raging storm, echoing through the house in steady rhythm. It was safe to say that Trisha's opportunity to leave had finally presented itself, and she wasn't going to waste even a second of it. She left her room, made her way down the steps, and found her mother's keys sitting on the kitchen table as they always were. As Trisha was leaving, she realized that she was about to leave without her phone. If she did run into a problem, it would be prudent to have it, even if it likely meant that she would be busted if she had to use it. She ran back to her room, so aggressively that she lost her footing and knocked over one of the various boxes. Paranoia consumed Trisha, and she froze in place. At first, silence filled the air, and she wondered if she should dive into her room, throw herself under the covers, and pretend to be asleep. Thankfully, the snoring resumed, and it was time for everything to continue. Trisha grabbed her phone from the room and left the house.

She was surprised by how brisk it was, despite it being summer, but she certainly wasn't going to go back for a jacket; she had a job to do. She pressed a button on her mother's keys, and a beige van, the size of which could accommodate ten people, lit up to indicate that it was now unlocked. She opened the front door and sat in the driver's seat. She had driven before, and through some miracle even possessed her license, even though she got into an accident with a mailbox the very first time she ever drove. She had never driven this van without her mother before. Most of her hours before her test, were logged in Nita's car, and she ironically hadn't obtained many more since then.

She put the key in the ignition and turned it; the roar of the engine taunted her slumbering neighborhood. Another occurrence that could have snatched her mother from the realm of dreams. With the car on, Trisha proceeded to back out of the parking spot, a procedure which took far longer than she would ever admit to anyone. The van was huge, and the dimensions of the parking lot were small. It was anyone's guess how her mother maneuvered this area so elegantly, while Trisha was left to struggle. Eventually, she was out of the space and on her way out of the neighborhood. She pulled over shortly after, ready to wait for her que.

Perhaps, it was her faulty imagination, or it was just her eagerness to get started, but Trisha expected police sirens to reverberate through the city every minute of every hour. That's what it seemed like on any other night, but so far, nothing had happened. Five minutes turned into ten minutes, which turned into fifteen minutes, all of which felt longer because Trisha was sitting in a car in the middle of the night with only the sounds of insects to distract her. The stillness provided the opportunity for her fantasies to develop again, and she was waist-deep into one when her phone buzzed, tearing her entire world of joy down and instantly replacing it with one of dread and terror. Why was her phone buzzing this late? Nita was never up by now because she was incapable of it. The pastor might call if she needed to say something at this hour. Trisha didn't allow any of the crew from her school to text her past the midnight hour unless it was an emergency. That left her mother as the prime candidate. She must have awakened, seen Trisha missing, and then discovered that her car was gone. Now Trisha was in an uncomfortable position. Should she answer it, or ignore it? If she did respond, would she then return home or continue with the plan? Even in the cold, Trisha was sweating, knowing that her mother would have nothing good to say. She took a breath and looked at her phone to see what the damage was, and to her surprise, it was a notification from her 'Spades' app asking if she wanted to play a game.

Trisha was simultaneously relieved and infuriated, but with nothing better to do, she tapped on the app. Trisha was on an expensive table and watched as the cards passed from player to player. As soon as she saw her hand, she gasped. She had all the aces, kings, and highest spades of the game. This was the type of hand that players dreamed of having, and she had literal seconds to enjoy it before she heard a police siren. The temptation of waiting until she finished the game was strong.

"How badly do you want to be a hero?" Trisha asked herself.

She tossed the phone aside and started driving. Her neighborhood was rather confusing, with many twists and turns, but she had walked them and driven them for years. She knew exactly where to go to get out, and based on where she heard the sirens, she knew which route to take to catch up with them. Trisha did in fact reach one of the exiting points of her neighborhood, just in time to see the squad car pass by. She tried to keep up with it as best as she could, but this car was speeding well beyond the speed limit. Wherever it was going must have been a real emergency. Not only did Trisha run the risk of getting pulled over herself if she tried to match speeds, she wasn't even entirely sure if her van could go that fast. So, she slowed down as her ticket into heroism got further and further away.

Soon after, another one came from behind her, presumably going to the same place, but it was traveling at a more manageable speed. Trisha tailed this one as well and was doing a pretty good job of keeping track of it. She stayed behind it just enough to keep up, but not be noticed. The officers inside had more important things to worry about anyway. Then, her plans were once again shot when she got stopped by a red light, and the police car continued its way. It wasn't a complete loss yet, as the light could be a short one, and she might still have time to catch up, but as time went on, that became less and less likely. Then, Trisha realized that she was going about this the wrong way. She didn't need to keep up with the car, she just needed to get close enough to one of the officers to get the information she needed.

When the light turned green, Trisha wasted no time. She followed the path for as long as she had been able to see the car, and right when the trail was getting too cold to be followed, another car was seen. Whatever this was, it was serious. She began to follow the third car, but this time she used her powers. Being careful not to pry deeper into the mind than she needed to, Trisha extracted some information related to where they were all going. The first thoughts she came across was 'B14 and B8'. Trisha had no idea what that meant so she probed a little further into those terms. She discovered that they were the Baltimore police codes for spousal assault and kidnapping, respectively. The first night out was a trip into the deep end of the pool, and Trisha began to think that it was too far out of her league. However, she was sure that she could end this peacefully if she acted quickly. She got the address from the officer, and then slowed down and allowed the police car to leave her behind. From there, it wasn't too far. No matter how this ended, at least she now had a more efficient idea than chasing down every car she came across.

Trisha drove by the house, noting the three police cars parked in front, and all the curious bystanders gathering to see how all of this was going to play out. She needed to make sure the car stayed a fair distance away from all of this. So, she parked a few blocks up, and walked back, ducking behind trees, bushes, and other cars. The pillow case was on her head, but no one was going to be able to convince her that she didn't need to hide, in fact the way she was dressed made her look like she might be an accomplice to whatever was going on. When she reached the neighborhood where the house sat, she took a peak at the gathering crowd. She knew all of them lived in the immediate area and figured that one of them must have known something about the residents of the house.

She started scanning minds for information related to the address of the home. She wasn't sure exactly how her powers worked, at least the telepathy, but it seemed as if it worked more on a subconscious level, though she had learned to consciously direct it. She used to do a lot of research on the brain, eager to learn what the scientific explanation was, but when she discovered how the brain truly operated, she knew that there was no way she was consciously doing all the work that her powers demanded. The sheer amount of will power that she would need just to send a single signal through her own body, let alone another person's mind, would have driven her insane. That's how she concluded that she must have been able to filter the kind of readings she got. Focusing on a single idea helped her brain to know what she was looking for, and while her brain was certainly efficient enough to take all the information in, it was likely that it stored all the excess somewhere in the back of the mind, while making the relevant information immediately available. Trisha wondered how much she knew about everyone without even knowing.

Soon, she got answers to the questions she was looking for. None of them knew what was going on, but a few of them knew who lived there. It was a four-person household known as the Mitchel's. The mother's name was Lilian, and the father's name was Mark. There were two children, a daughter named Melanie, and son named Seth. After probing a few cops, Trisha discovered that they were called by Seth. She also learned that they had attempted negotiation but had received no response from anyone. With that information, Trisha filled in a few additional gaps. Whatever dispute happened between Lilian and Mark turned violent, and now Mark was holding Lilian captive. Trisha shuddered to think where the children must have been. There was one more thought that she picked up, one of the officers was determined to kill the assailant. Trisha thought back to her own father, and how satisfied she would be to have him in any capacity. This family was going to be whole when this was over, even if that meant visiting Mark in prison.

Trisha ran to the back of the house, which had a porch that she planned on using to gain access to the house. That plan wasn't as straight forward as she would have liked it to be, as there was a cop posted by the door. She read him to figure out why he was just standing there, and she found out that he had not yet been given clearance to go in because of the hostage situation. He was also ready to kill the assailant as soon as he saw him. Trisha tried sneaking and got right next to the steps of the porch, but then stepped on a twig.

"Who is there?" the cop asked angrily. "If you're the bastard we're here for then you better give yourself up quietly." Trisha saw enough to see that the cop's gun was drawn, so direct confrontation was out. The only other option she had was to wait, and she didn't have to wait long before the cop came her way. With the aid of darkness, Trisha was able to get the drop on the cop, disarm him, and get her hand over his mouth. He kicked and tried to elbow her, but she didn't so much as flinch. This was where her other power came in handy. She was able to manipulate kinetic energy to a degree. Any that was incoming, her body reduced, which essentially took all the power out of this man's meager attempts of struggle. Any energy that was outgoing, she could enhance. So, it was child's play to out-muscle the cop.

"Don't worry, I'm here to help." Trisha said. She then rendered the cop unconscious. Now, she knew she was getting in too deep, but she needed to save lives, all the lives. She could negotiate all of this without violence, while the police would simply shoot to kill, and having already lost her father, there was a chance that she could appeal to the parental side in Mark. She jumped onto the porch and tried to slide open the door. Of course, it was locked, but it opened when she forced it to.

At first glance, the house was decorated nicely. This door led directly into the kitchen, which sat across from the living room, a huge tv taking up the span of its wall. A few feet forward were steps leading to the basement, and a few feet beyond that were steps leading upstairs. This is also where the door leading to the front yard was situated. Trisha tried to move as quietly as possible. There was no telling where this crazed man was in this house, and she had not ever had the opportunity to learn if her powers protected her against bullets. She hoped for her sake that she would not have to find out. The home was eerily quiet, given all the commotion going on outside, but it made it easier for Trisha to listen for voices. She didn't hear anything and concluded that the people she was looking for were not on this floor.

So, she needed to go upstairs or downstairs, and she knew that if she needed to hide, she would have picked the basement.

The home must have been newer than Trisha's, because it made no sounds as she took step after step, unlike hers which would creak even when a mouse moved across its floors. Once she was in the basement, she saw a closed door to her right, and assumed that she had guessed correctly. She opened it up, and it was completely dark, but throwing the lights on, even if she knew how, would probably have been a bad idea. Likely no worse than what she did next.

"Anyone in here?" she asked. There was no answer at first, but then a shaking male's voice pierced the air.

"Are you an officer?"

It must have been the voice of Mark, and Trisha's heart rate started racing. She was in a dark room with a kidnapper, and suddenly she could understand the shoot first mentality. Her fear wanted to drive her to take this man out before he hurt anyone, including her, but she came here with the intent to save, and she needed to maintain that.

"I'm not a cop, but I do want to help. There are a bunch of them outside ready to kill you, but I think if you give yourself up, you can walk away from this." Trisha said, her voice breaking multiple times during her delivery. Hopefully, Mark was as frightened as she was, otherwise she had shown a weakness that would be exploited.

"Close the door and do it quietly." Mark said.

Trisha had her reservations, but there was no telling what Mark had, or who he had, and she needed to play by his rules for now. So, she shut the door as quietly as possible.

"The switches for the lights are right on that wall where you're standing. There are three of them. Turn the middle one on." Trisha did as she was told, and when the light was turned on, she was shocked by what she saw.

Mark was a skinny white man, nothing threatening about him. There was nothing in his hands, no weapon of any kind, and the two children were clinging to his legs. There was a bruise on his left eye, presumably from whatever struggle had taken place, but all the signs pointed to him being the victim, rather than the assailant.

"Why would anyone try to kill me? I'm just trying to keep my kids safe. And who the hell are you?"

Mark stepped back, and tried to shield his children, and that's when Trisha realized that she looked even more threatening than she initially thought. She was still trying to accept the fact that Mark was not the enemy. Besides the original shock, it presented an issue that was going to make negotiating a little harder. For now, she thought it best to answer Mark's question, and that's when she noticed that she had not taken the time to come up with a name, hero or otherwise. With no other options, and no time left, she threw out the first two names that came to mind.

"I'm Natalie. Natalie Bowman. I uh…haven't really chosen another name yet, but I'm working on it." She said nervously.

"Is this a joke!? She's coming after me and my kids and you're making jokes? This isn't the time to be playing hero. You said there are cops outside; let them handle this, if they gotta chase her down, I'm guessing they won't run out of breath."

She ignored the rude comment. "They've been outside for a while now. No one has come in to save y'all yet, except me. If you want to wait for the supermodels to burst through the door to save you, then be my guest…they might be a while. But I'm here right now, and no one is forcing me to be. Now, I get that this is startling and weird, but I really am trying to help. So, maybe tell me what happened, and we can work something out."

"You're wearing a pillow case." Mark replied.

"Focus. Tell me what happened." Trisha said. She was thinking about reading his mind but showing her concern would help to ease the tension and reassure him. The conversation would likely help him remain calm.

Mark took a deep breath. "My wife Lilian always gets home by seven, nine at the absolute latest. It was midnight when she came home in a bad mood. She's never had a drinking problem. Hell, I've never even seen her touch alcohol, but she was out of her mind when she came through the door. She's been going through a rough time lately, both of us have, to be honest. I've been in anger management, she's been dealing with her own issues, and the kids have been getting into a lot of trouble at school. My boy, Seth was suspended last week for fighting. So, family life hasn't been its best. We got into it pretty bad tonight, I guess she had no idea how to handle herself under the influence. She's always been peaceful, but she was cursing, yelling threats, and causing a general disturbance. When I tried to calm her down, she punched me in the eye. By that point, the children were awake and scared. I knew things could only get worse from there, so I got them out of bed, and told her I was going to take them to a hotel tonight. Guess she didn't like that too much. She got a hold of my gun and held me in our room. I guess one of them called the police. As soon as we heard the first siren, she took her attention off me and posted up against the window. I ran out of the room and grabbed the kids, ready to run outside, but I panicked and came down here. We've been waiting for something to happen ever since. When I heard the door open, I figured it was either them or her."

Trisha pulled the pillow case off her head. "We're going to fix this. It sounds like this is a lot of aggression that's built up over time."

"I'm not letting her hurt my kids." Mark said. "They're the one good thing that I've done with my life; she's not coming near my kids!"

"We're going to sort all of that out. You said you were in anger management. Can you tell me why?" Trisha asked.

"Because he's an abusive pile of garbage." Another voice said, belonging to a woman. Immediately following that, was the cocking of a shotgun, and that changed Trisha's entire world. Now, she truly was in the room with the assailant, and while she was afraid when she first heard Mark's voice, there was a certain bliss in the ignorance of not knowing what she had stepped into. He could have been armed with a knife, gun, or nothing, and not knowing offered a dimension of peace. This time, Trisha knew exactly the kind of danger she was in, and it was horrifying. "You got about five seconds to get out of this house. I suggest you do it, so I don't have to put a hole in you. There's no way I could miss."

The offer sounded nice, a chance to walk away without the possibility of dying would appeal to anyone in her situation. But that was the thing that separated those who fought for others, and those who only looked out for themselves.

'How badly do you want to be a hero?' Trisha thought to herself. She turned around and looked Lilian straight in her eyes. Lilian was about as tall as she was, with maybe an inch separating them. Her eyes were puffy from crying, and she reeked of Hennessy.

"My son has those same eyes." Lilian said. "Something you wanna tell me, Mark? I wouldn't be surprised."

"Come on, Lil. He doesn't even look like her, and she's too young. You're not thinking straight." Mark said.

"Shut up!" Lilian yelled.

"Everyone needs to take a breath." Trisha said. "Why are you doing this, Lilian?"

"I don't have to explain anything to you!" Lilian asserted.

"True, but there are a bunch of guys out there who would have already turned you into swiss cheese if they were standing where I am, and I'm just trying to talk to you. I'm trying to give you a chance." Trisha pleaded.

"I'm not the bad guy here." Lilian insisted. "I do what I'm supposed to do. I pay my taxes, I'm on time for work, I nurture my children, give to charity. I do everything I can to help. And don't even get me started on holding *him* up. Even after everything I do for him, he still thinks it's okay to put his hands on me, repeatedly. Then my job wanted to cut me loose because it was more cost effective, and my kids can't keep themselves together. So, I guess I'm just a failure everywhere. And, he thinks he's so great cause he got himself into some therapy. That doesn't erase what he did!"

Trisha read Lilian's mind to confirm the story. There were memories of being fired, and several incidents of Mark putting his hands on her. This forced Trisha to reevaluate her original judgment of Mark. Even still, it didn't justify murder. As far as she could see, it was a few slaps, and one time, he bruised her arm. The most he deserved was a divorce, and no visitation until he got himself together, perhaps even some jail time, but not death. There was too much death in the world already.

"What is killing him going to accomplish?" Trisha asked.

"I'm not just going to kill him." Lilian confessed. "He was a good man once. I loved him, and I still do. He tried to raise these children, but life has gotten to him. He's not a good man anymore, but I don't want to lose our family. We all go out tonight, and we can find the better part of ourselves again in the next life."

"You're insane, lady!" Mark cried.

"Be quiet." Trisha said to Mark, and then she turned back to Lilian. "I know that he hurt you, and I know that you don't trust him. Maybe you think that you're to blame for what is going on, but you aren't. What happened at the job is a result of how evil people can be, and what happened between you and Mark…that's on him. He has a lot to answer for, a lot of growing to do, and it's going to be a long road before you can trust him again, but he's trying. That's more than you can say for a lot of people in his position. You have a chance to rebuild your family. You both can find the better parts of yourselves right now in this life, and your kids also. They're young, they are going to make mistakes, but your family is not in shambles, and you are not a failure. Please, put the gun down."

"No. I have to do this. This life is pain, but we can dodge it in the next one." Lilian said.

Trisha used her powers again and found the hesitation in her mind. She was afraid to pull the trigger because she knew it was wrong. She was afraid because she didn't want to hurt her family, and she was simply scared to die. But, deeper than the hesitation, Trisha found that this lady had the conviction to kill. There were parts of Lilian's mind that were fully committed to becoming a murderer and a suicide victim.

"I know you are kind and sweet, and right now you're horrified that you're doing this. That goodness in you is what you need to focus on. Keep that, find it in Mark and your children, and everything will work out. Please. No one wants to see anyone get hurt."

To her amazement, Trisha saw that her words were having a positive effect. She watched as Lilian lowered the gun and threw it down. Trisha moved slowly towards the gun, and grabbed it, moving it away from the woman. She tried to console Lilian, who was sobbing uncontrollably. Trisha told her that everything would be alright, and that they would get through this together, and as she turned to face Mark with hope in her eyes, she heard the shot gun go off, which propelled Lilian into the wall. She was dead before she hit the floor, and Trisha was frozen from what had just transpired. She saw Mark holding the smoking gun and knew what had happened. She could barely speak, but she managed to get out one coherent sentence.

"What was that!?" Trisha exclaimed.

"I told you, I wasn't going to let her hurt my children."

Trisha knew that officers would be swarming the place in seconds, if they weren't already inside. She felt like she couldn't move, but if she was still here when they arrived, her whole life could come to an end. She forced her body to obey her will, effortlessly pushing Mark to the side to retrieve her mask, and then taking off for the steps. As she was running up, she came up against two police officers, who she knocked down on her way out of the house. From there, she ran into the darkness without looking back.

Chapter 5

What Were You Thinking

Trisha couldn't bear to look at her television any longer, but her mother's eyes were glued to it. The local news station was covering the incident from the previous night, and as far as the masses were concerned, a mysterious woman in black had intervened. However, Trisha knew who they were referencing, and judging from the disapproving glare coming from her mother, she knew as well. The news didn't seem to say anything negative about Trisha's antics from the previous night, although one police officer stated that they were going to open a public investigation. Trisha began to worry, and her only consolation was that she had not given Mark her real name. Her fears were lessened even more when Mark was interviewed on television, saying that he had no idea who the woman was, and that they had never spoken. The story was made to look like Trisha appeared out of the dark, stopped the children from getting shot, and Mark in defense of his children delivered the deadly blow, a story that was playing well with the public.

Trisha's mom was not as enthusiastic. With each passing minute, she grew more upset, which was made clear by the fact that she had not yet said a word. When Trisha had gotten back in the house after her stunt, her mother was still asleep. Trisha was free to grieve on her own, without having to explain anything to anyone, and it was a grueling process. Sleep was impossible for her, and apart from taking her clothes off, she had not moved from the spot on her bed for the next few hours. She was first summoned when her mother turned on the tv to watch during breakfast, something she made a habit of. So, Trisha got dressed, picking out nothing special, just whatever was laying around, and went to join her mother. As soon as Trisha heard the distinct voice of her mother's favorite reporter, she knew that she was going to have to confess to what happened. She was ready to tell her mother everything, including the parts of the story that the news was getting wrong, but her mother would not speak. She could not imagine a worse form of torture in this moment then allowing the tension to build. Trisha felt as if she was going to explode, and she had to force herself to stay calm.

Finally, her mother turned off the tv, as coverage of the story had already reached its climax. She went into the kitchen, leaving Trisha alone with her thoughts, a sadistic hell of human creation. Trisha could only imagine what her mother was going to have to say, and she didn't have any sort of defense. Her outing was a complete disaster, and if things had gone even slightly differently, there could've been a basement with a dead family. There was not much time to be lost in her own thoughts as Trisha saw her mother coming back from the kitchen. She had a hot cup of tea in one hand, and a plum in the other which she sat in front of Trisha gently.

"What were you thinking? I used to imagine having a talk like this with you one day, and I always knew exactly what I would say when this day came." Trisha's mom said. Trisha could relate, as she did the same, plenty of times. "The first thought that came to me was being at work and having some cop call me. 'Miss Annetta, we regret to inform you that your daughter Trisha was found dead this morning. And, she ruined a perfectly good pillow case.'" Annetta said in her best impression.

"I know, Ma."

"No, you don't. You think you know, but you don't. You ain't never been no mother before."

"Yeah, but I have been a daughter before, looking at the clock as it gets later and later, and my mother hasn't walked through the door yet. You went to sleep with me here and woke up with me here. Do you have any idea how many times I've passed out with absolutely no idea where you were, or what man you were with?"

Annetta struck Trisha across her face. "You mind your mouth when you speak to me, young lady. You think it's been easy without your father next to me at night?"

"I never said that." Trisha said, her vision obscured by the tears.

"You don't know a damn thing about what I do when I leave here, and it isn't your business either. I know exactly what you went out to do, and that is terrifying! You could have been killed last night, and then what?"

"I wasn't killed."

"But you could have been. Did you ever find out if you can even survive a gunshot, or were you just planning on winging it? This is real life, Trish. You don't get a replay, or a second or third chance. It's way too dangerous for you to be running out into the world, without knowing what you're doing. At the very least, you should've taken time to learn the full potential of your abilities. You beat up a cop for Christ's sakes. You think there won't be any consequences for that? They're looking for you."

"I didn't give my name, and no one except Mark saw my face. Doesn't look like he's talking."

"Maybe fifty years ago that would be enough, but nowadays? All they gotta do is get your fingerprints off anything you touched, what if someone saw the van?"

"You knew about that?" Trisha asked.

"Oh please. You think I thought you took the bus there and back? You get a little unpredictable sometimes, but that's not hard to figure out. I still can't believe this happened. Are you that unfulfilled that you have to throw your life away?"

"I just wanted to do some good. God gave me these powers for a reason." Trisha said desperately.

"I'm sure of that, but there are other ways to use them that don't involve you picking fights with people with guns. Doing that is no different than transferring. At least there's protocol there, but you just want to go off on your own. I can't lose my daughter, especially when it's senseless violence. I'm supposed to protect you."

"People are supposed to protect each other. We shouldn't be afraid that someone else is going to intentionally hurt us." Trisha defended. "Yet, all over the city, people are getting hurt and killed by other people, for no reason at all. If that can be prevented, then it should be. Someone should stand up for them."

"Plenty of people do." Annetta rebutted. "You have the police, support groups, government agencies. There are people whose jobs it is to run into danger, take in the worst of the worst, care for the people who have seen all the crazy stuff in the world. If you want to help, then help, but not like this, not like some untrained overeager running target. They say you got the drop on that woman last night, but what happens when you don't? What happens when you're staring down the barrel of a gun? What good have you done if you get killed? If you had died last night, what would your memory be? Would you be satisfied with how things ended?"

"I'd be satisfied knowing that my concern, even at the end, was trying to make sure someone else was okay."

"A bunch of people have drowned trying to get other people to shore." Annetta. said. "There are so many things out in the world trying to kill you. Illness, natural disasters, crazy people, and there is no cure for these things. I just wish you could understand that. My world changed drastically with a phone call, and then fell apart completely after a meaningless surgery."

"So did mine! You're not the only one who loved dad."

"That's my point! You're what I got left. Maybe I do get over zealous with these men; my loneliness gets the better of me, but that's just a bad coping mechanism. You're the one I love."

"You don't understand, Ma. I can't just sit on my hands when I know that there is something I can do to help the world. Sorry you can't support that." Then Trisha stood up, grabbed the tea and leaving the plum behind, ran out the door.

While she sat on her porch, she examined the patch of sunflowers that sat in the shade of her home. In a moment of objectivity, Trisha knew that what she had just done was wrong, but the moment was short lived, as all her personal feelings got in the way. She whipped out her phone from her jean's pocket and called Nita. There was a voice on the other end immediately, already prepared to meet, and was in fact already on the way. A few minutes after that, the familiar blue car pulled into the neighborhood, which Trisha got into immediately. She asked Nita to pull off quickly before her mother decided to come outside to see if she was still there, and Nita complied. They were out of the neighborhood a few seconds later.

"How did you know I was going to call?" Trisha asked.

"Who else would you call? Can't believe it took this long. What were you thinking?" Nita asked. "You tryna get yourself killed now? Are you a freaking idiot all of the sudden?"

"So, I'm guessing you saw it?"

"Are you kidding me? I wasn't looking at that garbage, so I could listen to them talk bad about you and probably say a bunch of crap that isn't true. Miss Annetta called me as soon as she found out, asked me if I knew anything about it. You're lucky I was feeling nice today, or I would've just left you on your own to get yelled at."

"Thanks, Nita." Trisha said shyly.

"Shut up. What happened to rescuing cats from trees? Where did this sudden Rambo act come from?" Nita asked angrily.

"When I stood up to Sandra, I felt strong. I felt like I was making a difference. There are people who got a lot more to worry about than being called fat. There are bullies everywhere."

"Scaring Sandra and being Batman are too different things." Nita said.

"It's just so hard." Trisha began. "I just want to do some good, and the first chance I get, I mess everything up."

"Stop with the pity party, Trish; it's insulting to the rest of us who actually care." Nita jerked the wheel to avoid hitting a car and slammed on her horn as if the other driver was in the wrong. "Look at this, you got me driving like a maniac. Anyway, chill out. You know that was dumb. You can't even fight."

"I didn't know she would have a gun." Trisha said.

"Seriously?"

"Sorry, but you sound just like my mother."

"Girl, I'm glad I do. You're so caught up in your own self-righteousness, that you can't see things for what they are. You think everything is good because you say you just want to help people, but your foundation isn't pure. There's too much of you that feels like there's something to prove." Nita accused.

"You don't know that." Trisha said.

"Geez. It's plain as day. How much time have you put into figuring out another way to get close to the dean?" Nita asked.

"The only option is a school function, and I don't have a good idea for one. She hardly approves anything."

Nita pulled the car over immediately. "That's exactly my point. You've been talking about this woman since last year. She's an evil person, like old school evil, and every day you ignore it, is another day she gets to walk. That's another student whose tuition is suddenly gonna disappear, or a test score altered so no one figures out how low quality the education is around here. Hell, under her we might even have another suicide. She don't care about the students, Trish and you're the only one who knows everything she's done. If this was as pure as you claim it is, you wouldn't rest until you figured something out."

"I'm sorry." Trisha said weakly.

"You freaking better be. Honestly, I don't even think I would say you should never do it again, but you gotta have a better plan, and some priorities. First, it would probably be a smart idea to learn the limits of your powers, whether you could even take getting stabbed or shot. Secondly, you gotta learn how to fight. You think the people out here don't know how to throw hands? I told you I would show you some stuff. I don't know about your mother, but you know I've been supporting your crime fighting from the beginning, but this stuff is real. There are real fiends out there, and next time you might not get so lucky."

"Last night was one of the worst nights of my life, Nita. You and Ma are going on about how lucky I am that I wasn't killed, but what about the woman that was? I've never seen anyone die before, and she got a hole blown through her right in front of me. Never mind me, I wanted to save lives, and someone died. I will be fine, but it's people like her that will keep me up at night."

"Look, I don't have all the facts of what happened, but most of them aren't relevant. Most of this comes down to you not being ready. You want to sneak out at night? Fine. You want to pick fights with the biggest and baddest? Be my guest. Heck, if you need me to help you come up with cover stories for your mother, then I'll do that. I'll drive you to the different sites. But if you're gonna be doing it, and if I'm gonna be out here lying, then you need more skills. You need to take a few months, let me teach you some moves. Let's figure out your powers together. Let's sit down and find some of the major problems of the city and see how we can apply your powers to them. Let's come up with a freaking plan, and then you can do what you feel you need to do for these people, but it can't be about you, like it is now."

"It's not about me! I put on a pillow case and ran headfirst into a hostage situation…a pillow case, Nita. I don't care about my image, or proving I can do this, or anything that you're saying. I just care about the people."

"My God, you're so stubborn Trisha. Answer me this then. If this isn't about your own personal demons, why are you so against getting help?"

For a few minutes, no one said anything. Trisha once again had to be honest with herself and accept that Nita had legitimate points, as well as her mother, but it was coming as a culture shock. Trisha had always known Nita to be blunt, so her unabashed honesty was nothing new. However, Trisha figured the day she finally acted, if anyone was going to be in her corner, it would be Nita.

'She is in your corner.' Trisha thought to herself. 'She just wants you to be careful.'

"You're right, Nita."

"Well, it's about time you listened to someone." Nita said. "For real, I'm sure last night probably sucked for you, so we don't have to talk about any of this stuff no more today. I'm gonna hit up Amaya, and Dominick, and we can chill at your house tonight."

"I'm not really feeling that. Plus, there's no way Ma is gonna be down for that, ya dig?"

"Come on. She loves me. She won't say no to me."

An exasperated sigh fell from Trisha's mouth. "Fine. I guess, but can you take me by my church? I need to talk to pastor. She's usually there in the mornings."

"K."

Not much was said for the rest of the ride, except for a few bits of conversation here and there about music, school drama, and pop culture. Trisha spent most of the time looking out of the window. The morning had greeted her with warmth, but also brought with it gray skies and rain. Now, it was a light rain, but she wouldn't be surprised if it picked up. She tried not to let the weather affect her mood, but it was difficult not taking it all personally.

When they arrived at the church, Trisha was relieved to see her pastor's car in the parking lot, but there was another surprise that awaited her. Sandra was standing alone, covering her head from the rain with her trademark leather jacket. This was the second time that Trisha had seen her posted up near her church alone, and it concerned her as to why.

"You seen her driving lately?" Trisha asked, drawing attention to the young woman.

"I don't really pay attention." Nita said, barely even looking in Sandra's direction. "I'm gonna call them and go pick them up. I'll scoop you from here when I'm done. Should only take about an hour."

Trisha nodded and then exited the car. As much as she didn't want to, she couldn't help but give Sandra a second look. There was anger and irritation on her face, and a certain sadness in her eyes, all which Trisha found nearly impossible to disregard. She thought about reading her mind and seeing if there was any problem that she could help with, but she wasn't convinced it was necessary. Even if she offered her hand, Sandra wouldn't take it, and she didn't deserve it. Trisha thought back to all the things Sandra had said to her since they met, all the things she saw Sandra say to other people, and the encounter they had over Dominick. She was always on top of the world. If she was going through something now, it was about time. Besides, Trisha was here for a specific reason that had nothing to do with her. She went inside of the church, refusing to look back.

Once inside, it was a matter of finding where the pastor was. She wasn't in the sanctuary which made her office the most likely place. She found it, knocked twice, and announced herself. In a matter of seconds, the door flew open. It was then, that Trisha truly accepted the gravity of what she had done, and what she had endured. All night she was focused on the memory, but she was trying to stay strong because she knew that it was something that she would need to do as a hero. When her mother was scolding her, she needed to stay strong because she was loyal to her convictions. When she was facing Nita, it was strictly driven by pride. She wasn't going to allow her friend to see her in a moment of weakness, not when this was something that she had been asking for. But as she stood face to face with Pastor Pauline, none of those self-imposed restrictions existed. She didn't need to hide anything, and so she didn't. Anguish overtook her, as she fell into the pastor's arms. Pastor Pauline held her up, and pulled her into the office, helping her to the couch. Then she closed the door and sat down at her desk.

Trisha lost track of how long she had been crying, but she was relieved to know that she was free to do so. There would be words exchanged soon, and it was likely that she wasn't going to like them, but for the moment, it was enough to know that she could show herself without a mask. In fact, having this certainty did a lot to push her to get herself together. The pastor didn't make her act like she didn't have feelings, and out of respect for that, Trisha figured she should try to be strong. She reached for her nose to wipe it, but Pastor Pauline stopped her.

"Here, use a tissue; I hate messes. Bad enough having to live with a man, definitely not putting up with it in my own office." She said as she retrieved an unopened box from one of the drawers and tossed it.

"Thank you. I appreciate your time."

"I'm always available." The pastor responded. "Now...what were you thinking?"

"Does everyone know it was me?"

"Not at all. Just the people that know about your talents. To say it was someone else would just be blind denial. Why were you out there, Trisha?"

"I thought I could make a difference."

"It was stupid, and irresponsible, no two ways about it. But, you made a difference, and there's no two ways about that either."

Trisha looked up in confusion.

"Mark and Lilian took marriage counseling from a friend of mine, I knew them pretty well, performed the wedding ceremony in fact. Lilian came to me a couple of times after Mark's…we'll call them incidents. I'm sure he wasn't thinking, but it doesn't make his behavior any less despicable. That's no way to treat a lady. I'm rambling."

"So, you *do* know everyone, huh?" Trisha asked.

"I get around. Anyway, when I heard the news, I knew it was you, and I knew where this started before you got involved. Based off what they were saying on tv, I firmly believe that Lilian would have killed that man in her emotional state. I can't say either way about the children. I'm more inclined to believe that she would've realized what she did to Mark and stopped there, but that's what I want to think. If I'm being perfectly honest, she probably would've killed them too. People take a lot for granted, forget that the line between held together and out of control is thin. So, where does that leave us? That leaves us with three people who are alive that would not be if you hadn't arrived. Outside of that, you showed tremendous character in risking your life for someone who arguably didn't deserve it, and who you had no actual attachment to. You certainly showed, that to at least some degree, you have the mentality of a hero. For that, you should be commended. I cannot condone your approach, the sneaking out, the ill-equipped nature, grand-theft auto and assault of a police officer. I can't argue your results either."

"I'm thinking I should just give the whole thing up." Trisha said.

"Maybe you should. But it's not because of your size, or your looks, or whatever else you've put inside your head. It's because this is not the way your talents are to be manifested, at least so far as you've been told. Have you sat down and spoken to God about what you should do? He gave them to you, I'm sure He has a pretty good idea of how you should use them. What does your mother think about all of this?"

"She wasn't a fan, but I knew she wouldn't be. She wasn't trying to listen to me, so I walked out. Even Nita offered to help me; it would be nice to get some support from my mom."

"That's not right. She's your mother and you need to respect her. If you don't agree with her, then that's fine, but you should never behave like that. She's trying to make sure nothing happens to you, and I must agree. What you did was dangerous. How do you think she would feel if you didn't come back?"

"Devastated."

"Exactly. The first thing you need to do is go home and apologize to her because you owe her that much. Then you need to spend a lot of time with your bible open, and even more time on your knees talking to God. If you want clarity and purpose, it needs to come from Him. Not you, Nita, your mother, or even me. Whatever you do, make sure you have spoken with Him.

"I've never seen anyone die before. I've been to funerals, but I've never been there when it actually happened." A chill went through Trisha's body.

"I haven't seen it since I got off the streets, but I used to see things like that every day. There's nothing glamorous about it; just be grateful it wasn't you. You used the talents you have, but you didn't use them in the most constructive way. You'll find success when you begin to think things through and when they're used to serve the right purpose."

"Like taking the dean down?" Trisha asked.

"If that's what you think they are there for, but even in that, you must be careful. Apply wisdom and discernment to any and everything that you do."

"I've already discerned that she needs to be dealt with. It's her job to look after the students and faculty. Did you know Edward approached her office several times about how much pressure he was under, and she didn't even reference him to any of the guidance counselors. She ignored him entirely because she was afraid that if he started talking that people would start asking about the state of the workers at the school. All that to protect a reputation and Edward ended up killing himself. She buried the story, said it was due to issues at home and a refusal to accept help from the school."

"And she should be punished for that. Just keep in mind that the day of confrontation will be different. It's not going to matter if she deserves to be exposed or not. All that is going to matter is whether or not you have the resources to get the job done."

The advice was much needed, and to Trisha's surprise, she wasn't harangued as badly as she thought she would be. She was even starting to feel better, more like herself, until she went back outside and saw Sandra still in the same place as before. The bitterness of past experiences was still eating away at her inside, but then Trisha thought of what her pastor had just done. She was praised for having the qualities of a hero and knew that she would be betraying everything that she wanted to be, and everything that she was already thought to be, if she decided to be selfish because of her personal feelings. So, she put the past out of her mind, and with no regard for how things ended before, or how they could end now, approached Sandra.

"I gotta say, I prefer the purple hair to the pink you had last time." Trisha said, commenting on Sandra's change in appearance. The second she said a word, just like last time, Sandra quickly put her jacket back on.

"Do you ever give up?" Sandra asked.

"There's a big part of me that wished I did, but not usually. You make it really hard to talk to you, ya dig?"

"Could be because I don't have anything to say to you."

Nothing made a college rivalry look more insignificant than having a gun shoved in the face. The usual fear that Trisha felt around her decreased. There was still a fair amount left, but not so much that she couldn't continue talking to the girl.

"The other day when you were out here, you dropped a flyer for some competition coming up."

"You saw that? I knew I lost it. Don't get any ideas; they don't tend to pick people that look like you." Sandra said slyly.

"If you're going to insult me, you're gonna have to do better than another fat joke. I've heard them all, and you tried it last time. Show some originality."

Sandra's face went to that of confusion. "What? I don't care about your muffin body. They wouldn't want you because you're too dark. They probably wouldn't even take me if I wasn't drop dead gorgeous."

"So, that's what you think of yourself. Do you do this kind of thing a lot?"

"I've been modeling since high school. My parents always made sure that my picture was being sent to someone. How do you think I got so much money? My face is a dream come true, honey, and all these curves...breathtaking. This competition will be the easiest thing I've ever done, then my career will launch, and I'll be kissing this dirty city goodbye."

"Seems like you got all of this planned out. I can't even really argue with you. Since you're on your way out, how about telling me what your problem is with me and my friends?"

"You and them just rub me the wrong way, that's all. My friends are always talking about y'all."

"Nice how you get all of your information about us from everyone except us. I'm sure that's reliable." Trisha said. "This is the second time I've seen you here. Who are you waiting for?"

"Someone who obviously isn't coming. This has just been a complete waste of my time. I guess I better get home then." Sandra looked at Trisha and then immediately looked elsewhere. "Stop talking to me."

The pain that Trisha felt from Sandra last time was back, and it was clearer than ever before. Something was being hidden, but she didn't know what, and she didn't want to use her powers. She was already feeling bad about the way she believed she was going to have to use them from now on, if this hero business was going to work. So, she wanted to enjoy the last time she would be able to let it go. Talking like a friend was working perfectly well.

"How about this, since you're not doing anything, why don't you come chill with us? You won't have to be alone and standing in the rain."

Sandra laughed. "That's cute. You can do what you want; I got better things to do with my time."

"At least let us take you there when Nita gets here. It's raining and it will probably pick up soon." Trisha had no idea until now how hard it was to get people to accept help. After a long pause, Sandra accepted the offer and the two waited for Nita to arrive.

Once Nita was there, Trisha walked up to the car with Sandra and asked to take her home. Dominick and Amaya were against the idea, while Nita held no real opinion. Trisha pushed harder, saying that it was important that they show that they can be decent, even to someone that treated them badly. She knew that a lot of how she thought right now was being pushed by her softer side, but she wasn't in the mood to fight against it. She was relieved when Nita approved, and before anyone knew it, the group was on their way.

Plus Size

Deeper than Skin

Chapter 6

Saint Victoria

"You gotta come up with something better." Trisha had began telling herself repeatedly.

Even without her questions of morality, there were other consequences of that night that kept Trisha uneasy. The police had said that they wanted to find the woman that was in the house. Every day, Trisha feared that her home would be raided, and she would be taken in for any number of crimes. She didn't know the law well, but she knew that what she had done was illegal; she knew that she could probably serve time, and she knew what the color of her skin was. It was likely that she would find herself with an even harsher sentence than someone else would, had they been the one to do what she did. Days went by, and then a couple of weeks, and nothing happened. There was no way for her to walk past a police car, or an officer posted in a store, without getting nervous. She didn't even know which ones were at the house that night. Perhaps she passed them by without ever realizing it. There were a couple of times when she would be right next to one, and she had to force her body to stop shaking, force her legs not to run off without her. As two weeks turned into three weeks, her near psychosis decreased drastically, though never fully arrested.

Going to school during that initial period was difficult. She found herself struggling to focus in class, constantly looking at the other students to see if any of them knew her secret. No one ever said anything, but she couldn't help but feel like someone knew something. One thing she noticed was that she had not seen Sandra around since the day she took her home. Her crew of friends were quite prevalent, but not the girl herself. She reasoned in her head that Sandra was probably devoting all her time to getting ready for the competition that was a week away, if she remembered correctly. Even with all the distaste Trisha had for the girl, she hoped that Sandra would win.

"Ho probably got what she deserved." Amaya would say.

"Yeah. Maybe she's pregnant and don't want no one to know. And it probably ain't even Justin's kid." Dominick would add.

"I hope it is. Both of them have it coming." Amaya claimed remorselessly.

Trisha ignored the hurtful comments. In between all of that, she was working to repair her relationship with her mother. Coming home after speaking with the pastor and apologizing immediately did a lot to jump start the process, but Trisha could see her mother's concern every time their eyes met. It reminded her of when her dad died. The bright side of this situation was that her mother would continue to speak to her. Very few things Trisha did resulted in her mother growing distant. They spoke during breakfast and often laughed and joked. Her mother continued to make candid comments about her personal life. There were a lot of passive aggressive jabs about what had happened, but that was to be expected. Once Trisha figured out what she wanted to do with her powers, she sat down and talked it over with Annetta, who still wasn't fully satisfied but could compromise.

"Please run it by me first." Anetta requested. "And don't run into any actively violent encounters. I'm sure plenty of them will escalate, but if it's already a bad situation...you know they're armed, they've already assaulted someone or anything like that...just call the police."

"I can agree to that." Trisha said as she shook her mother's hand.

She met with her pastor regularly, always informing her of what was going on in her personal life. She reassured Pastor Pauline that she was conducting herself appropriately and she was telling the truth. She had taken the advice and given all her problems and concerns over to the Lord. She had not used her powers on anyone during this process. Trisha demonstrated great restraint in curtailing her powers. She decided that there would be no action on her part until she had been adequately prepared. This posture did well to keep her out of trouble, and it made her feel better about the entire ordeal. There was room for her to use her powers for good, and once she got her message, she took it to her pastor.

"I had this dream last night that I was in a garden. There were a bunch of people with me with water and they were looking for flowers. We were surrounded by them, but only I could see that they were dying so I watered them myself and when I couldn't, I asked them to." Trisha explained.

"What do you think that means?" Pastor Pauline asked.

"I think it means people can learn to solve their problems, if someone is there who can point them out." Trisha affirmed.

"Do you think it's from him?" Pastor Pauline asked.

"I do." Trisha answered.

They spoke about it at length, comparing what she was saying to what the bible said, to make sure that Trisha wasn't confusing one message with another. Once they both concluded that this in fact could be the sign Trisha had been waiting for, she left the pastor with her blessing.

She realized that it would take the words from all the people around her to fully grasp what she was supposed to do. Her mother told her that she needed to know the limits of her powers and she had been working to figure them out. She wasn't going to use anyone else as a test subject, so she focused on herself. She dug through her mind to see how deep her powers could go inside someone's head. She uncovered memories that she had long forgotten, tapped into emotions she didn't know how to express and even learned that she could see signals to other parts of the body through the mind like a code. Trisha could tap into and read the code. If she focused, she could read the process of her mind telling her legs to walk, or her hands to clap. The only limit that this power seemed to have was that it was observatory. She could see into the mind, but she could not manipulate it. She even discovered that she could read a mind up to a block away. As for her other ability, it was harder for her to test.

Trisha had consulted her math professor at school once, describing a character she was creating with the ability of kinetic energy manipulation. She used some of her own experiences to lay out what the character could do, in hopes that the professor would be able to tell her how powerful this gift was. This was how she had discovered that she reduced any incoming kinetic energy by half, and increased any outgoing kinetic energy by three times. As for testing the limits of her outward powers, that was no issue. She examined how much she could lift, how hard her punches would be. She tore through trees, with her fists, and almost made it through a brick wall. She could lift her mother effortlessly, but it seemed heavier things like cars would still not make it off the ground...much. When it came to what she could endure, she was simply too afraid to look into that. She struck herself with baseball bats, chairs, a butter knife once. For the most part, they had no effect on her, though the metal chair did leave a slight bruise. However, the more dangerous things like a real knife, she kept away from, and she had no access to a gun to test that theory. She wouldn't be able to pull the trigger anyway.

She even finally took Nita up on her offer to teach her to fight. She planned on engaging specific criminals in fairly controlled environments, but there was no telling what life might throw at her, and she wanted to be as prepared as possible.

"Let me teach you how to throw a real punch. Cause whatever you got going on is depressing." Nita teased.

This activity alone took hours the first day and seemed to need correcting at the beginning of every session. However, it needed less and less correcting as time went on.

"You're lucky you have those powers or else you would've really messed up your hand with your suckish form."

In addition to that, Nita taught her basic stances, a disarming technique and a proper kick. Trisha stated that she wanted to keep learning until she was just as dangerous without powers as she was with them.

Those weeks had been filled with a lot of self-examination and growth, and Trisha was happy for it. Now that she felt better equipped to handle the world, and she was getting over the fear of being hunted by the law, she was ready to move forward with her plan. There was a park in her city called Saint Victoria that she used to frequent as a child. While she no longer visited it as often, it was still quite popular among the rest of the community. It was refreshing to see that, despite the violence and crime that plagued the city, there was a place where that didn't happen. Saint Victoria was notorious for being a place to escape, as if there were some sort of unspoken rule that everyone was to leave their problems outside of its perimeter. That's how Trisha figured out how she was going to help. Just because people didn't bring the issues they had inside of the park, didn't mean they didn't have them. There was no telling how many were wearing false smiles and hiding dark troubles. There would be a need for Trisha to use her powers in an unsanctioned fashion, which was something she was trying to avoid, but the nature of them required that she not wait for permission if she was going to do any good.

She would enter the park, find a specific bench that was closest to the center, and then wait. People were friendly here, with no shame in getting close to one another. Outside the park, it seemed like people were overly sensitive these days, and would go to great lengths to avoid being near each other. Within the territory of Saint Victoria, people would share benches, strike up conversations and act as social as human beings were designed. The bench opened the possibility for the most interaction. She was here mainly to talk, but she kept a mask in her purse just in case she needed to be her alter-ego.

Getting the hang of her routine was tricky at first. Figuring out a person's problem was the easy part. The hard part was starting a conversation and getting it to the issue naturally. That required subtlety that Trisha didn't possess, and at times she would just have to go with a more direct approach. This made for some awkward encounters, but she cared more about addressing the various problems and finding solutions, than she did about how she looked in the eyes of the other person. She told herself that there would be no need for violence if this was her approach, and for the most part there wasn't. But on occasion, she needed to get physical, and thanks to Nita, she was ready for it.

The first time, she found out about a dangerous stalker following one of her unwitting clients. When she discovered this, she didn't need to share any words. What the man looked like, where he lived, and what he had done were all present in the young lady's mind. She found out that he liked to park outside of the lady's house at night and wait for anything to happen. That night, Trisha found the man's house, and waited for him to come outside to begin his procedure. Before he could make it to the car, Trisha got her hands on him. She continued to wear all black, but instead of a pillow case, Nita had bought her a ski mask. It didn't do anything to change the criminal look she was portraying, but it couldn't be helped. She felt the desire to really hurt the man, as his behavior made her sick. After reading his mind, she found that he had perverse intentions if he ever caught the woman alone. This was something that Trisha could not allow to happen, but she still found the difference between what was necessary, and what was self-indulgence.

"I'll remember your face." Trisha asserted. "And I'll be watching you. If you ever lay your hands on her, I"ll know and it won't end well for you."

Then she relieved him of his keys. She spent some time writing warning notes and putting them on the houses in the neighborhood, so that everyone would know. Afterwards, she traveled to the woman's house and left a note on the door, assuring her that there was nothing to worry about anymore. As an added precaution, she left warning notes on the houses in her neighborhood, too.

The second time, she found out a woman was thinking about robbing someone. She had a drug problem and had no money to pay for more. She was getting so desperate that she was going to steal. Trisha knew the nature of things like this in the area she was in, and chances are things would get out of control if this woman went through with it. Either, she would get hurt or she would hurt someone else, and Trisha didn't want either of those two things to happen. So, she tried to have a normal conversation with the woman while they were at the park. She began to discuss the woman's problem, telling her that she noticed her appearance and behavior. It helped her recognize that an issue existed. She then assessed the situation to see if anything she said may have helped. The woman was still very conflicted, so Trisha followed her around that night, once again using what she found in her mind to locate her. Unfortunately, the woman ultimately decided to try something, but Trisha intervened. The woman had a knife that Trisha took from her and then flipped her on her back. That was enough to send the woman running. Later, she returned to the woman's stomping grounds with brochures for various rehabilitation facilities, with numbers attached.

"Anyone can change, but you have to want to." Trisha said out loud.

Finally, she learned of a corrupt landlord that ran a tenement building near the park. He heard complaint after complaint about people living there, sometimes in unsafe conditions, but took his time to change those conditions. He often raised prices of rent illegally, and preyed on some of the helpless women there, threatening eviction if they didn't satisfy him sexually. This was a man who Trisha decided was going to have to pay severely. She went to his building, knocked on his door and waited.

He answered the door angrily. "If this ain't a booty call, you got no business waking me up this late."

"Are you Riley Cruze?" Trisha asked, though she already knew the answer.

"Yeah, so what?" He asked.

Trisha pushed him inside and closed it behind her. Just looking at the way he was living brought into question why he was acting the way he did. Trisha figured that he was exploiting others to better his own life but other than the physical pleasures he was receiving from unwitting victims, there didn't seem to be other benefits. His home was a rathole to say the least, and it seemed to be as messy and unkempt as the man himself. After being pushed, he began to curse and holler at her, accusing her of breaking and entering. Trisha did not care. She took him by his throat and threw him into a wall. Then, she tossed him across the room. As he struggled to get up, she placed her foot on his chest to hold him in place.

"People like you should be dead." Trisha said. She tried to make herself sound as threatening as possible. "That' not really my call to make, but don't think I won't cross that line if I have to." She wouldn't, but Riley didn't have to know that.

By this time, Riley's bravado had vanished, and he was a helpless victim. "What do you want from me?"

"I want you to do your job and fix these people's homes. I know you have no shortage of complaints. I don't care how long it takes. You keep working until it's done. These are things you should have tended to a long time ago. Then, once that's done, I want you to turn yourself over to the police and admit to every vulgar thing you've done."

"Are you serious!? They'll lock me up for the rest of my life if I tell them." Trisha had done such an amazing job of instilling fear in him that he didn't even bother to lie.

"Yet and still, it'll be better than what I'll do to you if I have to come back." Trisha grabbed the man's arm and threatened to break it, but stopped short. "Ya dig?"

These were the unfortunate things that Trisha took upon herself to see to. Learning about all these problems meant that she was becoming part of the issue if they didn't get solved. Some people like the stalker, simply needed a forceful warning, while other people like the landlord needed to feel some of the pain that they caused others. She wished that she could be rational with everyone, but it would be naïve to think that everything would be solved with letters of protest, or reasonable conversation. She wished that it would be this easy to deal with Isabelle Dreyfus, but that was a much more complicated path. If she was going to go after such a high-profile target, she was going to need more than just what she read from her mind, and her strength. That was an issue that she would deal with another time. For now, she was still in the park on the bench.

A child sat next to her, which Trisha liked. Their problems were usually less complicated than others, and this child was no different. She had gotten into an argument with her father. For the last week, she had gotten lazy with her school work, and her grades had begun to reflect this. As a result, her father had relieved her of her game system. The father was a single father and was doing his best to raise her. Looking through the child's memories revealed that he didn't punish her often, even when she did deserve it. Considering this, it came as a shock to the child when the father put his foot down which led to the fight. The child lashed out and said that she hated him, and that was the end of the discussion. At the beginning, Trisha rolled her eyes, certain that this girl was stewing over not being able to play her game. Trisha couldn't imagine saying such a horrific thing to her own mother, but that's when she dug a little deeper into the girl's mind. She didn't care about the game at all. She didn't care about the fight. She was broken up over the fact that she had said what she said to her father.

"You like this park?" Trisha asked.

"Yeah, I guess." The little girl said.

"Me too. I used to come here all the time when I was your age. I don't really come as much anymore, but I still come if I'm feeling sad, or I have a fight with my mom."

"You fight with your mommy?"

"Not often. My mom is like my best friend, but friends fight sometimes. We had one recently, and I said somethings I don't think I should have said."

"Me and my dad had a fight. I said bad stuff too. Now, he won't love me anymore."

"Oh no. That's not true at all." Trisha said. She didn't want to cross any boundaries, but she felt the desire to give the girl a hug. "Mommies and daddies know that children say things they don't mean. That doesn't mean they stop loving us. Talk to your dad and tell him you're sorry. I promise he'll still love you, and before you know it, you won't even be thinking about this anymore. Oh, and keep up with your studies. School is important."

This interaction between child and could-be mentor was a long-forgotten art form nowadays. There were so many twisted people in the world that no one trusted children around adults anymore, unless it was their own child. It was a shame, because it took away from the larger sense of community that people used to share with one another, but situations like this served as a pleasant reminder. The warmness that could be shared between two people, the joy and hope that a child could bring, even in the face of hardship, were both things that Trisha missed. As an adult, and sometimes even earlier than that, people got in their heads that forgiveness was too much of a chore. Once something was said, or done, no matter how trivial, things could never be the same. People lacked the strength to forgive and move on; they invested instead, too much stock in holding grudges. This child reminded Trisha that forgiveness is important and how rare the ability to repair bridges is.

A teenage boy sat down at the bench, who was dealing with a classic case of loyalty to a friend above doing what was right. He was holding onto alcohol for his friend, who had strict parents. He didn't want to be considered uncool, or risk the relationship with his friend, so he agreed to hold onto the contraband, even though he knew it wasn't right. He wanted to tell his friend he couldn't do it. More than that, he wanted to tell his friend that he shouldn't be drinking in the first place, but he couldn't find the courage to do either one. Trisha of course got involved. Once she got the kid talking, it wasn't long before the issue came up. Trisha explained that if he wanted to be a real friend, he needed to confront the other boy. It wouldn't do any good to sit by and watch him ruin his life, especially if it left the possibility for both of them to get in trouble. Trisha told him that he didn't necessarily need to tell anyone, unless his friend didn't stop. For his friend's safety, this boy would need to inform his parents of the drinking problem. At the very least, he would need to get rid of his current stash. Satisfied with the advice, the boy left.

One time a kid was sad cause he couldn't afford anymore dog food to help feed a stray that hung around his home. Trisha left a bag outside of his house with a note attached during the night. As much as she liked fighting crime, doing things like this made her feel good too.

There was a lot to be said about a person who had the strength to mind another person's business. At a point, it was called being nosey, but right before that line was crossed, it was called being responsible. This was yet another thing that people had forgotten about as time went on. Now, half the people were far too private, and the other half were too passive. That bad things that could be avoided were happening on the regular was because no one knew about it. Trisha was starting to realize just how much she was harming other people by sitting on this power of hers for so long. It was enough to have rules. It was enough to only use it so long as it was strictly to find ways to help people. It was unacceptable not to use it at all because she was afraid of getting involved in other people's problems. There would be times when she wouldn't be able to fix it, like when she found out about a man who was struggling with the knowledge that he had HIV. She couldn't cure it, but she could be there if the man needed someone to talk to. The more she did this, the more she discovered the small ways of being a hero. Being a shoulder to cry on was just as important as being a guardian angel in the cover of darkness. It was starting to get late, so Trisha checked her phone. She had spent the better part of the day at this park, sitting on the bench.

At one point, she noticed a group of girls looking at her and laughing with each other. It made her feel self-conscious, but as they were walking away she probed them. If they had problems, she wasn't going to shy away from them. That's how she confirmed what she had already assumed.

'She looks sloppy.'

'Girl that is NOT cute.'

'Nappy head ass.'

The only problems they had was picking who to gossip about. Trisha would not have been surprised if they were friends of Sandra. They didn't know who she was and yet they felt comfortable judging her based solely on what they could see physically. They didn't even have the nerve to say anything to her face. It frustrated Trisha, but she tried to stay focused on the reason she was here. Between talking to other people, and getting lost in her own thoughts, she had completely let time get away from her. That's when she saw Dominic and Amaya walking by.

"Well, don't you two just make the cutest couple?" Trisha asked. Both of them immediately got defensive.

"Gross. Don't even joke like that." Amaya said. She looked at Dominick who didn't seem bothered. "What are you doing out here?"

"A lot of thinking really. You?"

"We just saw a movie, and now we're here to have a bit of fun. Right about now the weirdos start showing up. It's hilarious." Dominick said. "Anyway, we'll see you around."

"Hell no!" Amaya exclaimed. Trisha examined what Amaya had just reacted so strongly to and saw Sandra coming from the opposite direction. She was alone, presenting herself as she always did, except this time her hair was red. "That girl won't give us peace anywhere."

"Not today, alright?" Trisha asked. "She's not bothering us."

"Her face is bothering me." Amaya insisted. "Come on, Dom. We can take care of this real quick."

The two stormed off to confront Sandra, and Trisha followed to hopefully stop any unwanted altercation. Even standing right behind them, she wasn't able to do anything before Amaya started running off at the mouth. Dominick seemed to be doing it too, though not as loudly or severely. Trisha thought for certain that she would have to stand tall the way she did the last time, but that's when she noticed something odd. She could see that Sandra was not defending herself, but she didn't look like a girl who had come under verbal attack. She looked like she was completely detached from the entire ordeal.

"I just want to get by." Sandra said, though she was ignored every time.

"Seriously, just let her pass." Trisha said softly and found that her request also went unheeded.

Sandra quickly balled her hand into a fist, and banged Amaya in the face. The moment caused Trisha to freeze up, not knowing what to do. One look at Dominick reflected a similar mindset. The punch was not enough to incapacitate Amaya, but it did cause her to stumble. In the interim, Trisha hoped that this would be enough to make Amaya leave Sandra alone, but of course it wasn't. Amaya attempted retaliation, but to no avail. Sandra bobbed and weaved around all of Amaya's blows, causing Trisha to reflect on the memory that Sandra was the only one amongst her friends that had been in a fight before. It was clear that Amaya was outmatched, but the continuation was only because of her. Every time Sandra dealt with her, she tried to walk away, but Amaya kept pulling her back in.

Finally, Trisha grabbed hold of herself and got involved. She held Amaya back and apologized to Sandra, who grunted and walked away. Trisha did what she could to avoid all the gazes coming from the others in the park who had seen the whole exchange. While holding onto the girl was effortless, trying to calm her down enough to stop the yelling and swearing proved to be another issue entirely. She enlisted the aid of Dominick, but neither of them were able to get a handle on the girl. It wasn't until Amaya decided on her own to be reasonable, that any sort of progress was made.

"You wanna explain that whole fake tough girl routine?" Trisha asked.

"Hell, you mean fake? She sucker punched me, that's all. 'Course she so sneaky, I shoulda seen it coming. If I had known she was gonna swing, I woulda dropped her."

"I don't know. She kinda whipped your butt." Dominick said.

"Shut up." Amaya snapped.

"Don't talk to him like that, just because you're mad. You could've just let her be on her way. She wasn't doing anything to us." Trisha argued.

"I don't care what she was doing. She hasn't said anything to me about what happened. She thinks she just gonna swoop in and steal what's mine, and then think she's gonna walk like ain't nothing happen? I ain't the one, and someone better tell her."

"Well, I'm telling you. Obviously, both of you are like 'zero and two' when it comes to Sandra. Maybe just lead separate lives. Before today, she hasn't said nothing to y'all except at school." Trisha noticed that Dominick looked down when she said this.

"You a little punk, Trish." Amaya said. "She treats you like crap, your friends like crap, and you don't do anything about it. But you'll come to her rescue. You make us sit in a car with her, like she don't got two legs that work. I see her, it's on sight."

"And what happens when she actually wants to fight you?" Trisha asked. "Today she was just trying to get by you, but next time she might want to hurt you. And she has like a bunch of friends she can get on you. You really want to be dealing with that? What if it happens and I'm not around?"

"Then you'll miss all the fun. Not like you would help anyway."

"I am helping by trying to make sure it doesn't happen again."

Amaya held her face. "Right. Just not when it's happening. I'll remember that for next time." Then she walked off, and Dominick reluctantly followed.

Trisha stared at them in confusion. When Sandra had threatened them at school, it was no chore for her to step in and shut it down. However, this time, it was Sandra who had come under threat, and Trisha was unable to find the will to act. She knew that she had her own qualms with the girl, but there was no question that this situation was not her fault. Amaya was in the wrong, and even though Trisha had found the courage to tell her that, she had not had the courage to take a stand when the fight was happening. That's when she realized that she never actually told Amaya that what she did was wrong. All she did was caution her about the foolish gesture but did not ultimately stand on any sort of moral ground. What she couldn't figure out was why. Despite the good she had accomplished in the park for other people, it was becoming apparent that she was no good at settling disputes in her own back yard. In such a short time, she had accomplished so much. Now, suddenly, it felt like she had accomplished nothing at all.

Plus Size

Chapter 7

Two Worlds

"Sounds like you've been pretty busy." Nita said.

The comment didn't register with Trisha immediately. She was reflecting on the events of the previous day, her conflicting emotions getting the better of her. "What was that?"

"Is it easy? Really wish I could be out there; some light exercise after class would be perfect."

"Light exercise? It's not a game, Nita. Well sometimes it is just some brat you gotta deal with, but other times, it's like a dangerous situation. I had to stop a woman from holding someone up once. You don't want to be in the middle of all of that."

"Trish, are you projecting on me? You can be the reluctant hero all you want. Sign me up. As a matter of fact, call me next time you go. You sit on the bench and handle all the *Trisha's advice after sunset* stuff, and I'll go out in the streets and kick behind. Don't want to spread yourself too thin."

"That's your pitch?" Trisha asked. "I mean, it's not the worst one you could've come up with, but you seem a little too eager to hurt somebody. Anything you want to talk about?"

The two girls laughed at each other and continued to talk. Trisha thanked Nita for the time she put in getting her ready, and they discussed how it was affecting her when she needed to use what she had learned. Trisha went on to say that it made her feel a lot more comfortable if she knew she was about to fight. Even with the limited things she had learned so far, it was monumental in placing her on a pedestal above most of the people she was coming up against. For a moment, she considered telling Nita about the fight in the park, but the time together was filled with positive energy, and she didn't want to ruin it.

After that conversation, Trisha listened to Nita talk about her plans for the next couple of years. The semester had just started, but this was her penultimate. By this time next year, she was going to be transferred to a university. There were a lot of debates about where she wanted to go, as her remarkable performance in her academics and extracurriculars had paid off in the form of scholarships to three different institutions. Trisha was happy for her, but worried how the last year at Dreyfus would be without Nita. On top of that, she wondered what life would be like at whatever university she herself decided to attend. This would be the first time since they met that they would be going separate paths. It had almost happened at the end of high school when Nita was offered a position at Stamford, but it was without scholarship and she lacked the finances to pay for it. So, they both ended up at the same school yet again. This talk that they were having reminded Trisha of how imminent their departure was this time. They would have to begin two completely different walks in life; even a year in advance scared her.

"Once you become Crystal on the big stage, I'm gonna be at your show every day." Nita reassured. "And hey, if I have to punch anyone's teeth out for being like your director, well, then at least I'll know how to fix them."

"How did that even happen? You hate the dentist." Then Trisha returned to her point. "You think I'll be able to balance a life on stage with a life in a mask?"

"It's like I said: famous actress by day, superhero by night. Speaking of which, have you thought of a name yet?"

"I'm not going to have one. It just means that there will be an identity for people to start tracking, and that'll bring a whole bunch of attention I don't want. Beating up a sleazy apartment owner, or would be criminal when you don't have a name is easy. It's not like they can really go to the cops, because they ask questions, and with no name or identity, who they gonna look for? If I had a name though, they would start telling stories, and then I would be on someone's radar."

"But people will still talk. At best, you'll just be a ghost." Nita countered.

"I'd rather be a ghost than a face."

"Can I take the credit then?"

"Stop it." Trisha said.

When the two arrived at school, there was a struggle to find a parking spot, but not nearly as much as the day of the campus festival. When they found one that was open, the two of them spotted another driver that was about to attempt to take it. Trisha sat back as Nita crossed the solid yellow lines painted on the ground to get to the parking spot first. The spot left Trisha far from any of her classrooms. It didn't matter though, as Trisha did not have class today. She simply didn't want to sit in the house alone all day.

The two of them parted ways, and Trisha was left to search for something to do with her time.

Trisha began to wander the campus with no goal in mind, however, she wasn't going to be able to leave until Nita was finished with all of her classes, so she would need to find something to do until then. The student lounge sounded like a good idea, but at this point in the day, none of her friends would have been there yet, and she was not good at making new friends. So, she walked around until she found herself in the arts building. She hadn't been a fan of her director, or the building in general since their unfortunate exchange, but old habits were hard to break. There was no other place on the entire campus that felt as natural as this place anyway.

Since the regular hours were in effect right now, the auditorium was in use, and so Trisha would have to find another place to reside. The building had three floors, all of which she had visited at some point. The third floor was reserved for the visual art students. Their work was displayed on the walls, and their classes were held in the rooms reserved for them. Trisha had spent the least amount of time here during her tenure. Not only did it not relate to any of the classes she was taking, she didn't have any friends in the field either. The second floor was for all the music students, which Trisha loved. She frequented this floor for her coaching lessons. She took pride in her voice, and signed up for every singing course she could. She had spent countless hours in one of the practice rooms, working on vocal exercises and mastering some of the classic movements. Time spent here was surpassed only by the time she spent on the first floor: the crown jewel. Acting classes, productions, stage management, and everything that could be taught about the theatre setting was taught there. She wouldn't even begin to imagine how long she had been there.

While she did not have access to the stage, one of the many classrooms was bound to be open. She intended to find one and settle down with a nice book for the next couple of hours, there was no shortage of them around. During her search, she crossed paths with Theodore Henry, who was rushing to class, folders, and books in hand. His fluster suggested that he needed to get where he was heading urgently, yet the second he saw Trisha, there was a pause. Trisha did not have any classes that he was heading this semester, so with their relationship on thin ice the way that it was, they had no reason to speak or see each other. Now, it seemed like fate was conspiring to put them together.

"Hello, Trisha. How are you?" Professor Henry asked awkwardly.

Trisha held her breath, waiting for something to happen, while simultaneously battling inside herself about whether she should speak. The moment, which likely lasted less than two seconds, seemed to drag on and on, threatening to drive her mad. She could feel the temptation to read his thoughts to find out what was coursing through his jumbled mind. She resisted that urge, so all she had was her own thoughts. She felt anger, sadness, resentment, and even a little bit of hatred that she needed to tame quickly. There was no reason that she should have still been concerned about what had transpired, and yet all the emotions that she had gone through the day it happened felt fresh. Before she had sorted through all her confusing sentiments, the moment was gone, and the professor was on his way. The entire exchange made her incredibly nervous, and she ran into the closest bathroom.

By the time she made her way into a stall, the feeling had subsided, and she was left feeling rather foolish. She hoped that no one had seen her frantic episode just now and reassured herself that she had not seen anyone. As she was getting herself together, she heard something. She had spent a lot of lonely nights in her room, and it had refined her ears to the point that she could tell when she heard crying. She didn't know who it was, but she knew she couldn't leave it unaddressed. She called out, in hopes of getting a response of some kind. There was no answer, just the sound of heartache, so she tried again, and yet there was no answer. Now was the time. She could use her abilities without regret. So, she took a peak into the mind of her mysterious guest, just enough to find out who it was, and the revelation was less than she could have expected.

"Sandra, is that you?"

Still there was silence, and Trisha began to question if she should even proceed. If she was going to try, and have her efforts ignored, then what would be the point? She exited her stall, and washed her hands. While she was drying them, her eyes were fixed on the door. Once she walked through, this situation would be left in the past. She couldn't quite figure out why she didn't want to go the easy way and just search for whatever was plaguing this girl. No one could stop her. She could have all the answers she needed in seconds, but there was a hesitation in her that she couldn't explain. Strangers in the park were one thing, it was likely that she would never know anything was wrong if she didn't read them. But Sandra wasn't a stranger. Trisha shouldn't have had to read anything, because she was willing to help, and she was willing to preserve the integrity of this young woman that she knew very little about. She moved toward the door, her hand pressed against the flat surface, her body and mind having already committed most of her will to leaving. But that small bit of her that couldn't bear to leave anyone behind, held her in place, and drove her to try once more.

"Come on Sandra, I'm really trying here." There was a short pause.

"I never asked you to try." Sandra finally responded.

"Sometimes you should just try because no one else will. Can you open the door, and talk to me?"

There was another moment of silence, longer than any of the previous ones they had shared, and Trisha was certain that their brief discussion had come to an end. Then, she heard the latch of the stall, and the door swung open. Out from the stall, came a vulnerable Sandra. This social icon who ruled the school any other time of the year, who commanded a small battalion of mindless girls to hang onto her every world, who always carried herself as if she stood above all others, was nothing more than a girl in desperate need of help. Her makeup was smeared, and Trisha knew that she had missed the climax of her crying, but that wasn't what caught her attention. This was the first time that Trisha had ever seen her without her trademark leather jacket, and she knew exactly why. Her right arm had been defaced by cut marks, most of which were old, but one, extremely close to the wrist, was fresh.

"Is this what you wanted to see so badly!?" Sandra yelled, holding her arm high in the sky. "Let's hear it. I'm sure you got plenty of jokes you could hit me with. So, come on, it's payback time. It's my own fault for being a bitch. Come on!" Her blue hair was covering one of her eyes, which only made her look more helpless.

"Do you think this is a joke? Because I don't." Trisha said. "How long have you been doing this? Why are you doing this?"

"I wouldn't expect someone like you to understand."

"Try me." Trisha challenged.

"Why would you even care? I'm always mean to you and your friends. I've never said a good thing about any of you. This should be a dream come true for you. I'm sure you were head over heels when Amaya was screaming my head off yesterday. I woulda been."

"Not at all. I tried to stop that before it started."

"No, you didn't. You just got a front row seat. If you had seen me doing that to one of your friends, you would've made a show. But since it was happening to me, you just ignored it. Why are you talking to me and not walking out the door?"

"It's the right thing to do. Is there really a better reason than that? Obviously, you're hurting, so tell me why."

"Right. Guess we'll just pretend what happened yesterday doesn't have anything to do with it. I just wanted to mind my business, and instead I ended up in a fight…again. My knuckles are bruised, and I don't have any time for stuff life that. It's just more that I'm gonna have to cover up."

"She shouldn't have done that. At that point, she was just being a bully. Is that the only thing bothering you? You just haven't seemed like yourself for a while, and honestly, I think I would prefer you being a douchebag than how you've been acting." Trisha admitted.

"What do you think when you look at yourself, like what you look like?" Sandra asked.

Trisha didn't know if the girl was intentionally changing the subject, or going through a roundabout way of answering the question. "No one has ever asked me that before." She started. "And to be honest, I have always been afraid that someone would. I've never told anyone what goes through my head about myself, ya dig?"

"Can you tell me?"

"I can." Trisha replied. "But you have to promise answers to some of my questions."

"Fine." Sandra said.

"Sometimes, I feel invincible. Sometimes I feel like I look good, always have, always will, and no one will be able to stop me. I see how people sexualize my look, I mean people like me have a whole specific category on the internet. I know that people secretly want the dark skin girl, if only for the credit of saying they tamed one." Trisha rolled her eyes.

"I know people want what I have, and I like what I have, and what I've worked at, and when I focus on all of that, I feel like I'm on top of the world. That's when I know that I'm enough, in fact, I'm more than enough. But then there are other times when I go to specific stores to find something in my size, or my clumsiness knocks something, or someone over, or I see a movie with someone who looks like me and its just one long gag." Trisha was becoming more downtrodden.

"Times like that, I feel like I take up too much space. I look in the mirror and see that two people could stand where I stand alone. I try to take pride in my size, and my skin, but the very same people who label me BBW, or Ebony, the very same people who can sexualize me without a second thought, shame me in everyday life. In the streets, I'm too fat. In the streets, I'm too dark. I'm too this, or that. I'm too much. In the real world, I'm too much of an inconvenience. And when I get to thinking like that, my heart starts to break, and I wish that I could shed all of this. I wish that I could be thinner, or lighter. But even then, I wonder if I wish that because it's what I want, or because it's what I've let society tell me I should want." Trisha took a few steps back before she tried again.

"When I go to the gym Saturday mornings, or have vegan Tuesdays, or run a mile every Sunday after church, are these things I do because I take pride in them, because they interest me? Or, somewhere along the way, did I let the world get to me, and I started doing them because they are supposed to fix something that is inherently wrong with me? I love to eat, but a big girl can't love food without it being expected. Some stereotypes I don't fit. I don't sweat easily, I love being physically active, and my butt is big because of my squats, not just because of excess baggage. But the stereotypes I do fit, are not because of my size. How do you combat all these conflicting ideas when the central problem is that the world believes my size is what defines me?"

"Your body can be a prison sometimes." Sandra said. "That's what's bothering me, and what has been bothering me for a long time."

"What would you know about it? You're a supermodel. You're probably the prettiest girl I've ever met. I'm sure you have problems, everyone does, but I don't think I can sympathize with any aesthetic concerns you might have." Trisha asked.

"And why not? You think it's all fun and games looking like this?" Sandra asked. Her tone revealed how offended she was.

"You don't think that I notice that I'm described as sexy, and you're described as good looking for someone your size? I see the bull-crap standards society puts on us, too. I won't act like I know what it's like for you, but don't pretend to know what it's like for me. I got four girls who pretty much follow me everywhere I go, who know everything about my favorite clothing choices, but not the first thing about me. I've got a phone full of numbers of people I'll never talk to, who will never talk to me because I'm not interested in having sex with them." Sandra looked away for a moment and then back at Trisha.

"I see you and Nita, and I see two girls who couldn't be closer if they had the same mother. And it's not because y'all are always together, it's not because you share the same interests. You two have a genuine connection that I don't know how to put into words. I've seen it since I got here. I never knew what that felt like, and the one time I got a chance to find out, I messed it up. You think those girls would bother with me if I didn't look as good as I do? They hang with me because they can roll up to the school in a convertible instead of a bus. It's just clout."

Sandra punched the stall. "Damn it!"

"They're children pretending to be women, the same way I have been pretending all my life. I wish I could decide to dress lazily, or even comfortably and it not be a big deal. No, I won't get chastised for it, but it bothers me that it should even be mentioned. I wish I could talk to a boy without him wondering what it would be like to sleep with me. I wish I could decide to hang with you and your friends without anyone asking why. I hate that when I tell people that I model, they expect such a thing. And I despise, more than anything, that someone like me has a better chance at being Crystal than you, strictly because of what I look like. Yeah, I heard about that. You think if I had half your talent he would've hesitated with me? The odds would've immediately been in my favor the moment the two of us walked into that theatre to audition. So, yes, my body comes with problems of its own. I love to eat too, but I don't eat much in front of people because I want to avoid the jokes where people like you are the punchline."

"If that's the case, then why do you treat us so horribly?" Trisha asked.

"Because you have courage, and I don't. How many people in the world do you think have ever heard me talk like this? You are the second. It's easier to pretend for the sake of having friends, even if they aren't real. It's easier to feel better in my own skin when I can make someone feel worse in theirs. Yeah, I know how to think on a deeper level, but I'm too scared to act on it, and I hate myself for it. I come in here, or wherever I can be alone, to have pity parties, and talk down on myself for acting the way I do, but always know that I'm not going to do anything to change it. Those girls were the first people I met at this school, and it took five minutes to see that they were douchebags, but they accepted me, they liked what I could do for them, so why would I give that up?"

As Sandra continued to talk, her emotions grew further out of control, but just as it seemed like she was about to go into hysteria, she calmed down.

"Every time I'm on a catwalk, trying to get a little bit of money in my pocket, trying to make a name for myself, I'm dying a little bit on the inside, because I don't have the strength to say that I don't want to do it. I've been jealous of you since the day I met you. You literally pick which talent you're going to use each day. I would love to sing like you. I would love to be an actress. I would love the chance to be a marine biologist, or a musician, or a writer, or a mathematician, but I can't. All the time that I could have devoted to learning any of those things, went to learning how to paint my face, walk erotically, be flawless, because it was the easiest path to walk. That's why I'm in this competition now. The money and the career opportunity could set me up, but it's the only chance I have, because being pretty is the only thing I'm good at."

Trisha struggled to find words. She was typically understanding when it came to other people, and had a unique ability to always see the world from someone else's perspective, but never had she misjudged someone so completely.

"Ya know, there are times when I envied you." Trisha finally confessed. "Everything seemed to just fall in place for you, while I had to work for it. Sure, I developed my talents, but I had to work even harder at them to make up for what I looked like. I work insanely hard for things I feel my invested time has earned-"

"While you watch people like me get things you know we don't deserve." Sandra concluded.

"And it impacts every part of life, like you said, right down to romance. People think that when I say I want to find love, I mean that I've never found anyone who likes me before. Plenty of guys have wanted me, but for all the wrong reasons. I was with a boy for six months, dude named Wyatt, who liked me for how I looked, but I had to end it because he *only* liked me for how I looked. My body is part of the package, not the package itself." Trisha bewailed.

"I've been with a guy for the last year, and I don't feel any closer to him now than when we met. Both of us play by the rules of a game we never agreed to, because of things neither of us can control."

Sandra showed her arm again. "If you repeat this to anyone, I'll make your life hell."

Trisha nodded in compliance.

Sandra took a deep breath. "That's what the cutting is, the only way I feel like I can cheat at the game. They would never accept me, my friends, the modeling agencies, the world, as what they believe me to be if they saw my arm. But I wear the jacket, and I use a lot of makeup, to make sure that they continue to use me, and they'll never know. They love me because they think I'm perfect, but that just means they love all the flaws they don't know I have."

"Do you hate yourself so much that you have to cut your arm up every day?" Trisha asked.

"Do you hate yourself that you gotta cut open your heart?" Sandra countered.

"What do you mean?" Trisha asked defensively.

"Why are you friends with someone like Amaya?" Sandra queried. "She's just like me, except she's being real. She means to hurt people, she means to manipulate them. That day you saw me with them, you would've known that's what she was doing if you had bothered to look. Your boy wasn't keeping his mouth shut because I made him feel bad. He was doing it because he's afraid to go against her, and so are you. And it hurts you every day that you let her get away with how she acts. And why? Because it sucks being by yourself. And without Amaya and Dominick, you pretty much would be."

"That what you think is going on?"

"It's what I know. Looking at you is like looking at a mirror, a fun house mirror, but it's a mirror all the same."

Trisha chose to ignore the mean comment. "So, when you win this thing, you'll just spend the rest of your life being miserable?" She thought it was better to change the subject than have the difficult conversation about her passivity.

Sandra took the bait. "Hopefully, one day, I'll be bold enough to be something else. But these opportunities will set me up so that I'll have the time and money to go another way. Right now, this is the only chance I have at any amount of comfort. So much of my life I hate, so much of what I've done makes me disgusted with myself, but I want to change things one day. I gotta get my foot in the door though, and I need the money to take care of myself. My parents messed up their lives, smoked all their savings up, and sold my car just to get what they needed to keep our house. So, I hope it's not the rest of my life, but these are choices I made, so I'm going to be unhappy for a long time. That's why stuff like that fight pisses me off. I really need to win this thing. The arms are easy to hide, but not my hands. If they know that stuff like that happens to me, I'm done."

"You don't have to live like that at all. And you're no one's prisoner. Listen, kick this competition's butt, but don't let it define you. Don't use the past as an excuse to keep doing what you have been doing. I know that's way easier to say than it is to do, but you *can* do it. You just need some real friends who will encourage you, and have your back when you're down....and a positive environment. You're right, Nita and I do have a connection, because we both know how to carry each other when we need to."

"It's been so long, I wouldn't even know what to do with it. I wouldn't know how to treat an actual friend. I've always bought my friends."

"That's the second time I've heard you mention that. What happened?" Trisha asked.

Sandra paused, and wiped a few tears from her eyes. "I was in high school; it was my junior year. I was just figuring out the way people acted, and it was making me really nervous. When I walked in on my crew talking horribly about me, I didn't really know what to do. Those were the only friends I had up until that point, but they didn't even like me. They thought I talked too much, was into nerdy stuff, and called me dumb because my grades were always bad. So, when I met this boy, Allen was his name, I wasn't my best self. He was a loner, mainly because of how other people treated him, and was probably the nicest person I have ever met in my entire life. He always walked me home, called me when I told him I was sad, sat with me at lunch when I was sitting alone, and even tutored me to help me pass. He was doing his absolute best to be my friend, but I wouldn't let him in. I couldn't trust him because of the way my last group of friends had turned out. Then I started modeling. It was small time, but I was making money, so much that when I got my license, I could put up half for a car; my parents put up the other half. So, I bought the convertible. People at the school saw it, and wanted to know how I got it, so I told them. Of course, all the people who talked about me wanted to be cool again, and I missed them. I should've stood up for myself, but I didn't, and I let them back in. They treated Allen like dirt, and he told me that they were no good, but I was too afraid that he was just as phony as they were. I was scared that I would let him in and get hurt, so I picked them over him, and sent him on his way. By the time I realized I chose wrong, he didn't want anything to do with me. I was heartbroken after that. I haven't made a real friend since, figured this is just how I'm meant to live."

"We all regret something." Trisha said. "But like I said, your past doesn't have to define you. I know I sound like a broken record at this point, but if you want a chance to try again, maybe to see what a real friend looks like, come hang with us. We can go to the house, order some food, and just talk. Nita, and Dominick, are really nice people, I promise."

"I'm sure they are, but they probably don't want to see me. No one who actually knows me likes me, and Nita probably isn't my biggest fan right now, Dominick either."

"If I can forgive you, they can too. I think you need this, and I'm willing to try if you are."

Sandra pondered it, but finally gave in. Trisha hugged her and promised that things were going to get better. Then she asked her to meet her at the bus stop after class, and they would go find Nita together. Trisha exited the bathroom and had never felt more like she was living in her purpose than in that moment. Even the time she was starting to invest in the park had not made her feel as fulfilled as this conversation in the bathroom just had. For the first time since she had met Sandra, Trisha could think of her in a positive way.

Chapter 8

Homebound

When Trisha pitched the idea of a night with Sandra to Nita, she knew that her friend would be less than pleased. Of their small group, Nita had the least amount of reason to harbor animosity towards the bully, with almost zero personal involvement. However, Trisha's social circle tended to carry a hive mentality. If one person was bothered, everyone was bothered. Fortunately for Trisha, Nita was the easiest person to start with because she also believed in letting go once the person who had been wronged had moved on. Trisha had been the main target for Sandra since the beginning, and she had the most to look past, but since she was arguing that she could, Nita followed her lead. These types of things made Trisha smile, as she knew how hard it was to get through to Sandra in the first place. She didn't want to compromise her breakthrough by making being around her an unwelcoming environment. There was still Dominick and Amaya that needed to be addressed, but Trisha made a few calls on her own. It was her house, and she was free to have whatever company she wanted to have. Still, she was no fool. After smoothing things over with Nita, the easiest battle was behind them. The harder bouts were on the horizon, and she would have to work overtime to make sure this night succeeded. However, if she could pull it off, a long-term rivalry would at last be put to rest, and Trisha will have made a strong connection. It was one that would certainly be pivotal in travailing the yet arduous journey of growing comfortable in her own skin. She had made tremendous progress even in the last couple of weeks, and the conversation in the bathroom was a huge step, but there was more to be done.

The car ride to the house was easier than Trisha thought. Though Sandra didn't say much, and it was mostly limited to the usual antics between Trisha and Nita, the lack of any hostile interactions was a welcomed relief. The last thing she wanted to do was push anyone further into the muck that she was trying to pull everyone out of. However, even without poor dealings, there was a visible discomfort all over Sandra, but whether it was because she didn't want to be there, or knew that there were others who didn't want her to be there, was a mystery yet to be solved. When they arrived at the house, Trisha sighed at the sight of a vehicle parked directly in front of her home. It was at this moment that she realized she had forgotten one of the most crucial aspects of any black woman's home: the mother. Trisha had taken her problems to her mother on more than just a few occasions, and by now she knew who Sandra was. Trisha had to start devoting all her brain power to figuring out how she was going to make introductions, and keep her mother from saying anything that could be perceived as rude or cut throat. Then she concluded that it was a waste of effort. Her mother was going to say whatever she wanted to say and that was going to be the end of it.

Trisha and Nita both got out of the car, but Sandra stayed put. After noticing this, Trisha signaled for Nita to make her way to the door, while she stayed back to deal with the situation. She had Nita toss her the keys, then climbed back in the car and closed the door. There were still traces of Sandra's episode, and while she had cleaned up a little bit, she had not gotten the chance to fully get herself together.

"I would've gussied up a little more, but the school don't got what I need." Sandra said almost apologetically.

"Don't worry about it. I'm sure I can find you something in the house." Trisha consoled. "You want something more comfortable to wear?"

"I think I'll be fine with my jacket. Besides, it's not like I'll be here long." Sandra said.

Trisha had a tendency to pull this move herself. Agreeing to any social event was the path of least resistance and offered the smallest headache. After that, she would only need to stay for a short time to show she was a team player, and it would likely defuse any attempts at further pressure. She couldn't blame Sandra for doing the same thing she would have done if the roles had been reversed. Yet, she hoped that she would be able to find a way to make Sandra want to stay, so that she could have an opportunity to show her that things can be different in the company of people who care. That's when she caught a glimpse of her mother letting Nita in. Even without looking directly at the door, Trisha felt the lingering gaze her mother gave the car. Had Nita told her who was in it? Did her mother assume it was a boy? Of the two, she couldn't decide which would make for a more awkward encounter.

"So, you ready to go in?" Trisha asked as she took her earrings off.

Sandra stared out of the window for a moment, and placed her hand on her cheek. "This feels like a really bad idea." She adjusted her trademark leather jacket.

"Don't worry. Momma might bite your head off for a little bit, but after that she's an angel; I promise."

"She know 'bout me?" Sandra asked with an innocence Trisha had not experienced until now.

"I tell her everything, so yeah she knows. She's gonna be surprised to see you, but she'll ease up. I got your back, ya dig?" Trisha threw both of her thumbs up in reassurance, and then both the girls were out of the car.

Trisha had met someone whose nerves rivaled her own, yet for the sake of the evening, she could not admit it. The walk from the car to the door was petrifying. She was walking into a gang's neighborhood wearing enemy colors. Trisha had prey with her, to be set upon at any given moment.

She was in the house now, with Sandra, and she had allowed herself to forget about the state of her home. All the boxes, and mess that she had become so accustomed to, that Nita and her friends had grown attached to in a way, was so normal that it didn't register as something that might have needed to be mentioned. She was mortified the second it hit her, and the door slammed shut like a jail cell. She was trapped inside, with a twelve-hour sentence, with an explanation expected. Whatever reason Sandra had to be on edge, was dominated by Trisha's many reasons, the most important at this moment being the pig sty that she had walked a relative stranger into. Now, all those times she had promised herself that she would clean the house, became cruel mockeries. Regret and shame were the daunting giants, taunting her from the impenetrable forcefield of the past. What would she say? Was there anything she could say to justify what Sandra was seeing? As more time went on, hope gushed from her body like blood out of an open wound, and hope was the only thing keeping her on her feet right now.

"This is where you live?" Sandra asked out loud.

Bam! The trigger had been pulled, the shot got off, and the bullet raced through the sky until it found its target in Trisha. A headshot with no chance of survival. How was Trisha to know that the thing that would bring this evening to ruin would be her own obliviousness? How was she to know that the sniper she truly needed to watch out for was in her own camp? It was her job to know. She began to beat herself up, as this was an easily remedied problem if she had just remembered, instead of being caught unawares and being subjected to friendly fire. Now that her life was over, she saw fit to use whatever was left to pray for the soul of Sandra. If her mother caught any sense of an insult from what had just been said, it was an almost mathematical certainty that it would be over for both of them.

"It's way nicer than my spot. Must be cool having so much that you don't even know what to do with it." Sandra said.

What was this? Was this mercy being granted by some guardian angel going unseen by mere mortals? It didn't matter. Sandra had just offered a modicum of hope that Trisha had been in desperate need of, and she was not about to squander this gift. She needed to gather her wits, and get her head back in the game so that she could take control of this situation before it spiraled beyond her influence. Yet, she remembered that she had not been given the reigns yet. Her opportunity to take control had been in the beginning when she walked in, but she froze and allowed someone else to speak first. She let Sandra take the ball, and after her statement, it had been thrown into the air. Trisha wanted to go for it, but her mother was taller than she was.

"So you're just a comedian, huh?" Annetta asked.

The beginning of the end. It had in fact been perceived as an insult, and everyone in the room was sorely out of their depth when it came to facing off against the mother. To add to this already impossibly uphill battle, Annetta had home field advantage. She could say anything she wanted, and if things didn't go her way, she could banish everyone present to the outside world where further battle would be impossible. Trisha's mind scrambled for a way to deescalate the situation before it turned into a slaughter of a young woman who never knew what was coming. All the preparation in the world could not have readied anyone for the raging beast they would have to quell if they got off on the wrong foot. The creature had been awoken from its slumber, ready to feast and Sandra stood alone in a damp cave with an extremely dim torch. Resistance was futile.

"Oh...no...I wasn't...I mean I...I didn't mean...I was just..." Sandra stumbled over her words like a blind man on an obstacle course.

'Wave the white flag' was the sentiment that kept repeating in Trisha's head. The fight was lost, the hunt secured, but perhaps there was a way to appease the hunter. With each incomplete and incoherent sentence that escaped the mouth of the victim, she was falling further into the trap. Trisha didn't know whether to run out of the house, find solace in the basement, or try to stand in between her mother and the girl. What she did know, was that if she chose solidarity, she would be facing the same consequence that Sandra was about to be exposed to. It was merely a question of whether she was ready to lay down her life with the girl who had not a single kind word to say about her even a day prior. The decision was made, and Trisha moved to stand up for Sandra, her heart rate equaling a metronome at full speed. Now, she needed to find something to say without falling all over her words.

"I'm just kidding." Annetta said. "Thanks. We've been saying we were going to take care of this for years now, but there's always an excuse. Can't you just see the excitement on my face?"

If she had ever doubted her self-control before, Trisha needn't do it any longer. The fact that she just resisted the urge to fall over in sheer relief spoke volumes, and she would be using this example to motivate herself for years to come. Starting off with a joke was a great way to ease tension, and the sound of a few giggles coming from Sandra, Nita, and Annetta gave her the kind of feeling she imagined the Israelites would have had when they saw manna falling from the heavens. She was so focused on saving the night, that she almost lost it. Now she could put all her efforts into enhancing it.

"Me and Trisha talk a lot. I didn't like you much, but I didn't raise a fool. If you're here, then I know that Trisha has made some intelligent decisions leading you here. So, if she don't got a problem, I don't got one either."

'I love my mom.' Trisha thought to herself.

Annetta declared that she was going to the kitchen to fetch them some drinks, and before anyone knew it, the three girls stood alone with each other.

"So, is anyone else sweating? 'Cause I feel like I need to change my shirt." Nita asked.

"Who are you telling?" Trisha asked. "I thought she was about to go off." Then she turned to Sandra. "I had a feeling that the real you wasn't as bad as you like to make people think. My mother is a harsh judge of character, if she felt anything bad coming off you, she would've said so just now. You don't even know how good you got it for real. All you gotta do is not mess it up."

"Is that your way of giving a motivational speech? 'Cause I gotta tell ya, it could use some work." Sandra said. "Wait, uh...is that okay? I wasn't trying to come at you or anything? I just...damn. I'm sorry."

"Relax. I've got a thick skin. If I can shake off all the other trash you've thrown my way when you were trying to hurt me, I can handle an innocent little joke. And it's cool; I'm not Braveheart."

"Y'all done?" Nita asked. "Cause I'm really hungry and I would appreciate it if we could get some food. You got any sandwich stuff?"

"Nah, but I'm sure we can get something together." Trisha answered.

"I got a few bucks. I can order us a couple of pies." Sandra said.

"Please tell me you don't mean pizza." Trisha said nervously.

"Yeah...why?" Sandra asked puzzled.

"You done messed up now." Nita said.

Out from the kitchen ran Annetta. She had one glass in her hand which she promptly put down in the first available space she could find and then she walked up to Sandra directly. If it had been anyone else, it would have been a hilarious sight, as she stood only five feet and Sandra boasted six.

"It's called a pizza! Pies are totally different things. Who even does that? You don't refer to corn as spinach and expect everyone to know what you're talking about. So why would we do that with pizza!? Geez, don't mind me, but seriously...it's weird. No one else thinks that's weird?"

"I think you're alone on this one." Trisha said.

Annetta returned to her previous activities while Sandra took out her phone to call the closest pizza restaurant. Trisha told her that she needed to check to make sure that they delivered to her house, but was surprised to see how well Sandra knew the area. She didn't even have to search for the number. She listened to Sandra on the phone. It was strange hearing the contrast in the many depictions of this girl. One was a nervous wreck who couldn't form a complete sentence, one was a cruel sadist who lived only to see other people suffer, one was an insecure girl who was only looking for an escape and this one was a confident strong individual convinced that she ruled the world. Even in something as mundane as this, Sandra showed her range. She enunciated each word clearly, ending every sentence with a hint of authority, and padding everything with years of practice. Trisha was saddened to realize that she couldn't even order for herself this smoothly. Four pizzas were ordered, one with cheese, one with pepperoni, one with sausage, and one vegetable. She assumed that the range was an attempt to cover the interests of everyone, though she wondered why Sandra didn't ask everyone else so that she could be sure. Trisha attributed it to her being used to running her own crew. She didn't imagine that there was much of a democratic vibe.

"She's got great taste." Nita said.

"She ordered swine, but I guess I can let it slide." Trisha responded.

After the order was done, the three girls went to the basement, with Trisha leading the way. Given the precarious state of the rest of the house, it was reasonable to assume that the basement would be in the worst condition of all. It was the first line of defense when it came to storage, and the fact that the rest of the house had fallen victim to it meant that the basement was too small. However, Trisha and her mother were not like other families. This basement was the only room in the entire house that was completely taken care of. Not a single box was seen, there was a couch beautifully decorated, a couple of air mattresses folded next to it, and an entertainment display in front of it complete with a television, a game system, a host of movies ranging from kid friendly cartoons to violent gore fests unsuitable for anyone. The rest of the basement included a bathroom, and a laundry room. Nita, feeling right at home, dove onto the couch, while Sandra stood in a corner waiting for something to happen. Trisha assured her that it was okay to get comfortable, but she received the adjustment of the trademark leather jacket as a response.

"Just watch your step. We keep the cat down here, and she tends to run wild." Trisha said.

"You have a cat?" Sandra asked.

"Absolutely not. My dad had a cat and he left her to me. I always wanted a dog, but momma said one pet was enough, so until I get out of here, I'll have to settle for Rocket."

"So, what's on the activities list?" Nita asked.

"I don't know actually." Trisha answered. "I thought they would be here by now. I guess we can watch something while we wait."

"You got 'Die Another Day'?" Sandra asked.

"What do you know about James Bond? I wouldn't take you as the type to watch movies like that." Trisha said.

"Are you kidding? I love all his movies. Usually I go for Noir films, but a nice lighthearted spy movie is cool too. What do *you* know about James Bond?" Sandra shot back.

"Other than a game he had a long time ago, not a thing. I don't watch a whole lot of movies, unless someone drags me to one, and I'll watch any musical, but I'm a book person. I'd rather read all day than watch tv all day."

"I never picked up reading the way I wanted to, but I'm a fiend for mystery novels. I'll tear through one of those." Sandra said.

"You gotta be dead inside, Trish." Nita interrupted. "How can you not like the movie going experience? All the posters of what's out, and what's coming out, meeting in a room with complete strangers that have gathered with one singular purpose, the ambiance. Watching previews is great just because everyone becomes a critic, and then the movie itself is almost interactive. If you have the right audience, it's an experience you just don't get reading books, and you know I love a good book."

"I don't think Ebony counts." Sandra countered.

"Ah, with the jokes. That's cool. Imma let that one go." Nita said.

Trisha returned the conversation to the original point. "My mom is a huge Bond fan though, so I'm sure it's around here somewhere if you want to look for it."

"You are tripping. I'm not going through your ma's stuff." Sandra said as a matter of fact.

"Okay good point. I'll do it then." Trisha said.

Yet another surprise that she would not have believed if she had not been present to witness it. Since she didn't watch a lot of movies on her own accord, besides the Disney films, and fifty shades series, she didn't know about trends, and what everyone thought was great or terrible, or what movies were considered things that had to be viewed at least once. However, she did know enough that she thought she could make a few general assumptions, especially when it came to things like James Bond and girls like Sandra. It excited her. What other secrets was she going to discover as the evening went on? That's when she remembered that she needed to make sure Sandra had every reason to stay, at least long enough to feel like it was something she could benefit from doing again.

As she looked through the movies, she thanked her mother silently for being such a fan. It was easy to find the collection of movies because they were all together. Everything else sat on the shelf in no particular order, and finding any one movie could be an adventure, but not the Bond films. Trisha couldn't believe there were so many, and found herself hoping that when she finally got herself a boyfriend again, he wouldn't be into them. If she had to sit through this many movies about the same guy, everyone would be attending her funeral far earlier than they had expected. She noticed however, as she went through them, that she did not see the one that Sandra had mentioned. She had a habit of overlooking things though, so she went through them again, slower. The same result. So, she tried a third and final time, but to no avail. This revelation was even more shocking than finding out that Sandra liked these movies. If there was a Bond film out there, her mother had it. The only explanation was that Sandra got the title wrong.

"I don't see that one. You got the right name?"

"Yeah. If she don't got it, I'm not surprised. A lot of people say it's the worst one, but it's my favorite."

"Why?" Trisha asked.

"Because everyone else hates it." Sandra responded. "I don't know. I guess I'm just wired that way."

"So...you're a hater." Nita said. "I always knew it."

"Is that your payback?" Sandra asked.

In that instant, Trisha heard the basement door open, and time froze. The moment of confrontation was at hand, and there was no telling what was about to happen. The feelings that she had been experiencing when she first walked through the door were returning to her, as her entire body fell back into its base fight or flight mode. Once again, the past began to haunt her. Would it have been better for her to just tell everyone exactly what the situation was? Would it have aided in mending fences, or would it have just ensured that this night never happened? Trisha was shrinking back into herself, her sure footing collapsing under the weight of self-doubt. It only intensified when Dominick and Amaya showed their faces. They were smiling, until they reached the bottom of the steps and ran directly into Sandra.

A standoff yet again. Last time all of them stood in the same area, Sandra was the enemy and Trisha was going against her. Now, Sandra was an ally, invited by Trisha herself. Trisha was unsure how to proceed. She knew that she needed to avoid making the same mistake she made last time, and take control of this situation before someone else did. She needed to speak first and secure dominance, because once someone else took that from her, she would be on the defensive again. She stepped forward, ready to assert her power, but her mind was still searching for the right words to say.

"What the hell, Trish." Amaya said.

Too late.

"So, were you gonna tell us about this or nah? 'Cause like, if you were gonna bring another girl, you could at least have gotten one I can smash." Dominick said.

"You're revolting." Sandra said.

"Say it to my face." Dominick dared.

"And dumb apparently." Sandra quipped.

Trisha was at a loss. Where did that random burst of cruelty come from in Dominick? It wasn't unlike him to say out of pocket things, but he always followed Amaya's lead. Was he so comfortable with her around that he could now start things on his own? It wasn't going to make things any easier and Trisha knew it.

At school where it was neutral, victors were decided by who stood stronger. However, here, the company that frequented the house had the most power. Trisha could see that Sandra, being the only one with no strong positive relationships, no crew to back her up, and no field advantage, was completely at the mercy of Dominick and Amaya, though she wasn't going to show it intentionally. Trisha needed to step in, and even though she now was tasked with responding instead of declaring, she could still fight her way back into a position of power. After all, the ultimate home field advantage belonged to her.

"Look, it's kind of a long story that I'll tell you later. I just thought she could use a friend, ya dig?"

"That's bull." Amaya stated. "I'm not about to sit here all night with her. Tell her to leave."

"What? No." Trisha said softly.

"It's fine. I knew this was a dumb idea. That's what I get anyway." Sandra said, as her bully persona began to take over.

"We not at school, ho!" Amaya yelled. "I'll beat you down right here if you come at me again. Don't nobody want your dirty ass here anyway."

"Bet. 'Cause that worked out so well for you last time." Sandra proclaimed.

"Can we calm down? I was just trying to get us all in a room, so we could get to know each other." Trisha said. She was ignored by everyone except one.

"I know everything I need to know." Amaya said.

Everything was out of Trisha's hands now, and the only way she was going to get control back was to do something drastic. She ran up the steps and closed the basement door, hoping to keep her mother from hearing the altercation that was growing louder by the second. They were cursing and threatening each other, and the only thing stopping them from outright fighting was Nita who jumped in between them and was doing her best to hold them both at bay. Even though she was able to break up a fight, Trisha wasn't confident in Nita's ability to keep one from happening completely. So, she decided that it was time for her to make her move, if one was going to be made. She jumped down the steps and shoved Sandra up against the wall. Her friend Nita followed her lead and restrained Amaya. Dominick tried to intervene, but Trisha shut down his advance with a cold look.

"Look, let me tell y'all something; I'm not feeling the nonsense tonight." Trisha said. "Sandra, I want you to be here, but you gotta leave that 'hood-rat' at the door." Then she turned to Amaya. "And you don't freaking live here. So, if you think you're gonna come in here and start stuff just because you don't like her…that's dead. I should've said this to you at the park. If it's so bad between y'all that you can't even sit in the same room without wanting to kill each other, then I guess y'all can both leave. However, I'm not about to sit here and choose who gets to stay and who's gotta leave because y'all wanna be immature. You're better than that. All of us are. We been in college acting like kids for way too long, and I'm not with it anymore!"

"Whatever. You got any food?" Amaya asked. Nita let her go after being certain that she could be trusted.

"We got some coming. In the meantime, I thought it would do us all some good if we talk to each other, and figure some things out. Confession hour is what I'm thinking." Trisha declared.

"Seriously?" Dominick sighed. "Those things never go well for me."

"First time for everything, come on. You and Amaya can gossip and whatever else later. Let's do something constructive." Trisha said.

"I'm game." Nita agreed.

"You're actually a lot stronger than I thought you would be." Sandra confessed.

"Yeah well, I eat a lot of protein." Trisha replied. Then she let Sandra go.

She left their company for a minute to go to the laundry room. Her mother had a small assortment of covers and blankets. Some of them were strictly for decoration, but others were for personal use. She grabbed five of them and returned to the others. She made sure to keep them folded, and set them up in a circle, asking each one of them to sit on one. She told them all to leave the blue one untouched, as that was for her alone. Her friend Nita requested the black and yellow Steelers blanket. Once they were all sitting in the circle, she explained the rules for Sandra.

The idea was that everyone would go around the circle and confess something to every individual in the circle. This was a chance to say whatever they needed to say, but they were not allowed to be rude about it. After someone made their confession, the person they confessed to was then permitted to respond to the confession and could either confess in response or move on. It took away the need for secrets and did well to help people sort their problems out in a controlled environment without having to resort to less rational means such as fighting. Trisha noticed Amaya and Dominick rolling their eyes, upset that they would even have to hear the instructions again, but she was more concerned with the collective whole, and everyone present needed to know how this worked.

Now that the stage was set, Trisha could take a minute to breathe. She had been on edge since the beginning. Telling Nita was the first, and then the encounter with her mother, and finally the near fight that had taken place. But now, all of that was behind everyone. The only thing left to do now was what Trisha had intended to do from the very beginning. She was content with how she handled the situation and was also a little astonished that she was able to put her foot down in such a way, even against her friends. Times like this reminded her that it was sometimes more difficult to fight friends than it was to fight enemies. But, the skirmish had been won, and now the war was entering its climatic battle upon the hill. There was no telling what revelations would come to light when the confessions began.

Chapter 9

Confession Hour

The history of the Confession Hour was not an intricate one, but it was an interesting one. Trisha and her close friends now treated it like a tradition, but there was a time when it did not exist at all. When the college life first started, Trisha allowed herself to be dragged to every party imaginable by Amaya. There were times when she didn't want to go, but her friend was quite insistent. Most of the parties went the same way, with loud music, drinking, smoking and a lot of gossip. Sometimes they would get out of hand, but usually they remained contained. Trisha didn't find too much enjoyment at these parties since the people did not interest her. She kept to herself, preferring not to engage in their activities. She never smoked a day in her life, and when she occasionally drank, it was a small amount: not enough to forget her own name unlike the others. As a result, she went out less.

However, her friend Amaya wanted her around, so she began to host get-togethers of her own. Because this guaranteed that her closest friends would be there, Trisha didn't mind going, and with Nita there, and the people she began meeting at the college, the lunacy that had become a staple of their endeavors became less frequent and then discontinued completely. These gatherings became more like social kickbacks. Trisha would never forget the day Amaya decided that she wanted to liven things up and had everyone play Truth or Dare. It descended into chaos quickly. The dares went from goofy, to sexual, and Trisha was far beyond anything she wanted to be a part of. She left with Nita and didn't look back. To this very day, she still heard about some of the things that happened that night, including the breaking of one of the toilets.

When it was Trisha's turn to host something, the idea of Truth or Dare came up again.

"Look. Ya'll not turning this into whatever it was last time." She said.

To quell this fear, she asked why there wasn't a version of the game that only involved admitting truths to people. Everyone agreed to give this method a chance, and soon, people were saying outlandish things to each other. It wasn't the truth, and everyone knew it, but that became the fun of it. Whenever Trisha was with the crew, that game was played at some point and it became known as the Truth Hour. The word confession was introduced when her friend Ace used it as an excuse to admit his attraction to one of the other girls. Trisha asked if anyone else wanted to confess anything, and thus confession hour was birthed.

Recently, within the last year, they played late into the night, and the confessions went from jokes to emotional vulnerability. People took it seriously, to the point where some were driven to tears. The group that Trisha now frequented was born that night. It was a night that Trisha would continue to reflect on for dire reasons. Edward had been there that night, and while everyone poured their hearts out, he remained silent. Trisha often wondered why he didn't say anything. Did he not feel safe? Even while everyone was showing their cards, did he not trust them? It wasn't long after that day that he committed the wretched act. But why didn't he reach out? Nevertheless, Trisha saw how the Confession Hour could be used as a therapeutic device instead of a running gag. Whenever two or more people were at odds, there was a confession hour. Whenever someone was struggling emotionally, and they needed support, there was a confession hour. And now, in the face of her persecutor and friends, there would be a confession hour.

Trisha looked around the small circle that she had formed, anxious to find out who was going to share first, but there didn't seem to be any volunteers. So, she did her best to move things along by first addressing Sandra.

"So, I'm guessing that since you know how this works, you know that everyone probably has something to say to you, right?" Trisha said in as nice a voice as possible.

"I don't care. I promise you; I've heard worse." Sandra replied.

Trisha needed to get her back into the good mood that she was in before the drama was introduced. "I think we'll have Nita start first, because I'm sure she'll be sensitive, and she's the fastest."

"What's that mean?" Sandra asked.

"Dom, you're shallow. Amaya, you feed off drama. Trisha, you need to believe in yourself more. Sandra, stop being a douchebag, and we'll actually like you." Nita said.

"Uh, that's what I mean." Trisha said, hoping that Sandra would quickly adapt to how Nita carried herself. It appeared that Nita always had new criticisms.

"What do you mean I'm shallow?" Dominick asked. Amaya raised concerns about her evaluation as well, but Nita said that she would go into greater detail later. There were more important discussions to be had.

"And how come you don't ever tell us any of your deep dark secrets? Always got something to say about us, but you never tell us anything about you that we don't know. At least, nothing interesting." Amaya complained.

"Well, most of my secrets you know." Nita said to Amaya. "As for everyone else, I like to be private." Nita said with a smile, showing off her dimples in full.

"You mean secretive." Amaya declared.

"No, I mean private." Nita corrected.

"Well, that was relatively harmless. Who's next?" Trisha asked.

"Guess I'll go." Dominick said. "Sandra, you're an asshole. I don't even know why you bother coming anywhere near us if all you're gonna do is treat us like crap. I already know I'm fat or whatever, without you having to come tell me. I'm not dumb, and I'm not blind. And what you did to Amaya was messed up, and I can't believe you walk around like it's all cool. You just lucky Trisha is my friend, or we wouldn't even be talking right now." He neglected to say anything to anyone else, which Trisha figured was going to happen. She could see Sandra doing her best to keep her composure. The part that wanted to lash out was being held back, but it was unclear how long it would last. Trisha was second guessing the decision to have this Confession Hour. There were perhaps too many potent feelings for it to go over smoothly, but before she knew it, it was moving on.

"Me and Amaya got our own beef but stop acting like what I said to you was out of the blue. Y'all started it; I just clapped back." Sandra argued.

"Anyone wanna clue me in?" Trisha asked.

"Your so-called friends ain't tell you about everything that happened that day on campus. And, I guess you were so caught up trying to be their enablers that you never thought about anything else!" Sandra said with righteous fury. "I was with my friends and Amaya ran into me. I would've snapped on her, but I had more important things to think about, so I kept walking. She wanted to turn nothing into something and came at me. Of course, her cheerleader Dominick had to get involved, so I faded them both.

Guess your boy is a bigger punk than I thought 'cause he caught an attitude. Then he kept acting like a cry baby when you showed up. I'm thinking it 'cause he knew you was gonna assume what happened. Amaya wasn't gonna set nothing straight and he don't got a mind of his own."

Trisha had reason to doubt this version of events, but she had to be honest with herself. She hadn't searched Sandra extensively during the encounter, and there could in fact have been more to the story. She used her powers and confirmed that Sandra's story was accurate. Feeling like a fool, she offered an apology.

"Oh please. You're gonna believe her just 'cause she said it?" Amaya asked.

Nita interrupted Amaya. "Don't bother; she knows..." She looked at Trisha. "...trust me."

"You know what? I've done a bunch of petty stuff to you, but I'm not gonna sit here and get trashed for something I didn't do." Sandra declared.

"Well, that answers one thing. We still don't know why there's this constant bickering between them though. She never trusted me with that much. What happened?" Nita asked.

"Justin happened." Dominick said.

"Justin Howard?" Nita asked. "I thought he cheated on Amaya."

"He did." Amaya said angrily. "I caught him with this heffer, and he said that he wanted to try other things. I at least thought that she had a little bit of self-respect and would leave him once he insulted her like that, but they still smashing."

"That true?" Nita asked. Her blood was boiling. "You did my sis dirty like that!?"

"Most of it." Sandra answered. She addressed Amaya. "When I met Justin, I didn't know that he was with you; I swear I didn't. He doesn't go to the school, and we never talk to each other, so how was I supposed to know you even knew him? I found out the same time you did. And the only reason I'm still with him, is because he came back and apologized, and said that he wasn't 'that guy' and he's been proving it ever since. I'm sorry that happened to you. I'm sorry he did that to you, honestly. But what we have now, really don't got nothing to do with what y'all had then."

"Are you serious!?" Amaya exclaimed. "So, you really think there's nothing wrong with that? Shouldn't be surprised. You can't even keep your legs closed, so you'll just take whoever is giving it, huh?"

"Screw you. Just cause you gotta mark someone for life doesn't mean I have to. Sometimes you just gotta show someone that you believe they can change, especially these dudes out here." Sandra stated. Even Trisha was impressed that she didn't lose control right then.

"Okay that's enough." Trisha said. "Here's something for you. It was almost half a year ago at this point. If you're never going to be friends with her, then fine, but let it go. You disappeared on us for like the entire summer, over a boy you were with for two months. And you're still bitter about it for what? Nothing is gonna change. Stop acting like Sandra is the sole source of your pain. Has she done some messed up things? Of course, to all of us. But none of us are all that innocent either. We've all done something petty at one point or another. And carrying each other's grudges is just a way to fuel more hate. Hey, Dom. Did she steal *your* boyfriend? Oh, no? Then stop cheerleading. She and her friends came at your weight a couple of weeks ago. That was wrong for sure but get over it. She's said a lot of awful stuff to me, and you don't see me whining about it. Besides, look around you. I don't see any of her other friends here. None of them seem to give a crap about any of us, but Sandra is here, trying to be a little different. It's already gonna be hard enough, considering everything she said and did. She doesn't need to keep being insulted and talked down on."

"I...well actually...that makes a little bit of sense." Dominick said.

"For real?" Amaya asked.

"Look, I'm sorry." Sandra said. "Like really sorry. I know I'm a jerk, but Trisha is so sweet and kind, she makes me feel like I can be a better person. Where I grew up, you couldn't be second best. There wasn't any room to come in second place or be anything other than the hottest thing around. So, that's what I try to do. Whatever people think is cool, or attractive, I become that. And, I hate being alone, so when I found people who would hang with me, I did whatever I could to make them happy. To be honest, not being in control, or being less than the best, it scares me. I know one day I'm gonna run into someone who looks cuter than me, or have this game mastered, and I'm terrified. Trisha makes me feel like I don't have to be afraid. You got a great friend."

"Of course, we do. That's why we put up with that annoying laugh she has." Nita said.

"Bite me." Trisha said.

Trisha laughed after she said it, which proved Nita's point, nasally complete with a snort, and when she caught her breath, a volumetric screech similar to that of a banshee. She was going to say something else, but she wasn't able to, because of Dominick.

"You know what, Trisha is right. I don't like the way I look…most of the time. And I was blaming you for making me feel that way because it was easy, but it was only one time. I know most of your beef is with Trisha. How I feel about myself is my business, and it's up to me to deal with it myself and build up my own image. I can get help from other people, but I have to do most of it myself. So, if you will try to be nicer to me, and my friends, I'll do my best to let go of what happened."

"That was surprisingly mature." Trisha said. It warmed her heart to see some progress being made, even if it was limited.

"Oh please. Obviously, he's just riding your wave." Amaya accused. "It's better when he listens to me cause I actually make sense."

"Quiet." Trisha said.

"I think we haven't been giving Sandra enough credit." Nita said. "I mean, which of us really knows anything about her life, or how easy or hard things might have been for her?"

"What is that supposed to mean?" Amaya asked. "When would things be hard for her? She got her own car, a nice one. She's always had money, great clothes, guys all over her, miss popular. Everyone thinks she's gorgeous, perfect and rich. People like her don't have problems; they make up problems to make themselves feel important. She don't gotta deal with nothing real."

"Is that really what you think? Guess you've forgotten, huh?" Nita asked. "Well, I never forgot. We had money, dope clothes, hottest albums, huge TVs, plenty of friends, the whole thing. We were the only ones in high school whose parents took them out of town for every single holiday, even the minor ones. We were the only ones who had ever left the country before, Amaya. And what did that actually mean? What did it mean when ma would come home drunk off her behind, and dad was up all night trying to calm her down? What was the point when she was beating us senseless for nothing, or humiliating our own father in front of us? 'Cause I remember being angry. I remember not caring about any of that stuff. Vacations weren't gifts; they were curses because it meant that there was no way we were going to get away from her. And both of us were happy the day the divorce was finalized. Then what happened? Depression, anger, abandonment issues, an empty hole where mom should've been, that no material possession or social standing at school could have possibly filled. You think having money fixed our issues, or the fact that that wicked woman ran off with all of it meant that the suddenly our issues were just starting?"

"Your mother took all your money?" Sandra asked.

"Pretty much every cent, because dad messed up one time and stepped out. You should've seen her. She milked the hell out of it, claiming that all of her behavior was a result of the depression he threw her in. He made this mistake before we were even born and she never mentioned it until it was time to settle. Dad was very open about his mistake our whole lives, always asking us not to take things for granted...praising this woman for her decision to forgive him. My whole life I never heard him say a bad thing about her. She talked about him like he was the devil, but not him. He stayed a man, and she used it to bring him down. You remember how you dealt with all of that, Amaya?"

"Does that really matter?" Amaya asked.

"How did you deal with it!?"

"Fine! I slept around, a lot. I slept with anyone who would, girls, boys, it didn't matter to me. I treated my body like it was an All You Can Eat buffet. Is that what you want to hear? I turned into a nympho." Amaya admitted.

"That's right. And I never dogged on you for it. I never called you a ho or tried to belittle you; I just tried to help because I knew you understood something not a lot of people could ever understand: that having money don't fix nothing. You know how I dealt with it? You remember. I tried dancing, fell in love with it, but it wasn't enough. So, I was just like Sandra. Mean spirited, flaunting my belongings around. I made sure everyone knew I was better than them; I made them believe that nothing bothered me, and if anyone was a threat to me, I tore them down. How many times did you see me make someone cry? And if words didn't do it, what came next? People got hurt. You think she's bad because she got together with a boy you used to like? We changed schools three times because of me, and it wasn't cause of something I said. So don't act like she's not allowed to have problems. And definitely don't pretend I wasn't worse than she was."

"My parents have a lot of problems too." Sandra said. "It sucks."

"I know it does." Nita said. "And I could tell from the first time I met you that you were dealing with something, no matter what it was. That's why when Trisha told me about this, I was so quick to agree, because you need this. At the same time, I knew that you couldn't be forced into anything. Circumstances have led you to build up walls, the same way I did. Trisha was always the one who knew how to get through barriers so I never even tried to talk to you. I'm sorry for that."

"Wait. You're apologizing to me?" Sandra asked, bewildered.

"Like Trisha said, we've all done things we shouldn't have done, or haven't done things that we should've done." Nita explained.

"I mean…I guess I accept. I don't think you did anything wrong. You're being nicer to me than I would be if I was you."

"Doesn't matter what another person would do." Trisha interjected. "Only you are responsible for your actions. So, when you get a chance to help someone and you don't, even if they wouldn't have helped if it was you, it is still up to you to answer for it. And sometimes, doing things like that helps someone to see something that they wouldn't have seen otherwise. I mean, you're here right now, Sandra. You wouldn't be if I hadn't tried to talk to you by my church, or in the bathroom. I know that you wouldn't have done the same, but that's because you don't expect anything from anyone. Your heart is not as black as you have people believing. In fact, it's probably made of gold. It's covered in dirt, slime, and a tangled web of lies, but once you get past all of that, I know it's made of gold."

"Right. When she ain't beating people up." Amaya snapped.

"You started that fight." Trisha corrected. "Are you mad that it happened, or are you mad that you lost?"

"I know I'm mad I messed up my hands. I got some stuff coming up and it's already a pain how much makeup I have to use." Sandra said. She wasn't getting a response from Amaya, so she turned to Nita. "Do you uh…still dance?"

"As much as I can. Usually, I use it as a warm up before I start my exercises."

"Do you think you could show me sometime? I don't dance, but I like watching it."

"What? I'll show you right now." Nita said.

Now Trisha was very intrigued. She knew that her friend danced, and saw bits and pieces when she walked in on it by accident, but she never saw her from start to finish. She was just as excited to see a performance as Sandra was. She got off of her blanket, and helped others up, tossing all of them on the couch, and making as much room for the dance as possible. Soon after that, classical music was playing from the phone, and she was watching a ballet performance. It was hard to imagine that someone with such a capacity for violence could also move so gracefully. She thought back to all of the times Nita got into a fight, or threatened someone, or pestered her to let her come out with her at night to fight bad guys. Watching anyone else do this would have had Trisha convinced that even *she* could scare them, but in all of her years she had never been able to intimidate Nita, and there was no telling who else was like that.

Trisha took an opportunity to look at Sandra and the others during the performance. Dominick was trying to watch, but it looked like it couldn't hold his attention. Amaya had checked out entirely and was texting on her phone, but Sandra was absolutely captivated. The fury and malice had subsided for the time being, and even though not everyone was as willing to mend fences as others, at least they had ceased trying to cause problems. Even with Trisha trying to be assertive, it was a welcomed aid having someone like Nita who could cover her when it was not enough.

"That was awesome." Sandra said.

"It was okay. I've done a lot better. But I guess I'll just keep practicing." Nita responded. "What did you think, Trish."

"Never seen anything better." Trisha said.

"Oh, come on; you're just flattering me. Are you afraid to give me your honest opinion?"

"Girl bye. The only thing I'm afraid of are spiders and bugs…and my head going under water."

"Wow. Me too. I panic whenever my face goes under. Scares the crap out of me." Sandra said.

"That's not even a big deal." Dominick said. "Try living with Trypophobia."

"What is that?" Trisha asked.

"You know how you'll see a bunch of small holes in a cluster and it really freaks you out?" Dominick asked.

"Dear God, stop it!" Trisha shuddered.

"Yeah, so I don't want to hear nothing about no spiders or water. What are you afraid of, Nita?"

"I've never seen her be afraid of anything." Trisha said. "She watches horror movies for the comedy value, walks through woods at night, loves touching reptiles and stuff. If you can name it, she's not afraid of it."

"Really?" Sandra asked.

"It's a waste of time being afraid of stuff." Nita replied. "All you gotta do is face it, and it's over before you know it. I don't like the idea of anything holding me back from enjoying life, especially something stupid like fear."

"That's a good point." Dominick said. "I'm still not going anywhere near them tiny holes."

"I would if it had a BLT next to it." Nita said. "It *is* my favorite after all."

"Steak. Definitely steak." Amaya said.

"I'm all about spaghetti, or any Italian food." Sandra said.

"Oatmeal." Dominick said. Everyone looked at him for a second, and he felt the need to defend himself. "I don't judge you for your choices. Oatmeal hits the spot for me, especially peach."

"I can get with a good burger, or a taco…I love tacos, preferably from Applebees, but I'll eat them from anywhere. Or a burger." Trisha declared.

"My ex loved burgers. He didn't meet my preferences anywhere else though." Sandra asked.

"Preferences? Don't make it hard on yourself." Dominick said. "She's gotta be hot, tall, got all the right curves in all the right places. If her sex game is whack, then I don't want anything to do with it. Talking is cool and everything, but if we can't get down when the time comes, that's a deal breaker for me. But I mean, look at me. There's no way I would ever land a chick like that."

"You could, but why would you want to?" Sandra asked. "You should be with someone who loves you for you."

"That's such a girl answer." Dominick said.

"You're right. The last time I checked, I have a vagina so…girl answer. I'm just saying, a partner should have some substance. They gotta be a deep thinker, confident in themselves. I would want them to be able to see me beyond what I look like. Financially responsible is a must. I don't care if they only have two quarters. If they know how to budget that fifty cents correctly, then I'm cool."

Trisha was once again surprised, both by how forthcoming Sandra was being, and what the layers were revealing. Shallow was expected of

Dominick, but Trisha was fairly certain that Sandra would be that way too. But the more that was said, the less accurate that assumption was. Trisha wanted to put in her opinion about the topic as well, so she went next.

"First and foremost, they have to be someone of faith. I personally don't think that people who don't share the same faith, or lack of it should be together. It's bound to cause problems at some point, because someone doesn't put as much importance on something that could mean the world to you. I also would like him to have a decent fashion sense. And he's gotta be a nerd. I don't get into it myself, but I love the atmosphere when you're around a bunch of people talking about comics and science fiction. If I could bring that home with me, that would be perfection."

"So, we're gonna act like Dom wasn't right?" Amaya inserted. "Look, I don't care what anyone says. Sex matters. Even if you're the type that's gonna wait until marriage, or whatever, it is still gonna be a part of the relationship. I don't know why you would want to wait until then, cause then you're taking a risk. Wouldn't you want to know that someone was good or sucked before the wedding? After that, you're stuck with them. Anyway, if I date someone, I don't have too many rules. Like I said, it doesn't matter if it's a girl or a boy, money or not, looks good, none of that. If they're down to go all the way to the altar with me, and they only touch me sensually, and never violently, we're good."

"So, sex is important to you?" Nita asked.

"Of course. It makes me feel great. What am I supposed to do, apologize for that? You thought. If he knows how to get me from the back…I lose my mind." Amaya said.

"Cowgirl is my favorite." Nita said. "I wasn't judging you; I was just trying to be clear. What about you, Dom?"

"What do you mean? Sex is sex. I don't ever think about the positions. I just do it." He said.

"You're crazy." Trisha responded. "I've been trying not to. I haven't really had sex in a couple of years, but the couple of people I have been with I've always liked-"

"Missionary?" Amaya teased.

"Uh no. It's like a spooning position. It's awesome. I kinda miss it, but I'm trying to wait for the right guy, and the ring. It's hard though, I'm only human, but it's important, so I'm gonna do my best. You got one, Sandra?"

"All that time with Wyatt and you never let him hit?" Amaya interrupted in disgust. "That's premium *first date man* right there. If I could get someone as good looking as him, we would've been at it every night, honey. Let me tell you."

"Trust me when I say I wanted to. He came over after practice, smelling pretty bad so I let him use the shower. He came out looking like a feast. Hardest no I've ever had to give." Trisha said.

"And why would you tell him no?" Dominick asked.

"Because I'm a Christian. I'm trying to do this right."

"Here we go with that junk again." Amaya rolled her eyes.

"Lay off alright?" Sandra interjected. "Everyone has to live by something. Who cares if she chooses to be religious?"

"Personally, I'm not putting my faith in any man-made thing disguised as holiness." Nita began. "But it works for some people, and Trisha is a dope person. If she gives credit to the bible then I say do whatever you gotta do not to be a trash human being."

"Awfully defensive there, Sandra." Amaya said. "Don't tell me you're a thumper too. Nah, couldn't be. Churches don't accept sluts. What's your favorite? I'm guessing there's too many to choose from."

Sandra paused. "I wouldn't know. I've never had sex before."

The room went silent in response to this startling revelation. Trisha had to be true to herself and admit that she was surprised, but she immediately felt bad once she made peace with that fact. What reason was there to be surprised? She wasn't involved in Sandra's personal life. She had seen guys around her because of her looks, but she had never seen one in her car, never saw Sandra arrive with one. Now that she thought about it, Trisha had never even heard any slut shaming rumors except when it came from Amaya and Dominick. How much of her perception was at the mercy of these two?

"Bullshit!" Amaya accused. "Justin loves sex. How are you with him and haven't done it yet? How do you look like you and have never done it?"

"I'm afraid to." Sandra answered. "I don't want to regret it or have someone use me or something like that. You never get your first time back, so I never did it. Honestly, it doesn't make a difference to me, not that I think anything bad about any of you…Amaya. But I'm so obsessed with the idea of love, like finding the right guy to settle down with and just build a life. I wish my life was like a romantic comedy. Sometimes the idea of not having it makes me sick to my stomach, just being alone, with no one to care for me."

"I understand completely." Nita said. "I was with a boy who I had no business being with, and I should have left him after about a week, but we ended up together for seven months. If I had a list of regrets, he would be on it."

"You never did let us meet that guy." Dominick said.

"Oh, I know." Nita responded.

Trisha remained quiet, but she could remember the boy well, as they had been given a few opportunities to meet. The first time, she was asked to vet him to see if he seemed like a decent person. The second time was during a baseball game when Nita brought him along without any heads-up. The third time was when Nita brought him to the house so that Trisha could read his mind, after she had grown suspicious. The final time was the worst. Trisha discovered the boy was hiding the fact that he had children. He lied about his living conditions. He lied about his job, and an unfortunate violent streak. He lied about everything, except his name, and up until she finally stood up for herself, Nita had been making excuses for it. But once Nita left, he came to Trisha for help. She refused to help him in any way, firmly believing that the split from Nita was his own fault, and that he needed to deal with the consequences. That's when Trisha saw concrete evidence of his temper and violent streak, but it was pointless to her. She could take him down easily. This was the one side that he had successfully kept away from Nita, and it was likely because he knew that he would get himself hurt if he ever tried that with her. Trisha was no weakling though either.

"Ya know, this is how things should be. We should all be able to come together and talk about things. It doesn't always have to be serious; it can be about anything. But there are so many things that we all share in common, and so many things that we don't, yet and still, we can be cool with each other. If we focused more on things like this, instead of concentrating on the stuff that makes us not like one another, I think the whole world would be a little brighter."

"You are being corny right now." Dominick mocked.

"That sounds great and all, but this ain't a cartoon." Amaya said. "We only stayed because you pretty much made us. It's not like any of us are *actually* gonna still be cool with Sandra once we leave tomorrow. And do you really think she's gonna suddenly like us and want to be buddies? Of course not. You can't fix bad blood with kumbaya circles and confession hours. You think anyone else would actually do this corny crap?"

"It's a start." Dominick said. "I do actually feel like me and Sandra could get along now."

"Yeah, with Trisha calling the shots." Amaya shot back. "You're getting caught up in the moment; I get it, but it won't actually change anything. Look at who you're talking to. She's the superstar model, and we're the fat girls...and Dom. Society don't *want* to see us happy, and it definitely don't want to see people like us with people like her. She so caught up in what everyone thinks about her, she finna go right back to how she was. We're all friends because we been through stuff, and we all know that in the heat of the moment, we would have each other's backs. You really think Sandra would give a damn about us if it came down to it? You think she would risk her image for us, or that this night would mean anything? Not at all; it's all a waste of time."

"I agree." Sandra said. "Society has done a great job at separating you and me just because of our shapes, and that shouldn't happen. Let's make sure it's more than one night. Let's make a statement...some kind of thing at the school. This time it can be about bringing awareness to people with poor self-image. Wouldn't that be cool? We could plan it, make flyers, get other students to talk about their personal insecurities...the whole nine yards."

"That actually doesn't sound like a bad idea." Trisha said. "Only one problem. You gotta go through the...dean."

And that's when it happened, the second chance. She was enjoying the comradery, but the mission was still in the back of her mind, and with Sandra's help she would be able to accomplish it. The idea was so inspiring that she knew she would be invested in the students as well, but the dean was taking precedent over everything. The thought of having to be in the same room as Isabelle Dreyfus disturbed her to her core, but the more she thought about Sandra's proposal, the more excited she got. Her mind was already putting together the event, and it was going to be amazing. The dean's final countdown had just began.

Plus Size

Chapter 10

True Heroism

Trisha's eyes popped open, and the first thing she did was look over at a pile of papers on the floor. There were scribbles, incomplete sentences, short hand, stray marks and even stick figures that covered what used to be plain white sheets of paper. The papers now were as chaotic as the jumbled ideas that had been thrown onto them. The others, save for Sandra, had fallen asleep before her, leaving the two of them up all night to start working on their ideas. Eventually, even Sandra gave into sleep, but Trisha continued. She left them in the basement and went to her room to keep working. The chaos she was looking at now was the various pieces of ideas she had tried to put together but couldn't make anything of. Tucked away in a manila folder was the work she and Sandra had done.

Already, she and Sandra had done more to invest in their idea than a certain naysayer thought they would. However, as Trisha turned over each page, and saw the disordered clumps of half-finished ideas, she became frustrated. If they were going to take this to the dean, then someone was going to need to sit down and turn this mess into a proper, well worded and concise proposal. She and Sandra both agreed that she would be better qualified to write the proposal, but that didn't make the task any easier, and currently she would rather have to watch paint dry then sit in front of a computer trying to make sense of her brain's random scribblings.

She showered, stared at herself in the mirror debating what she was going to wear, trying to decide whether she should try something different, only to ultimately pick whatever was next in the rotation. However, this morning she got stuck in the mirror stage of her procedure. The recent days of her life had been filled with more satisfaction than she had experienced in her entire life. Her activities in the park, her beating of would-be criminals and her interactions with Sandra, all served to fulfill her, and make her feel like she was living in her purpose. It was enough to distract her from the haunting memory of the wife who had gotten a hole blown through her chest right in front of her, and other unpleasant memories. Despite this, there were still issues she could not seem to overcome.

When she looked at herself in the mirror this morning, she didn't see the woman who had begun doing these great things, she saw the flaws. She saw the woman absent the mask she showed everyone else when she needed to be there for them. Even with all the things she had been trying to do, even training with Nita, practicing with Sandra, speaking with Pastor Pauline and venting to her mother, none of them could take away the thought that society had planted, watered, and nurtured for years inside of her head: she had the wrong look. Nothing that she accomplished, no matter how big or small recently, had done anything to change what she looked like, and none of it was going to.

She found herself angry at the world for trying to make her feel ashamed of what she looked like. She found that she was angry at herself for allowing the world to influence what she thought of herself. And she found that she was powerless to change either one. Her powers meant that no one could keep a secret from her if she didn't want them to, and yet it did her no good because using it likely meant that she was going to unearth the even crueler words that people dared not to say. Even if she wanted to use them, and probe everyone she encountered, how would it help her? Her powers also made her stronger than most, and more physically durable than most, and yet it couldn't protect her soul. It was still debatable whether a bullet would break her skin, or kill her, but words had already proven their effectiveness. Despite what she tried to tell herself, she still had no armor for that. The fact that she even needed a letter to address body shaming and self-image spoke volumes about the world she was in.

To quell herself, Trisha used a different aspect of her abilities, one that she had not told anyone, even Nita, that she possessed. She could peak into her own mind and find memories and feelings that subconsciously would be lost forever. What she was looking for was hard to find, as it was a fleeting moment in her life, but she was able to locate a memory, right around the time she turned four, when she loved herself completely. It was the first day of Pre-K, and her mother had dressed her in the school uniform. From the moment she met other students, society began its work. But that golden moment before she had stepped into school for the first time, was more valuable to her than any jewel could ever be. Were it not for her powers, she would never have experienced this memory again. She could feel how happy and gratified with herself she was. She wasn't a fat kid, or a thin kid, or an ugly kid, or a beautiful kid. She was just *a* kid, and a kid's life before meeting life was not complicated. Sadly, those days were gone, and a kid's life after meeting life only grew more complicated as the relationship matured. Judging people or being dissatisfied with her own appearance was something that Trisha had been taught. It was something that people were taught as they lived their lives.

She knew she couldn't stay in this memory forever, so she let it fade back into obscurity, and continued with her process. She grabbed a shirt, jeans, her brown short boots, and a head scarf, and was ready to go in a matter of minutes. She was about to leave the room when she realized she wasn't wearing the earrings that her mother hated, or her glasses and had to go back to retrieve both. The scramble was beginning to adversely affect her, so she stopped to take a deep breath. Then she did a mental check list, to ensure that she wasn't forgetting anything, once again using her powers for more mental clarity. Once she was satisfied that she had everything, she ran to her basement. Everyone was already gone, to her surprise, but it saved her some time. So, she left. On the way out of the door, she made a call to Minister Frankford. She owned a laptop, but it wasn't working properly, and she had not gotten the money to fix it yet. The minister always allowed her to use his house to work, sleep, or just hang out, but she wanted to call as a courtesy. When he picked up, she got straight to the point, and the call was over in less than ten seconds.

His house was not far from hers, which meant walking was both a practical and healthy option. While she made her way to his home, it gave her an opportunity to reflect on last night. The words that Amaya had uttered during their gathering had stalked her from the moment they were said to this very moment, and she did her best to make sure that they were grounded in nothing. Sandra's competition was now only one week away, and Trisha wanted to show her that she could take a genuine interest in her life. So, she and Nita agreed to get together with Sandra today to help her prepare. Sandra reluctantly agreed. Trisha knew all the things she would need to look for, including her walk, posture and body language, and her answers to generic interview questions that they would use to determine if they wanted her as their spokesperson. Working with Sandra would be a nightmare, as she seemed like the type to lose her mind over every insignificant thing that happened. She was a harsh judge on herself and left absolutely no room for error. Trisha knew a perfectionist when she saw one and was cognizant of the fact that she would have to be willing to accept that working with Sandra was like working with herself.

Realizing that she had not had an opportunity to involve Amaya last night, she called her while on the way. She invited Amaya to come with them, but the invitation was ruthlessly declined. The girl even went so far as to say that she would be keeping her appearances limited if Trisha continued to involve herself with Sandra. Trisha suggested that it was unfair to have to pick between friends, but Amaya insisted that she was making it easy. This made her sad ever so slightly, but she knew that there were presently more important matters to worry about than this difference of opinion. She couldn't figure out if Amaya was being driven by her anger that Sandra was even around, or if she was being driven by the fact that she might have been wrong. The fact that Trisha and Sandra were still trying to build a relationship was likely a blow to Amaya's pride. If this was anything like what usually happened, they would be back on good terms inside of two weeks. Until then, all Trisha could do was focus on helping Sandra and helping herself.

Even in helping Sandra, she needed to ensure that her lessons with Nita did not slow down or stop. She could tell that Nita was growing more aggressive in their sessions. Trisha was aware that there was nothing Nita could do to physically harm her, and Nita was figuring that out as well. As a result, she stopped pulling her punches and stopped treating her like a fragile creature. Nothing was more revealing about the gap between the two girls than when Nita fought with everything she had. The goal was for Trisha to further learn that her powers protected her from harm but wouldn't be able to help her all the time. Up until now, she used her strength and minimum skill to hold her own, and even with Nita holding nothing back, she was still able to occasionally gain the upper hand, just because she knew how to use her size and strength to her advantage. However, Nita consistently bested her due to an advanced prowess. On the plus side, not being hurt by Nita's assaults allowed her to train longer. The day would come when she mastered this art form, but that was a day far off in the future.

Before she knew it, she had arrived at the minister's house. It was protected by an electronic lock, with a keyhole that served as a backup albeit, a much less time efficient way of getting inside. She had a key, and she knew the code, but she preferred to act as any other guest would, so she knocked on the door. When there was no answer, she rang on the doorbell. As soon as that happened, she heard loud barking, and a booming male voice demanding that it quiet down. When the door opened, Minister Frankford stood in the doorway, just short enough not to have to duck down. It was always weird seeing him casually dressed. Either he would be in his work uniform, or dressed up for church. However, this was a day off for both, and he was treating it as such.

"Good Morning, Uncle Lewis." Trisha said. "May I?"

"Of course." He said as he moved to the side to let her in. She closed the door behind her, and heard the mechanism whirring up to lock automatically.

"I'm guessing everyone is at class right now?" Trisha asked.

"Everyone but the wife. She's out trying to find me a tie." His head turned to the side, and his face scrunched up, as he mouthed the words again. "You would think we could've stopped after we hit two hundred, but she' still buying them."

"Come on really? You have two hundred ties?"

"I might as well. If you account for the ones that I have no earthly idea where they at, then I'm in that ballpark by now."

"Shoot, I'm gonna be just like her. My man is gonna dress fine for me. I should start buying some ties now, just to get ready." Trisha said confidently.

"Tell me if you feel the same way when you start seeing the prices for some of 'em. She's gonna end up taking out a second mortgage on the house if she don't cut back, but she's the wife, so she gets what she wants, even if it puts us out on the street. I love that woman, but I'm this close to smackin' her upside her head."

"For real?" Trisha asked.

"Of course not. There's plenty of green left from the days when I was a smoke jumper, plus what I'm making now working for the post office." Minister Frankford said. "I got the computer all set up in there. Feel free to take as much time as you need, but you only have an hour, and of course you can help yourself to whatever you would like, but don't touch anything."

It was always entertaining for Trisha to listen to her uncle's many paradoxical phrases. The charm and appeal to him was his ability to find a way to complain about any and everything. There were countless times in the past where she brought friends over, and she had to explain to them the nature of her uncle. For anyone who did not know him, he could come across as a jerk who couldn't be satisfied with anything, but nothing could be further from the truth. He was surprisingly lenient as a person, but when it came to what he believed was right and wrong, he would speak up about it, no matter who got their feelings hurt. That was something that he attributed partly to Pastor Pauline. Though he always stood up for his principles, no matter what they were, he didn't possess the hardcore candor that he was known for today. This was one of her favorite things about him, because he was yet another person that wasn't going to lie to her or let her go down the wrong path passively. If Trisha wanted to act a fool, even if he couldn't stop her, she would hear about it.

As she sat down to begin her work, she acknowledged some of the décor. Movie posters from before she was born graced the walls, as well as records. She examined some of the paraphernalia he collected from various mediums that entertained him. Masks from the days he was into wrestling, decorative plates, signed records from some of his favorite artists, and no shortage of pictures of black role models. Maya Angelou, Ray Charles, Miles Davis, and even Shirley Caesar. The crowning achievement was what Trisha referred to as a shrine. It was set up in the middle of the living room designed to show off two stages of his life. The first side was reminiscent of his days in the streets. Clothes he used to wear, a bandana, the first watch he stole, and the gun he owned. It was encased in glass, and he had never touched it after he left the life behind, except to mount it. The other side was filled with things from his days as a firefighter. His uniform as well as awards he received, pictures of him with his team, and an obituary of the first friend he lost on the job. There was also a picture of him walking a woman down the aisle for her wedding. This picture was the most recent item of everything collected, and it marked the event that led to his retirement. He saved the woman from her home when she was a girl and knew that it was going to be the defining moment of his career. They stayed in contact for years afterwards. Once he was able to see her married, he had done all that he was ever going to do, and happily said goodbye to the fire department. Whenever Trisha heard that story, it inspired her. She wanted nothing more than to be as undoubtedly sure as he was that she was living in her purpose.

She didn't even notice that she spent so much time gawking over her uncle's things, that she let time go by without her accomplishing anything. Once she realized this, she forced herself to focus and got to work. The first couple of sentences as an introduction were easy enough to write, but her mind began to draw blanks after that. Every sentence she wrote down after that was either moved, restructured, or completely erased. No matter what she did, she couldn't find consummation with anything she wrote. It wasn't a skill that she lacked, in fact it was the only thing she could do that was almost as refined as her acting and singing capabilities, but she was so plagued by doubt that nothing else mattered. Between the ideas that she had, and the ideas Sandra shared, this should have been nothing but transcribing from her paper to the computer. However, she presently couldn't find solace in any of the wording. In fact, she was certain that she was going to have her idea blatantly rejected, and that was before even considering the evil woman that she was going to have to propose it to. An hour passed, and then two, and she still had accomplished nothing beyond what she already had. That's when Minister Frankford came into the room, armed with two cups of ice tea. She went to grab one.

"That one is mine. Take the one with ice." He said.

"I hate ice." Trisha responded.

"So, do I. My house, my rules."

Trisha thanked him for the drink, ignoring the fact that he placed ice in her drink strictly to be a nuisance. She tried to position herself in front of the computer screen, so that he would not be able to see her lack of progress, but there was no fooling him.

"Having some trouble, I see."

"I don't know what it is. This never happens." Trisha responded angrily.

"Well, how are you feeling today? What's going on with you?" Minister Frankford asked.

"I mean, nothing really. It's just another day." Trisha responded nonchalantly

Minister Frankford chugged his entire glass of tea, and then pardoned himself for the belch that escaped him. "Listen here, I done raised four kids, and three grandkids, and I've watched you grow up and helped when I can, so we gonna go ahead and throw you on that list too. You know what I'm saying? It's a waste of your time trying to catch me with a red herring. If you don't want to tell me, then say that, but don't pretend I can't tell that you're off."

"You're right." Trisha said. "I'm all the way off. Sandra and I came up with this idea to host something at the school for people like us who have a hard time with the way we look. And I think it's a good idea, but part of me just doesn't think it's going to mean much of anything. Then I was thinking about what you and me talked about. After we spoke at the church that night, I started doing what you said. I found ways to help the people I was trying to help, ya dig? But none of it is huge, or important. There's no way to really know if anything I did mattered in the long run. I can't find any significance in what I'm doing. I thought after I started making these moves, then I would be able to appreciate the person I saw in the mirror. But then I woke up this morning and still felt small, still couldn't see much value in myself. So, I don't even know if I was ever happy with myself, or if I just told myself that I was. And now, if the only thing I want to do adds up to nothing, then what's the point?"

"My first piece of advice for you would be to figure out what you want. Do you want to help people, or do you want your work to be important? Because those are two completely different jobs. No one ever helped anyone by just *being* important."

"What do you mean?"

"Well, it goes like this. Let's say I'm the head coach of a football team, and someone says it's gonna be my job to take the players, judge their skills, put them all into the right starting positions, or the bench if that's where they need to go, and everything else that concerns that title. That's an important job, and I'm an important face as head of this team. But when it comes down to it, I'm not playing the game for them, I'm not busting my butt in practice, taking ice baths, reworking the same play thousands of times for years of my life. I'm important, but they are the ones who are helping us reach our goal. The experts will know every name, every position, and every detail that the team is contributing, but the public will know the team as a whole, with a few standout faces. So, what is it you want? Do you want to be important, or do you want to help?"

"I want to help." Trisha said.

"Then you need to be prepared to accept that your contributions might go unnoticed, as least as far as anyone knowing that you're the one who did whatever was done. If your goal is really to help as many people as you can, then there's no time for questioning whether there's a lasting effect or not. For you, there's only the mission. Time will speak for what effect you had, but in the moment, that is not for you to think about. Someone pulls a gun on your family and you have a chance to shoot first, what do you do? If you hesitate because you want to figure out if this criminal has a family, or friends, or how court will go for you, or whether you'll miss, harm, or kill, your family might end up dead. You must do what you can in that moment to make a situation better and think about the big picture later. An extreme example for sure, but the concept is the same. Your work can be important, even if you aren't. The advantage is that typically doing positive things for the right reasons tend to produce positive results, even if they're small. Are you ready for yourself to mean very little?"

"That doesn't sound much like a hero." Trisha said solemnly.

"You ain't say nothing about being a hero. You want to be a hero?" Minister Frankford asked.

"Yeah like you. What's more important than saving lives?" Trisha asked.

"Believe it or not, the importance of saving lives, or anything, lies in the importance of whose life it is. I know my work was important to me, and the people I met, and God, but I just helped. My name isn't in papers, I'm not signing autographs. I'm pretty sure most of the people I met wouldn't even recognize me today, and I'm not sure I would recognize all of them. What I do is important; who I am is a nobody. You only get to pick one. That's why you must really decide if you want to be a 'hero'. Do you even believe in heroes?"

"What? Of course, I do. Don't you?" Trisha countered.

"The short answer is one word. Is that sufficient for you?"

"No." Trisha stated.

"I didn't think it would be. Most people don't know that a hero is someone with superhuman qualities, its origins found in Greek mythology attributed to individuals who had dealings with the various gods and achieved great feats that no mere mortal could ever hope to accomplish. So, a hero by definition is more than a simple mortal. Following that example: no one can be a hero." Minister Frankford explained.

"So, you don't." Trisha concluded.

"This generation has no patience." Minister Frankford responded.

"Sorry." Trisha then sat back to listen.

"I never liked comic books, or fantastical movies growing up. I couldn't feed into those things because they were too depressing for my taste. I was a weird kid. Everyone loved stuff like that because it couldn't happen, but that's why I hated all of it. I always wanted someone to dress up and clean up my neighborhood and beat down all my bullies and what not. Never happened. So, I decided that I didn't believe in heroes. Sure, there were cops, and firefighters, medics, and all those other jobs, but they were still just people. They weren't bullet proof, couldn't fly, or shoot lasers. So, what made them any different than anyone else?"

"They run into danger when everyone else runs away from it." Trisha responded.

"So do white people." Minister Frankford unapologetically said. "It wasn't until I was first starting my career that I met this kid, cool little kid who said he didn't know what he wanted to do when he grew up. He sounded a lot like you, saying that he just wanted to help people, but it was too broad of a statement. I didn't think I would ever see him again, but I thought about him a lot, often wondered what he did with his life. I was hoping that he found a way to make his dream come true, but he probably moved away from that and found something else to do. I didn't know, and as the years went on, I forgot about him. Then, one morning, I woke up earlier than usual, restless and unable to sleep. It was bizarre, because I have never had trouble getting to or staying asleep. Anyway, I wasn't getting anywhere inside, so I walked outside to get some fresh air to see if it would help, and I saw these boys throwing my trash in the back of the garbage truck. I didn't know any of them, except one of them that looked familiar. Couldn't figure out why I felt like I knew him for the life of me. Then, again I had trouble sleeping. This became a habit, and I found myself outside every time they came around. I thought I was going to lose my mind, to be honest. But once I figured it out, I had to talk to him. It was the kid that I had seen all those years ago. I approached him one morning, asking if he remembered me, and he said yes. I asked him about his life and he told me we could meet later and discuss it. Gave me his number and that was that. It took a few days for me to work up the nerve to call him. It was kind of awkward between the age difference, and the fact that I really didn't know him. I didn't even know his name. Crazy thing is, I still don't know his name. We met in this little diner that has long been shut down, and I asked him what he did with his life, what he was working on. By that time, he was married, had a son, and lived a modest life. But he was a sanitation worker full time. I couldn't make sense of this, so I asked him if he got stuck in this job, or if he was in school for something more. He had *chosen* that path and said that he had no desire to leave. I was of course happy to know that he was content, but I couldn't help but ask why this was what he was doing. So, he took the time to explain. He said that life was full of influences that you couldn't control. He talked about home life, what is seen on tv, what is taught in school, how peers talk to each other. The point was that it was extremely hard to find a way to be at the center of what someone learned and experienced. The closest you could get was being a parent. As a parent, you were the first person your child saw, the person they saw most often and consistently. You decided the rules they lived by, and you heavily influenced their values, no matter what anyone said. So, he said that because he wanted to help people, which was a goal he held onto, it was imperative that he become a parent because he could do his best to mold a productive member of society. When he explained it like that, I was completely lost. I figured if he stayed with this objective his entire life, why didn't he set himself up to be something more? Why not be a teacher, or an officer, or a judge? He broke each of those three things down for me. He said that they were all necessary positions, but that he wasn't the one to fill them. He said once a child came into a classroom, their morning had already started. As a cop you were going to spend a lot of time trying to undo the thinking some guy likely spent years developing. And as a judge, you were just punishing people for things that they had already done. So, I told him that I had not considered things like that. You know what he said next? He said that people get caught up in trying to feel like they're doing good and meaningful things, they miss out on the small factors that affect people. So, he told me that the earliest influence he could have on a person on a day to day basis, was the condition of their immediate area when they came outside. Even if the rest of the day was terrible, even if the morning in the house was terrible, the first influence they would get from life outside of their home would be clean; the first taste would be positive. And through this kid, whose name I never knew, I learned the meaning of true heroism. So, I do in fact believe in heroes. I believe they're everywhere, going unnoticed, uncredited, and above all, unbothered by it."

"I'm not entirely sure I understand that." Trisha said weakly.

"And it may take years before you do, but one day it will make sense, in a way you never imagined." Minister Frankford concluded.

Plus Size

All Shapes and Sizes

Chapter 11

Isabelle Dreyfus

Trisha was blessed to have the kind of support system that other people typically imagined. Any goal that she made was backed by the people she loved, and who loved her as well. If she found herself without it, it was because she was pursuing a purpose that they thought was morally wrong, but she never had to worry about if they would believe in her dreams, no matter how unique or cliché they were. She attributed the completion of her proposal to her uncle, who, even though she didn't fully understand it, offered her some much-needed advice about her current situation. Outside of the park bench was her own life that she needed to live, and this was one of the ways she wanted to live it. After writing all of it up, she put it through the rigorous process of editing and rewriting, and allowed it to be vetted by both her mother and her pastor. She also ran it by Sandra to make sure she was satisfied. While she was certainly capable of fixing her own grammatical and structural errors, a different perspective was always necessary.

"There are a lot of punchlines in here." Annetta claimed.

"What do you mean?" Trisha asked.

Annetta eyed it again as if she needed to be sure. "It seems like every other line is a joke."

"It's a hard thing to talk about, kinda helps me cope." Trisha defended.

"Understandable. But I'm wondering if you might be losing some of the gravity of what you're trying to say. It's good to have some in there so you can keep the conversation light. But you want to make sure everyone knows that you take this seriously."

In the end, Trisha couldn't deny that her mother had a point. So, she reworded her proposal and limited the humorous nature. It was difficult for her to alter the tone in such a way because it meant that she would have to fully commit to what she was trying to say. She wouldn't be able to hide behind comedy if she were rejected.

After taking it to the pastor, there was more guidance to be given.

"This is good, but I don't hear your voice when I read this. It reads like someone who observed the issue from afar and did their best to report on it. You're pushing a message that you relate to. Keep the statistics and data, but put a little bit of *you* into it. Personal testimony will reach farther. Remember that this is as much for you as it is for them."

Again, Trisha could not argue the sense. She went back and made changes so that it sounded like *she* was speaking, and not a faceless voice of a broad movement. What both her mother and the pastor agreed on, was that there was nothing they could offer her in terms of spelling and English. Trisha had little concern in these areas, certain that she was competent enough to oversee them properly.

This was the first time she was excited to meet anyone in a position of power at an educational institution. Usually, she hated the idea of appealing to those types of people because they often thought that their experiences in the field gave them the answers to life, and there was no longer anything anyone could teach them. However, with the work that she had put into this, and the message she wanted to spread, Trisha was confident that she could sway the mind of even the most skeptic reader, and, in this case, it happened to be the dean of the college. That's when the cruel waves of reality washed over her.

As much as this was about her plans for the students at the school, it was also about getting close to the dean. If she got her proposal passed, this would give her the opportunity to learn about the person she was attempting to defeat. If she was going to best her opponent, she was going to need to know her opponent. She needed to know how she spoke, how she thought, how she moved, the type of relationships she had, the values she held. Apart from that, the hardest part was going to be figuring out how to prove to everyone else that this woman was not who she said she was. Given all the filth the dean had engaged in — like the time she erased evidence of sexual misconduct on behalf of one of her teachers in order to keep him employed --Trisha was sure Dreyfus had made a mistake or two along the way. All Trisha needed to do was tie Dreyfus to something, any of her many crimes, and it would at least have her removed from power. Trisha figured a crook like Isabelle had all aspects of her life rehearsed. She knew how to pretend to be nice and concerned, she knew how to lie, and what stories made the most sense, but no one knew how to be perfect.

When Trisha requested a meeting with the dean, she had not fully considered what she was asking for. The dean was always meeting with someone, either from the faculty, or various business expeditions from higher departments. That didn't include previous appointments made by other students, parents, and future attendees of the college. Once this occurred to her, Trisha began to lose a little bit of hope for any kind of immediate result. She would have words with the woman no matter what, but it was likely that it wouldn't be until later in the semester. That's why it came as the ultimate surprise when her request for an appointment was met with an immediate invitation. She had seen the email on her phone when she woke up to get ready for her classes, and almost fainted. It was apparent in the future that she was going to need to better prepare. She had not completely gotten her strategy together, because she had not expected a response for quite some time. However, now she needed to come up with everything she was going to do and say in a matter of hours. She had three classes today, all an hour long, and the invitation offered a meeting right after her final class.

Once again, the issue of fashion reared its ugly head. Getting dressed for an audition was one thing, but getting ready for a professional meeting with the head of her college was another matter entirely. Nothing in her closet was going to be appropriate for the situation, so she looked elsewhere. Her mother did not trust her with fancy clothes because of the condition she kept her closet in. That did not mean that Trisha didn't own any. She ventured to her mother's room, who had already left for work, and examined the main closet. This one was a shining example of what closets everywhere should be. Everything was hung without wrinkle, the shoes were neatly placed side by side, and properly organized, by function. The best clothes were kept in protective sheets to prevent dust from setting in. If Trisha had the capacity to keep her room like this, she would never lose anything again. Her section of clothes was in the back, as she only possessed a couple of outfits that both she and her mother considered formal. She found a long black dress that would be more fitting at a wedding reception than a dean's office, and the few other dresses boasted the same caliber. Since this was getting her nowhere, she settled on a pair of khakis and a buttoned-up shirt. She took a comb, picked out her hair, claimed her earrings and her glasses and walked out of the door ready to face the day.

The ride to school was the most entertaining obstacle standing in the way of Trisha and her current mission, but today it wasn't enough to keep her distracted.

"Today is the day, Nita." Trisha said nervously.

Nita, having known her intentions long enough, needed no explanation. "I'm here to help you if ya need it, girl. But please be careful. If everything you say about her is true, then this chick is ruthless."

"Got it. Don't worry; I'm not fighting her or anything. This is just about the proposal and a way to formally introduce myself."

Trisha had to reassure Nita a couple of times. Finally, Trisha was able to quell her Nita's anxious heart. Soon, Trisha was dodging questions about Nita being able to be there to beat Isabelle up once the entire thing came to light. Trisha told her that if she did her job right, no one would have to hurt the dean.

After the car ride, came the longest school day of her life. After that came the main event. Now was the time. She knew that to some degree, this was the beginning of her defining battle as whatever it was she was aspiring to be. And so, every part of her was focused on the task. She walked with confidence, kept her head up, and her eyes fixed on what was in front of her. The folder containing her proposal was secured tightly by her side, while her other arm swayed back and forth in rhythm with the rest of her body. She could feel the other students' nerves as she passed them, and she knew that her attempts at being intimidating were working. If she walked into the dean's office with the 'all-business' vibe exuding from her, she would be walking into the confrontation holding all the power.

She stopped dead in her tracks when she saw Amaya. It was the first time she had seen her in person for the last week. She had been so preoccupied with helping Sandra prepare for tomorrow's competition, as well as getting the letter together, that she had not given any thought to Amaya after the two spoke. Seeing her at the school was not nearly as shocking as who she was with. She was huddled with the group of girls that hung with Sandra. All of them were laughing, but Trisha couldn't tell what it was about. She had no desire to waste her power on something that was likely petty, so she walked by them without a word, and continued to walk until she was standing outside of the dean's building.

It wasn't as fancy as Trisha assumed it was going to be. It had four floors, none of which she had seen so far except the one she was currently on. The walls, and floor all looked aged, as if someone was waiting for them to be structurally unsound before they even considered tending to them. There was a front desk and a secretary. Trisha approached the young man, who was most likely a student trying to earn a little cash on the side. She explained what she was here for, and the young man reached for a phone to call the dean.

"Top floor, last door on the left." The young man said apathetically.

The stairs were also in bad shape, and every time she reached a new floor, she could see the consistency. When she reached the fourth floor, she paused in the hallway. The closer she got to the dean, the less time she had to change her mind and back out of this engagement. Trisha gave herself a pep talk and reclaimed her facade. The hallway wasn't long, and in mere seconds, only one door stood between her and her target. There was a large man who seemed to be standing guard. He wore sunglasses, and he looked unapproachable.

"Good afternoon, young lady." He said with a smile that never quite reached his cheeks. "I'm Drexel Sharpe, head of the dean's security. Feel free to go right in."

Trisha could only imagine the woman she was going to see behind the door. Being at the school for so long, she had seen Isabelle around campus before, dressed to impress, black short wig, giving speeches to students, or being involved with the various happenings at the school, and sometimes even away from the school. However, based on what Trisha knew about her, these presentations were fronts, and while she didn't have a chance to see who the woman really was while on the premises, Trisha would see the closest version of the real woman in this office. She pictured opening the door and meeting a woman dressed from head to toe in a beige suit sporting heels, or dress shoes shined to perfection, illuminated by a single lamp to the left of her. A solid gold bar engraved with her name and title would grace her desk, and the entire room would be painted a dark brown, or black.

This was a woman who didn't know how to smile, was strictly business all the time, and would likely attempt to be just as intimidating as Trisha was attempting to be. The only problem Trisha could see was that the dean had been doing this for a significantly longer time and held a position of considerably higher authority. The dean's act wasn't an act at all. At this point, Trisha was convinced that the dean would spin around in a large chair with a cat in her lap. She knocked on the door, and waited for those two iconic words, "Come in." Once she did, Trisha took a deep breath, and opened the door.

Every assumption she made was immediately proven false. The office was doused in a bright orange for starters. The room wasn't dark, but instead boasted of several environmentally friendly light bulbs in strategic locations to limit the amount. As for the dean herself, there was the most momentous surprise. The dean was leaning back in her chair, dressed in jeans and a t-shirt. Her heels were tennis shoes. With her legs fully extended, her feet rested on the desk. And there was no engraved bar, but she instead possessed a sheet of construction paper with her name and the word 'dean' spelled wrong, written in crayon. A pen cap sloshed around in her mouth, while she put all her attention into the cellphone which she was texting on. Without knowing what to do, Trisha cleared her throat to announce her presence. The dean didn't look up immediately, but instead finished her text message. Then she put her feet down, placed the phone on its back, discarded the pen cap, and looked at Trisha.

"Ah, you must be Miss Howard." The dean said.

"Actually, my name is Morgan." Trisha said without ever breaking eye contact.

"Oh, I know. It's just that my best friend went to Howard University, and I went to Morgan University, and even though those two schools aren't exactly arch-enemies, we had our own little rivalry going on. So, Howard is the opposite of Morgan now and uh…forget it. It's just a bad joke."

"Right. Well, like I said my last name is Morgan…first name Trisha."

"Yes, of course, and I gotta say it's really nice to meet you." She said.

Isabelle jumped up and offered a high five, which Trisha awkwardly indulged. She noticed that Isabelle's finger nails were bitten down to nubs. The woman's attitude may have been casual and playful, but her frame did not match. When standing, she had excellent posture, and evidence of a full-time active gym membership reached from her neck to her ankles. While Trisha wasn't fond of her choice of attire, she had to admit that the woman looked good. Her skin was almost perfect, except for a scar on her neck, and she was a shade darker than Trisha was, the tone that Trisha always wished she had been. Trisha had never gotten a good look at the dean's eyes, but now that she was close enough, she could see that they were hazel. Isabelle even sported a buzz cut. Trisha was sure that the dean would at least be sporting the wig she always saw.

"Sorry about that, I'm not really a handshaker. I gotta say though, you really overdressed for this. I'm the dean, not the president. If I didn't have the title, we'd basically be equals."

Was this all a part of the strategy? Trisha wondered if Isabelle was simply trying to break down her walls, and seize power. It would certainly have been

146

hard enough to keep her composure in the presence of the dean she imagined in her head but standing in front of her made it nearly impossible. She thought back to the threat she had made to Sandra once, about being able to bully her but choosing not to. Now, Trisha knew what it was like to be on the other end of that threat; the dean could snap her in half without even breaking a sweat. Still, Trisha tried to stay strong; it was the only chance she would have.

"I guess. Well, I have our proposal for you. Sandra and I came up with it together. I'm sure you considered her as well."

"Casandra Tyler? Yeah, I did my research. You wanna do something for people who look like beach balls. Gotta say, you're brave to want to be the head of something like that. When you wrote that you were a big girl who wanted to help other people claim confidence in their skin, I wasn't exactly sure what to expect. Although, looking at you now, I can say for sure you're not fat, at least not the way I would consider it. You're gorgeous."

"Actually, I'm gonna stop you right there for a second. I am fat, let's get that out of the way. I'm also gorgeous." Years of learning the art of method acting were carrying Trisha through a performance that was making her heart race.

"I can admire that." Isabelle said. "That must be that passive aggressive fat shaming that I read about. I'll be honest, once I read your email, I started doing some research. You never know how big a problem is until you use the internet, and your social justice task is one of the harder ones I've seen. It's fantastic though. It means that you'll be remembered fondly for what you stood for. So, I shouldn't act like any one physical stature determines beauty. Got it. Though, with everything being as politically correct as it is these days, what *can* you say? Oh crap, where are my manners? There are some folding chairs up against the wall there. Grab one and take a seat. Oh, and hand me that so I can read it."

Trisha missed the chairs on her way in but proceeded to claim one to sit down. She was trying to be cognizant of her posture, and crossed her legs to appear lady like. However, the dean told her to sit however she liked to sit. Trisha watched Isabelle reach for a pen, and at first thought that she was going to mark up the work, but she instead placed it in her mouth. That's when Trisha discovered that Isabelle mumbled a lot of what she was reading, and was likely not even aware of it. As time went on, Trisha became antsy, unsure of how long she would be able to keep up the act. So far, there was nothing in the way Isabelle behaved that would tip Trisha off to a more sinister creature underneath. In fact, if she had not already read the dean's mind once before, no one could convince her that this woman was dangerous. So convincing everyone else of her guilt was going to be immensely more difficult than she had thought. Before she knew it, the dean was tossing her work on the desk, and applauding her.

"That may have been one of the best written pieces of work I have ever seen, and I've met with a lot of English majors. You do theatre right? Dang. If I could write like you, I'd have a real job instead of sitting here bossing people around. Anyone could do this. There are a lot of points in here that I never even thought about. You want some candy? I got a bunch of candy in this drawer right here."

"I'm good. I just want to talk about this and see when we can start putting it together."

"You're assertive. We need more students like you. Unfortunately, I am not going to be able to do anything regarding this." Isabelle said.

"Wait, what? Why? You said it was great." Trisha was having flashbacks of her audition for Phantasm. Would this be yet another thing that her appearance would hold her back from? How could it? She was literally the target audience for what she was trying to push.

"It is. In theory, this is a great idea, and you should find someone who genuinely wants to do something with this, but funneling efforts from the school, the budget, the time, it gets complicated. We have a lot of projects we must choose from, and ever since that unfortunate business with Edward, we've been focused on bringing awareness to suicide prevention. In comparison, your problem really doesn't matter."

"You gotta be joking." Trisha said. "Suicide is a drastic action taken by people who deal with a bunch of other problems. You don't think self-image is one of those problems? I don't think everyone who struggles with themselves is gonna swallow a bunch of pills, but I have seen someone physically hurt themselves because of the struggles they were dealing with. Poor self-image was one of those problems. You could support this as well as support suicide prevention. Think of it as a sub-genre."

"I do support it, Trisha. And I want to see you succeed. However, getting this approved would be nearly impossible. Other people aren't going to see this the way that you do. Some people are going to see it as an excuse for unhealthy lifestyles to be supported, and to villainize anyone who speaks out against it. I'm telling you, I know how these things go. I would rather keep focused on what our school is already working on. Now, if you want to be a part of that, and can find a way to work it in, I'll be sure to find a place on the team for you, because this is really good work."

"No. Screw that!" Trisha stated. "I'm tired of people always trying to push me to the background, or use me to lift someone else's concerns up. What I deal with, and people like me deal with is important too. It's a huge problem that deserves awareness like anything else, not just a short column in the 'your body and you' pamphlet. You would never tell someone who thinks their life isn't worth living that they are exaggerating, or that their problem isn't big enough. Well here's the thing: we feel like that sometimes, and it stems from how we perceive ourselves when we look in the mirror. Do you really want to be the type of person who waits until someone jumps off the roof of a building before you start asking why….like you did with Edward?"

"Excuse me?" Was Isabelle's response.

Trisha either broke her rule because of her own personal anger, or because somewhere, she knew that the plan hinged on the time spent with the dean that would be granted if this became a school event. She read Isabelle's mind for no other reason except to find something that she could use against her. When she found it, her mouth started moving faster than her brain was.

"Honestly, I shouldn't be surprised that you said no, given all of the despicable things that you think about people like me. If you ever said half of that stuff out loud, you'd be out of a job. But of course, you know that, so you play nice." Trisha saw the look on Isabelle's face go from cheerful to concerned. "You're actually quite the mean-spirited person it seems, because you haven't had a kind word to offer me since I walked in, at least not in your head. I know how you got this position and what you do to keep it. I know that you've done awful things since you became dean of this school, and highly illegal things as well. I know all of it, and the only reason you're still sitting there is because no one can prove it. I was giving you an opportunity to use your position for good, like you do with the suicide prevention, but you're only saying no because you think I'm a joke. I'm not a joke." Trisha had not felt this powerful since her showdown with Sandra.

Isabelle's concern now relaxed. The playful side of the dean was still present, but it had become corrupted by the disturbed mind underneath.

"I think I was looking forward to this meeting a little more than you were." Isabelle avowed. "I had been waiting ever since you enrolled here for you to find the courage and the excuse to come see me. There was no way I was going to be able to keep anything secret from you. Although, if we're being honest, you could've come in whenever you wanted. I'm a huge fan of yours. Seriously though, that candy is still an offer. You need to calm yourself down anyway."

"What are you talking about? You don't even know me." Trisha said.

"You think? How does one 'know' a person? I mean, you're twenty-two, five feet tall, attended high school in the county, grades next to perfect, daughter of a single parent household and talented in many areas. Oh, and you've got those pretty purple eyes."

"Big deal. All of that stuff is on record." Trisha said. "You should be worried about the person who knows things about you that aren't on record."

"Rookie mistake, showing all your cards like that." Isabelle said. "You're trying too hard to come off as threatening. If it's really you, then your actions speak for themselves. As for how you know these things about me, it's easy to find out when you can read people's minds."

"How in the-"

"Yeah pretty trippy right? I can't read minds, but I knew that. How on earth do I do it? I've played this game a bunch of times, *Trish*. I already know how it's done. The difference between you and me is that I'm smart enough not to reveal all my secrets. Against someone normal, you would've made quite an impact listing off things only the person who thought it could know. But, I was expecting it. I've been expecting it from day one, so I only left a small amount accessible, just so you would catch the scent."

"Why would you do that? How did you do that?"

"Like I said, secrets. Though I'll tell you why. I'm intrigued by people like you, and I'm involved in a pretty lucrative field, which you may or may not know. It's a great business for 'miracle' children such as yourself."

"Miracle? Is that what you call me?" Trisha asked.

"What? No. I didn't coin the term, I just use it. How much of a beginner are you, really? You don't even know the world you're in, but you thought you were going to be able to use it to get one over on me? That's adorable. It was obvious that you were banking on the deal that the dean and student of any school event do most of the work together. That's when you were going to try and find evidence of my misdeeds right? It's what I would do. But you don't know me. You know things I've done, but you didn't take the time to learn your enemy. That's why no matter what front you put on before you walked through the door, you had already lost. But anyway, the reason I wanted to see you was because I wanted you to know that I have an opportunity for you. I can imagine that someone as morally upstanding as you wouldn't want anything to do with it, and that's fine. Basically, I know you're out there, and you can walk away and leave all of this behind you, and nothing happens. Or you can push the envelope and try to take me on, but I promise I'm far more prepared for this than you are."

"I doubt it. I'm not scared of you. I have enough credibility and talent to make it anywhere I go. The only thing you could possibly do to me is take away my financial aid, or straight up kick me out of this school. But I'm not afraid of that, so what do you have?" Trisha asked arrogantly. She was nervous about the dean's knowledge of her, but she was certain there wasn't much the woman could do to harm her.

Isabelle grinned. "This is amusing, so I'll play with you. I have the address of your church and the name of your pastor, Cynthia Pauline. That's just a start. You might wake up and find your church burned to the ground, your pastor a bit more postmortem than expected. I admire your drive. That's why I'll let you walk away and do whatever you want to do, on whatever park bench you want to do it on. Just keep out of my way."

Now, Trisha was without a rebuttal. There was a simple explanation for how Isabelle knew basic things about her. It was tougher to figure out how Isabelle knew about her powers, but it was still plausible. But how did the dean know about her life outside of the school? And was it a bluff that this was only a fraction of her knowledge, or did she really have extensive information on Trisha and other facets of her life? Without a means to battle this, it would be foolish to pursue it further. She would find a way to free this school from the awful tyranny of its corrupt dean, but the day would have to wait. She got up hastily and made her way to the door. She pulled to open it, but it would not budge. She tried again, this time adding her considerable strength and yet, it still did not open.

"Having some trouble there?" Isabelle asked.

"How? It's not even locked." Trisha said.

"You're right. Like I said, you didn't know about your opponent before the confrontation. If I was malicious towards you, I could really hurt you. It kinda sucks that purple eyes are the dead giveaway for people with powers, because it's not a natural eye color. So, you always know a miracle child when you see one. Nothing that colored contacts can't fix though. I love the hazel tint."

"You're like me?" Trisha asked.

"Well, I was here first, so really you're like me."

Isabelle reached into her drawer and retrieved a pair of scissors. After tossing them up and down a couple of times, she let go of them and watched them float in the air. Trisha was dumbfounded. She let go of the door and faced the dean.

Isabelle continued. "It's awesome being in a room with someone who also has special powers, cause then I'm allowed to show mine off, just like you are."

The scissors beamed through the air, directly at Trisha's right eye, stopping mere inches from impaling her. Trisha pressed against the wall in a panic, sweat forming everywhere it could. Her heart felt as though it was about to give out, and her legs were shaking enough that the very bones could crumble underneath her. She slid onto the floor, and watched as the scissors floated around her, occasionally taunting her by pointing the blades near her face. Before she could say anything, they traveled back through the air and into Isabelle's hand.

"Pretty cool right? I mean, it has limits like every power does, but I think it would be best if I didn't tell you. I hope this has been informative for you. I know about your kinetic manipulation, and I'm honestly not sure how it would stack up if I shoved these at your body with all my strength. So, leave this alone, or next time we'll test it, ya dig? Oh, and before I forget, you really are the best writer I've seen here."

The door forced itself open, and Trisha gathered herself enough to make it out of the office. Once the door slammed behind her, she once again fell to the ground. It was a wonder that she was even able to make it out in the first place. She was already thanking God for seeing her through the ordeal and blaming herself for not being better prepared. The world was a lot larger than she thought it was, and she recalled all the warnings that Nita, Annetta, and Pastor Pauline had thrown her way. Her confrontation with Mark and his wife marked the first time she couldn't save someone else. However, this was the first time she was incapable of saving herself. She was alive only because the dean allowed her to walk away, and that knowledge would haunt her for many days to come.

Chapter 12

Vengeance or Justice

Trisha lost track of time while sitting on the floor in front of the dean's office. All her focus was dedicated to maintaining control of her bladder and avoiding her heart exploding. She had certainly been afraid before, but this was the first time she ever felt petrified. Even if she had wanted to fight Isabelle after the revelation, she would not have been able to. Trisha's tenure as a small-time therapist/vigilante was fresh, but she had possessed her powers all her life, and had never come across another individual with gifts. She knew they existed but staring one in the face was an experience unknown to her until now.

Her body wasn't cooperating as she begged it to stand so that she could make her escape, and she feared that her rival would open the door and take back the mercy that she had just extended. Trisha couldn't begin to imagine what she would do if she had to take on the dean right now. Before, when she was just looking for a way to prove that Isabelle was the evil woman that she knew her to be, there was no threat. Even if she couldn't find a legal method of dismantling Isabelle, she could have taken matters into her own hands and done away with her physically. It wasn't something she wanted to do, and it would likely be far more complicated if she ever decided to execute the task, but it was a solid contingency in theory. Now, she had nothing.

'You're out of your league.' Trisha thought to herself.

Finally, her fear of facing Isabelle again trumped her paralysis, and she jumped up to make her way out of the building. On her way out, she considered Isabelle's offer. Would it be beneficial to let everything go and focus on her own life? She was already helping her fair share of people, even if it was small time. Perhaps they weren't life or death situations, perhaps she wouldn't be remembered, but someone's day would be brighter because of her. Even Sandra was in a better place than she had been before Trisha took an active part in her life. Maybe it was worth letting this case go in the pursuit of all the other good she could do. She got outside, and then immediately pulled out her cellphone. Scrolling through her contacts, she reached the 'P' section and dialed her pastor's number. She received an answer immediately.

"I messed up." Trisha said weakly.

She proceeded to explain her traumatic experience, but then needed to backtrack to explain the events that led up to it. As she expected, her pastor was not happy, and had less than kind words to offer. This time it wasn't about encouragement; it was discipline. The only words of comfort that the pastor could provide was the sentiment of being happy that she was alive. Beyond that, Trisha had to hear about how foolish it was to engage the dean alone, and without any previous preparation. It was everything that Trisha knew, but somehow it felt more legitimate because of who it was coming from. She tried to apologize, but the pastor insisted that there was no need for an apology. The only thing that was necessary was for her to start using better judgment. The call was brief and harsh, and yet there was still room for a heartwarming end.

"I love you." The pastor's parting words.

After the call, she walked aimlessly around the campus. With no real goal in mind, she struggled to find anything to do. There was an egregious difference in the way she carried herself now. Her body slumped, her eyes were fixed on the ground and her head was lowered. Every time she encountered another student, she jumped, fearful that it was Isabelle coming to finish the job. Every time it happened, she had to awkwardly apologize for nearly making a scene in front of people who were just trying to say hello. When she realized that she had no hope of keeping her composure today, she decided that it was time to go home. That's when she again came across an astonishing sight.

The campus was a friendly environment, setting itself up to be a great place to bring someone after class to talk, or just hangout. As such, there were plenty of places to sit as a group or individually, and it was at one of these stations, under the shade of a tree, that Trisha found Sandra's crew. However, she had not seen Sandra anywhere near them in any of the recent days; today was no exception. Who she did see with them, was Amaya. All of them were laughing together as if they were the best of friends, something that Trisha wouldn't expect from even herself as forgiving as she could be. For someone like Amaya who could hold grudges for months at a time, there was no explanation. Even though Trisha wasn't feeling up to any drama, she had already passed on this opportunity once, and she wasn't going to do it again. She approached them, but they were so loud that she could hear their conversation even before they saw her, and what she heard was undesirable.

"So, this is what we do now?" Trisha asked accusingly. "You gave me a bunch of mouth because I wanted to give Sandra a chance, while you're running with the girls who don't care about any of us?"

"I just ran into them. It was something to do." Amaya said.

"I'm not dumb, or deaf. And y'all are loud. You're trashing Sandra, and I heard them say something about me. Do you think that's funny? These are the types of people we said we wouldn't be like. They're bullies who brought their immaturity to college, and now you're acting just like them."

"You're a backstabber, Trish. So, I don't want to hear nothing from you. You had Sandra in your house, after all the times she treated you like crap. You just let her get away with it." Amaya stated as she looked away.

"So, because I forgave Sandra, you started hanging with the people she was stepping on us with?" Trisha asked.

"What can I say? I don't like her, and they don't like her either. Turns out, your friends get pretty pissed if you suddenly forget about them to go take some fancy pictures. Oh, and it turns out that real friends don't stand around and let you get beat up." Amaya said bitterly.

"You don't know what you're talking about. Sandra is going through a lot. She didn't abandon anyone, she just focused. But, I can see why she would leave all these girls behind. As for that stupid fight, I told you to leave it alone, but you wanted to throw hands. You got what you deserved."

"Big talk from a big girl, but it's always just talk. This is why people treat you like dirt. You got no backbone." Amaya stood up, showing no fear.

Trisha had the courage to confront them, but she was still too shaken to do anything now that it was escalating. She couldn't even bring herself to say anything else. So, she turned and walked away, fighting back tears, ashamed that there was truth to what Amaya was saying.

"See? Who lets people talk to them like that? Only you. You wanna be all big and bad in your basement, but not out here."

Trisha kept walking. She never looked back and tried to repress what she was feeling. Soon, she was standing on the bus stop waiting for her ride home. After a half hour with no sign of the bus, she left the stop and wandered the school some more. She figured that it would only be another twenty minutes before Nita was out of class, and then she could just get a ride with her. During this period, she came across another familiar face, yet this surprise was even less pleasant than the last one she saw.

It was Sandra, but not in her usual presentation. Even before she got a good look at her, Trisha knew something was wrong. She was sporting her trademark leather jacket, except this time it was completely zipped. Her face was bruised, one of her eyes was blackened, and upon closer inspection, obvious cuts were on her knuckles. Trisha was no ace detective, but she knew the signs of a fight when she saw one. She approached Sandra delicately.

"What happened?" Trisha asked in the most calming voice she could gather.

"Life freaking sucks! That's what happened." Sandra snapped. "What do you care?" Sandra backed away, clutching her purse unusually tightly, as if she felt threatened.

"Why would you say that? Of course, I care. Obviously, you're not okay. What's going on?" Trisha pleaded.

"Get away from me. I forgot the way this stuff works. I don't need you, or anyone else. If I had kept to myself, this wouldn't have happened." Sandra cried.

"I don't even know what it is that happened. Please give me something." Trisha pleaded.

"Are you blind!? I fell down the steps." Sandra said sarcastically. "Someone beat the piss out of me."

As Trisha's assumption was confirmed, there was only one question that she had left. "Who did it?"

"It don't matter."

Usually, Trisha would try to get Sandra to open, but things were happening fast, and she could sense that Sandra wasn't going to be talking much longer. So, she read Sandra's immediate memories, and more of her fears were reinforced. She watched the entire occurrence in her head, trying to accept what she was seeing as the truth, but no matter what petty things had been done in the past, something like this was beyond what she ever thought would manifest as reality.

Sandra had been on the way home the previous night, trying to stay focused on her imminent opportunity. She was so caught up in her own thoughts, that she did not even notice that she was being followed. She was pulled to the side by her former friends, and as such, she didn't expect anything bad. They started asking her why she wasn't hanging with them anymore, and she suggested that she was busy, and she needed to get ready for her event. Then they asked her why she left them to have to get to school on their own. Not wanting to tell them the truth, she insisted that her car was still getting repaired. They weren't satisfied with either one of those answers and asked her why she suddenly wanted to be around Trisha all the time. When Sandra told them that she didn't know what they were talking about, Amaya showed herself to be part of them, and completely sold her out. Amaya described the entire night to them, and how Trisha and Nita tried to fight her just to protect Sandra. Even though it was an oversimplification of what transpired that night, it was all that the other girls needed to hear.

They took it personally that Sandra lied to them and accused her of tossing them to the side for Trisha. Amaya said that it was okay, because Trisha was just as bad as she was. Then, Amaya said that she was ready to talk about Justin, and that Trisha wouldn't be there to protect her. Sandra found herself in a fight against Amaya, which she was better equipped for than Amaya thought. When it was clear that Sandra was going to win, the other girls jumped in, and collectively became more than she could handle on her own. Once she was too sore and weak to fight anymore, the other girls backed off and Amaya beat on her alone. Sandra asked her to stop, but Amaya ignored her. So, Sandra begged her to stop, and Amaya said that she never cared when she was making other people feel like dirt. Amaya was convinced that Sandra deserved it and kept hitting her to the point where the other girls got uncomfortable. Ultimately, they were the ones who ended the thrashing. Then, before they left, Amaya spit on her, and the other girls dragged her away. Sandra laid there for an hour before she was able to gather the strength to walk the rest of the way home. People saw her, but no one offered to help. That's when Trisha saw the darkest part of the memory. When she went home, she went to her room and found her pocket knife and threw it in her purse. It was the only reason she came to the campus today.

"Amaya did this didn't she?" Trisha asked.

"So, what?"

Trisha quickly took the purse from her and fished out the knife. Sandra tried to stop her, but she wouldn't have been strong enough at full health, let alone now. There was no time for Trisha to think of an explanation for how she knew the knife was there. All she knew was that she needed to stop a bad situation from getting worse. She put the knife in her pocket and handed the purse back.

"You know I can't let you do this, right?" Trisha asked. "This will get you kicked out of the school just for having it; you'll get locked up if you actually use it."

"I don't give a damn!" Sandra said as she tried to push Trisha out of her way. She was held in place.

"Please, talk to me. We can get through this. You don't have to hurt them."

"Get off me! You told me I could trust you, but that chick is worse than anyone I've ever met. Those are the types of people you hang out with? You think I'll be able to go to my competition now? I'll never have a chance, and that was the last thing I had to get me out of here. I don't care if I get kicked out of here; I won't be able to afford it next semester anyway."

"We'll figure something out, I promise. I'm not gonna leave you. You're my friend."

"Cut the BS. What the hell does friendship do for me? This is real life, and nothing you say is gonna help. Jesus, you're such a coward, Trisha. You let me bully you ever since you got here. You let those girls talk to you however they want, and now when I want to stand up for myself, you want me to let them get away with it. I'm not the one to play with like you. I thought I could count on you. For the first time in a very long time, I thought I had found someone who understood me, but you don't. If something doesn't go your way, you can just do something else. You screw up an audition, you can write yourself a book. The book don't sell, you can release an album. If no one wants to hear you sing, you can just finish school with your perfect GPA and scholarships. You could never understand my life, and I was an idiot to ever think you could. Now, give it back so I can settle this my way."

"I'm not giving it back. I'm not gonna let you throw your life away; that's what a real friend would do."

Trisha had to prevent a couple more attempts by Sandra to get the knife from her. Physically it was easy, but she was having a difficult time emotionally watching it. Finally, Sandra gave up and started screaming. Trisha had to listen as she called her every insulting and demeaning name in the book, and she wanted to give up just so she wouldn't have to hear it anymore. She wanted to throw the knife at Sandra and let her do whatever she wanted, but she knew she couldn't do that. Once the screaming stopped, she watched Sandra storm off. She tried to follow her, but she made it very clear that she didn't want to be followed, leaving Trisha alone. Almost immediately, her cellphone rang.

On the other line was Nita, saying that she was getting her things together and would be getting ready to leave soon. Trisha told her what had transpired, from seeing Amaya with the girls, to finding out that they jumped Sandra. Trisha was feeling particularly guilty for not doing something about it, claiming that she only ever had suggestions for what not to do. Even with her friend trying to console her, Trisha couldn't help but feel like everything that both Amaya and Sandra had said to her was right. When Nita asked her what she was going to do, Trisha hung up the phone without an answer. It was then that she decided that she was not going to search for a peaceful solution, and fear transformed into blinding rage. Now wasn't about peace; now was the time for action.

She put her phone back into her pocket, and stormed back to the place she had seen Amaya and the girls. They were not still there, but she knew of other ways to find them. There were plenty of students walking from place to place, and someone saw them, even if they didn't know it. She started reading the minds of whoever she came across, searching for the girls' location. Each student that had passed them, or even perceived them in any capacity, whether it simply be hearing, gave her a piece of the trail. So far, she knew that they had been seen going inside of the classroom building, and so she did as well. As she passed more students, she found out that they had walked through the classroom building to cut through the campus. She smiled at the idea of having cameras everywhere if she ever needed to access them. Of all the ways to use her abilities, this was one of the more interesting ones. Once she reached the end of the classroom building, there weren't many students left. The door that Amaya and the others exited led off the campus, but there was one boy that Trisha could try. She read him, and he had seen them leave the campus, and so she did too. Once she knew that they left the campus, there was only one place that they would be heading. None of them had cars, and the closest bus stops were on the premises. However, there was a strip of various stores nearby. Some of them were food, others were clothing stores, but she knew that's where they were heading.

When she arrived, it was hard to find a reliable trail because of the throng of people there. Even the minds that had seen them were overlapping with each other, and Trisha had not mastered juggling multiple minds at the same time. She couldn't confirm the time with any of them, so where they were at the time, they probably weren't still there. The prospect of checking every store was infuriating, but it appeared to be more reliable than trying to shift through the various mazes of thoughts in her head. As she was going to begin her long search, she remembered that her powers had range. It wasn't far, and given the density of people here, it likely wouldn't work, but she could attempt to isolate Amaya's mind by searching for thoughts that only she would have. Her powers could respond specifically to her conscious desires, and so she started searching the immediate area for memories of the night in her basement. At first, there was nothing. She walked through the strip, trying to keep her mind focused on the search, and then she began to get faint readings on the memory. From there, it was just a matter of following in the direction where she could get a stronger reading. It didn't have to be much stronger for her to read into Amaya enough to figure out where she was. She wasn't in any of the stores, but instead in one of the alleys with the girls. They were passing a blunt around, which Amaya was not partaking in, but was sticking around because she didn't want to go home.

When Trisha found the alley, and the girls, there were no words exchanged. Amaya saw her and tried to say something, but Trisha was too fast and had already delivered a powerful right cross. There was more strength in the punch than Trisha would usually allow, and as such it threw Amaya face first to the ground. The other girls jumped up and tried to protect their fallen comrade, thinking that what they did with Sandra would work again. As with Nita, Trisha found that these girls were faster than her. However, they weren't stronger, and they didn't know how to fight the way Nita did, so Trisha's abilities gave her enough of an advantage that speed did not matter. Their blows did little to harm her; she had already been prepared for something like this. When she was out at night, the purpose was protection. This time, her concern was settling the score. Throwing each of the girls off her was easy enough, but they were persistent, and she liked it that way. Even with all of them, they were little more than sparring partners. All of them were dismantled in a matter of seconds, and after the fourth time of getting knocked down, all of them stayed down. All of them, except for Amaya. It was fitting, as Trisha had the most resentment for her now.

"Sucker punching? That's low, Trish." Amaya said as she wiped blood from her mouth.

"Don't say anything to me. That was despicable what you did to Sandra." Trisha responded.

"She had it coming. She been treating us however she wanted since day one. Someone needed to confront her and shut her up." Amaya boasted.

"Except, you didn't confront her. You jumped her. Five of y'all and one of her, and then you took it way further than it should have gone. She would never have done anything like that to us; you're trash."

"Who the fuck you think you're talking to!? We not at school no more." Amaya threatened.

"I agree." Trisha said.

Trisha waited for Amaya to strike first, waiting in anticipation to make her look like a fool. Once the first punch came, Trisha let herself get hit, barely feeling it. Then she grabbed Amaya's arm and twisted it until going any further would break it. She heard Amaya's grunts of pain, but at this point she didn't care. She kicked Amaya to the ground and then jumped on top of her. Then, she declared that Amaya was going to learn what it was like to feel helpless. Trisha proceeded to strike Amaya repeatedly, in the same vein of Sandra, while the other girls just watched. With each blow, Amaya's face took on a new bruise, and Trisha's fists started to collect blood. Even when the lesson became life threatening, it wasn't enough to make her stop. Years of being told she was a joke, and her encounter with Isabelle was coming out of her, and it devolved from a task of justice for a friend, into personal validation. If she had been allowed to continue, it was likely that she would have become a murderer that day. Fortunately, she was pulled off Amaya by someone who cared about her more than she did any vendetta.

"What are you doing!?" Nita asked angrily.

In a fit of rage, Trisha tossed her off as well. "Back off."

Trisha found that Nita wasn't as easy to deal with as Amaya, and it was then that she realized that even with Nita not holding back in training, it still wasn't actual field behavior. With the adrenaline pumping, Nita proved to be an almost unbeatable enemy. Her pain tolerance could rival the resistance that Trisha's powers gifted her, and she was the clear superior in an actual fight. Every punch and kick that Trisha threw Nita's way was countered, or completely avoided. One thing that Trisha had not learned to do, was remain calm. She was lashing out in rage, while her newest opponent was clear headed, and solely concerned about her well-being. Trisha found that she could do nothing against Nita, and once that realization occurred to her, she gave up, just in time to receive a kick to the head. It didn't hurt, but it shocked her so much that it knocked her down. Nita took the opportunity to subdue her.

"Are you done yet?" Nita asked.

"Let me go! I'm a horrible person; I swung on my best friend." Trisha replied.

"You're doing the self-pity thing again. I can't really pity you, because you didn't have to come do any of this. Now, Amaya is a mess, and you can't undo that. Honestly, I don't care about what just happened between you and me. You lost your temper; it happens. But do you really think you were right to attack them? Was this really about Sandra, or was this just an excuse to hit someone? You've been saying for years that you just want to help. This right here isn't helping. Finding Sandra would help. Talking to her and making sure she's alright will help. Figuring out what y'all are gonna do now that the modeling thing is done will help."

"She won't talk to me. I've ruined everything. She wouldn't have even been in that position if I hadn't tried to make her talk to Amaya. And even if she would talk, I don't know where she went." Trisha explained.

"Shut up. And for once in your life, stop making me listen to you freaking whine! What kind of an excuse is that? How did you find them? Don't sit here and act like you're all out of options. You could be finding her right now, but instead you're wasting time trying to flex on people who don't matter. If this is who Amaya is, then we can just walk away from her, and be done. I'll deal with this, you go get Sandra."

"But I-"

"Get it done!" Nita demanded.

Trisha felt immense shame and disappointment, but she knew Nita was right. She could make up for her failure if she tried to act now. She stood up and hugged her friend, reflecting on how blessed she was to have someone like Nita, who didn't leave her behind, and who had enough love for her to say even the things that Trisha didn't want to hear. Nita let her go, and then Trisha stood up so that she could be on her way. As she was leaving, she heard one final taunt from the mouth of Amaya. That's when she knew. It was not cowardice that walked her out of petty squabbles, it was maturity. This time, Trisha knew that there were more important things for her to see to, and so she rose above the comment, and kept walking.

Chapter 13

The Reason It Didn't

Trisha spent the better part of the night searching for Sandra. Between calling her, and searching people's brains, she thought that she would have figured out something. Unfortunately, it never came to that, and Trisha returned home defeated. Guilt was consuming her, and she couldn't stop wondering what would have happened if she had focused all her efforts on tending to her friend instead of trying to match violence with violence. She did the best she could not to fall into self-pity by plunging into her work, but when she woke up, and realized she had failed the night before, she could not deny the despondency any longer.

She was sluggish this morning, lazy even. Her outfit for the day was whatever she could find that was clean, a decision that betrayed her usual unique style for one that resembled a careless teenager. Staring at her messy room reminded her of the things she had promised herself that she had not been able to accomplish. She told herself that she would help Sandra, and now she had ruined their budding friendship, perhaps irrevocably. She promised herself that she would find a way to bring Isabelle down, but had only succeeded in confirming that she was in over her head. After the idea for her proposal was discovered, she told herself that she would make it happen, but the dean didn't want to hear it. She couldn't help Sandra win her competition, and just recently, even her powers failed her in locating the girl.

Lately life seemed to present itself in such a cruel manner, endless moments of doubt, fear and self-hatred, interrupted briefly by superficial moments of hope and purpose. Trisha had convinced herself, or maybe she had let life do it, that she could be a hero, and that she was ready for all the things that came with it. But it was that kind of thinking that got her thrust into the middle of a basement staring down the barrel of a shotgun, or locked in a room with a woman who was stronger than her in every way…or simply heartbroken over a part that should have been hers, but was never going to be. Where ever Sandra had gone, and whatever she was going to do, Trisha simply hoped that it would turn out better than things had been. She wanted to pray that in some way she could be a part of those future endeavors, but she told herself that it was better for everyone if she stuck to doing what she had always done.

When she went downstairs to have her breakfast, her mother was waiting for her, having cooked an entire spread. Buttermilk pancakes as fluffy as the clouds, and eggs that looked like they had come straight out of a food artist's hand were only two of the things that graced the table. The sausage, toast, grits, and muffins were some of the other delicacies Trisha eyed as she plopped in her chair, and slouched. Even the bacon was crisped so perfectly that it almost made her rethink her stance on pork. It was a shame so much effort had gone to making all of this because Trisha's appetite had evaded her completely.

"That girl is okay." Annetta said between bites. "You won't be any use to her, ya walk around with an empty stomach. Come on, eat."

"More optimism than I'm used to from you." Trisha callously stated. She was going to read her mother's mind to see if it was her genuine opinion, but she decided against it, opting to believe in the encouraging side of her mother.

"And a whole lot less than I usually get from you. I hope that this is just a product of the moment. You're way cooler when you're doing the superhero thing." Annetta professed.

"There is no superhero thing! Everything I've done, I've messed up. You were right when you said I wasn't cut out for this kind of thing, that there were plenty of other things I could do. Everything is just blowing up in my face. Sandra dedicated everything she had into winning this modeling gig, and after what Amaya and those other punks did to her, she never even had a chance. If I had just left her alone, instead of trying to rescue her as if she even asked me to, then she would be fine right now."

"So, you're getting bent out of shape because of a few setbacks? Is that how you plan on carrying yourself through life?" Annetta asked furiously. "Your father died, and I shut down. I was afraid to do what I would need to do to move on and really heal. All of the things that used to be me, I don't do anymore because I've been in the same place since it happened. Not you. You dealt with it, got up, moved on with your life and continued to try to make your dreams a reality. I was terrified of losing you, so much that I was going to try to make you miss out on your calling. Was I right that you shouldn't treat life like a game? Of course I was. But I never said that you weren't cut out for this. No matter what you choose to do, whether you make a life out of this power you were given, or never use it again, there will always be setbacks. Things will happen that have nothing to do with you, and things will happen that are completely your fault, both good and bad. But you don't just walk away. You dust yourself off, and you get back to work. And I don't think you're finished yet."

"I don't even know what I'm supposed to do right now." Trisha responded meagerly.

"Then start looking. And get some food in you. I'd hate for you to lose that lovely figure."

Trisha found it hard to force herself to partake in any of the bounty, but her mother was right about everything she had said, so it was best to heed every bit of the advice. When she had stomached every bite that her mood would allow, she jumped up to hug her mother goodbye, and left for school. She had called Nita as soon as she woke up that morning, and told her not to pick her up. She then silenced her phone. The original plan was to use the time to talk down on herself even more. Now that it was clear that such a thing was not going to be tolerated, the time could be better devoted to something constructive.

As she walked she brainstormed ideas as to how she could find Sandra, and what she would say to her in an attempt to get them both on the path to mending their relationship. She was also thinking of ways she could find an alternative for Sandra, now that her immediate doorway had been closed to her. It would be difficult, but it was only a matter of time and effort before solutions to all of her problems would be found. Her more pressing concern was what she would do if news of her altercation with Amaya and the other girls reached the wrong ears. Most of them could pass off what happened as a bad fall, or some clumsy happening at their own homes if they didn't want anyone else involved. But Amaya had no chance at such a thing. The only way no questions would be asked in her case was if she stayed home. Fortunately, despite Amaya's natural inclination for drama, she hated for her name to be a part of it, and would never take a chance at giving people something to talk about. Trisha barely noticed that she had reached the school before she was being violently shaken. It was Nita.

"Where have you been!?" Nita asked frantically.

"What's going on?" Trisha asked, unable to gather herself.

"They shut down all of the classes. They won't let any of the students go near the arts building. Everyone is being sent home, but no one will go. I was calling you over and over. Why didn't you pick up?"

Trisha looked at her phone for the first time since she called Nita and saw that she had several missed calls that had nearly reached twenty. Her heart began to sink as memories of the last year resurfaced. The panic in Nita's voice, the urgent atmosphere, and the disoriented feeling she was now experiencing was all reminiscent of the last time Dreyfus Community College had experienced a tragedy. She wasn't ready to go through it again, and yet she had to muster the strength to ask who the student was. The words left her, but they were inaudible to herself, everything was filtered except Nita's words.

"It's Sandra. She's at the top of the arts building. A student saw her there about an hour ago and told security. She's been threatening to jump if anyone tries to come near her. The dean has been trying to talk her down for the last ten minutes, but she won't hear it from anybody. You gotta get over there."

She froze in place, as the knowledge penetrated her. Flashes of Edward shot pass her eyes. She did all that she could to move, but she had little control over even her most basic motor functions. Even in the midst of Nita's pleas that she was the only one who was qualified to help the girl, nothing worked. Desperate cries filled her ears, and a particular statement snatched her from her prison.

"You gotta get up there, Trish. You have what she needs, and you know it."

"I'm not a therapist! I don't know how to talk people down. I got someone shot the last time I tried to do that." Trisha said.

"But you *did* talk her down." Nita stated. "That man grabbed the gun in a frenzy and you didn't see it coming. You stopped her from killing him and those kids. You know you can use your power for this, in fact there's no situation where your powers would be better suited. Please, save Sandra."

Trisha looked to her left and then to her right, as if searching for another source to transfer the immense responsibility to. The increased stress on Nita's face did nothing to combat the guilt racking up against Trisha, knowing that she had absolutely no excuse not to try and help Sandra. Before she knew it, she was following her friend to the arts building, where a terrifying sight was waiting for her.

Almost every security guard employed by the school was present, as well as a few actual police officers. The squad cars were lazily parked next to each other, the shine of the lights dulled only by the much stronger shine of the sun. The area was generally blocked off, but there were several persistent students who were trying to stay up to date on the situation. Some of them had joined hands and were crying, comforting each other as best they could. At the top of the arts building was Sandra, pacing back and forth. It wasn't a terribly tall structure, but it was high enough that death was likely, and serious injury was guaranteed. The entire scene was a nightmare straight out of Trisha's darkest moments. Then she heard the voice of her dean, screaming through a microphone all the most generic words she could think of. It wasn't going to do anything to help the situation, although given the circumstances, it was difficult to know what would. However, Trisha knew for certain that she could get information that no one else could, and so had to acknowledge that she was the best candidate for the job. Unfortunately, seeing the dean once again caused Trisha to pause. Her friend came up behind her.

"What are you going to do? You think she's gonna let you through?" Nita asked.

Trisha focused for a moment, choosing to finally take the advice she had been given. "I think I have a bad idea."

As she tried to get closer to the sight, she was blocked by a couple of campus security guards, and Drexel Sharp. In the light of day, he seemed even more frightening than he did in the hallway. In the absence of knowing there was a more powerful threat behind him, Trisha was left solely with the man himself, and he was an unnerving physical presence, much like Isabelle. The two guards next to him looked more like warm ups than actual protection, and he was in fact the strongest of the three. He wore the same sunglasses as before.

"Good morning, Trisha. I wish we were seeing each other again under kinder circumstances, but there is a situation we are handling right now. We need you to leave. You may go home if you wish; classes have all been canceled for the day." Drexel said nervously, as if he needed to choose his words carefully.

"You don't understand. I can help." Trisha proposed. "Let me talk to Dreyfus; she'll hear me out." Even saying the woman's name was painful enough, but even more so when Trisha discovered that it was for naught.

"I'm sorry, but she has strictly said that no one is to be allowed near the site." Drexel responded.

"What about those students who are just hovering. I don't see you sending them away!" Nita cried out.

"They will be handled momentarily. Now, be on your way, or I'll be forced to have you escorted off the premises." Drexel snapped his fingers and the two guards gripped Trisha's arms tightly.

Trisha didn't move a muscle, but soon felt herself being dragged away. Powerless was a word she had become too familiar with throughout her life. And now, as she was being taken away from a situation where she knew she could make a difference, everything boiled over. No one else was going to pay a price because she was too afraid to act. No one was going to tell her what she couldn't do anymore. In a completely impulsive moment, much like what led her to attack Amaya, Trisha broke free of the guards' grasp. She pushed passed Drexel and made her way to the dean. Several others tried to stop her, including a couple more attempts by Drexel, but Trisha was not going to be stopped. Soon, she was standing in front of a surprised Isabelle, with a trail of defeated guards. Drexel took his place next to the dean, apologizing repeatedly for his failure. Isabelle waved her hand to dismiss him, and Trisha prepared for the reprisal.

Isabelle put the microphone down for a moment to address the new development. "Guess you aren't taking my advice?"

Trisha retrieved the microphone from the ground and spoke to Sandra directly. "Hold on. It's me, Trisha. Let me come up there and talk to you. We can sort all of this out."

"Stay away. I mean it." Sandra yelled.

"I owe you an apology. Just let me give it to you in person. I know you have a lot of pressure on you right now, unbearable pressure, and you blame me for a lot of that. So, please let me tell you how sorry I am to your face." Trisha pleaded.

"Come alone." Sandra yelled.

Trisha looked back at the dean. "I'm going. Don't try to stop me."

"Damn, I know grown men with smaller balls than you, in fact an entire staff worth, if that pile of insufficiency behind you is any indication. You know I could have you expelled for this. I could probably have you arrested." Isabelle claimed.

"Save it. I faked a lot of things when we met, but being indifferent about getting kicked out was real. Now, you were right about me rushing into stuff, and I don't know you well at all. But I know enough to see that you're an opportunist. You aren't going to turn down the offer I have for you."

"And what is that?" Isabelle asked.

"I'm going to go save Sandra. You know I can do it if I use my skills right, and I'll see to it that you benefit from it. You're trying to maintain the power, but you need me, and you know it. You must have been losing your mind when this came up and I wasn't here."

"You're thinking too highly of yourself." Isabelle shook her head in frustration.

"You can buy your way into this school. You can shift money around all you want to make sure you stay in power despite your small mistakes, but nothing is going to fix your reputation. And no amount of money or power is going to keep people believing in you after two students die on your watch. That's what the whole suicide prevention thing is, a chance to reverse your poor favor after it happened. But here we are, on the verge of it happening again. If Sandra loses her life, especially when all the facts come out as to why, you'll be finished no matter who you know, and you can't afford that. You could kick me out of this school, but you won't. You could probably force me to stay down here with the powers you have, but you won't. You need me to save your reputation, as much as Sandra needs someone to save her life."

"So, what are you suggesting?" Isabelle asked.

"What I'm *demanding* is those guards are going to keep quiet about what happened; there won't be any charges. Amaya and the girls who jumped Sandra the other day will be immediately expelled. I'll have names for you when this is all over. You'll see to it that Sandra receives the help she needs for her mental stability, as well as full tuition and a part time job wherever you have one on the campus for next semester."

"Why would I agree to any of that?"

"Because, in exchange, you'll come out with the story to the public that in the middle of this tragedy, you recommended me personally to reach out to Sandra. You had been taking such an interest in her, that you knew exactly what she was going through, and who could help. It will ensure that all the glory goes to you. You'll also announce the beginning of the proposal I handed you, except you will tell everyone that you have been working on it for a while and finally got approval. You'll use the pressure that Sandra was under to bring awareness, and you'll use me as your personal spokesperson while she recovers. You'll tell everyone that you convinced me to be a part of it by teaching me how to love myself."

"That will certainly boost my approval. Even if you pull this off, considering that you want so bad to bring me down, you're effectively committing suicide on that goal. You'll be making it irresponsible to remove me from power, since I'm apparently doing such wonderful things for this school. Not a smart decision at all."

"Maybe it isn't, but I care more about Sandra than anything. We'll deal with everything else later. Now I'm going. You just focus on what you're going to tell the school." Trisha said.

Then Trisha ran into the arts building to make her way to the roof. The bargaining had taken longer than she had intended, and she was sure that it was a decision that she would come to regret in some ways but ensuring Sandra's survival would not be one of those ways. Her only concern now was making sure she had something up her sleeve to keep her friend from making a choice that she would never be able to undo. She reached the roof, and opened the door for the final confrontation.

Trisha saw Sandra sitting on the edge. Sandra got up once she heard the door. That's when Trisha was able to see her as she truly was. There were no more wigs, or changing hair colors. There was no makeup or false smile, no trademark leather jacket. The facade that she had hidden behind for so long was no longer strong enough to conceal her pain, and it had finally disintegrated in the face of the truth. Her arm showed the scars that Trisha had already seen, with a few new additions. The bruises from her beating were prevalent, and her face was swollen. Trisha knew that she would have to tread carefully.

"I didn't know if you would actually come." Sandra said. Trisha tried to walk to her, but Sandra teased her fall by dangling her foot over the edge. "You come any closer and I'm going over."

Trisha read her mind, and knew that there was enough motivation in the girl to follow through. Once again, someone's life depended on what she said. She put her hands in the air as if she was surrendering, and sat down in a crisscross position. "That's fine. I'll talk to you from here. I looked for you last night. I wanted to talk to you."

"Not surprised at all. You never know when to mind your freaking business. Why can't you ever just leave people alone? I would've been fine if you hadn't talked to me. I would've been fine if I didn't try to be your friend. That bitch bashed my face in. This isn't the face of a model. My face is as fat as yours is. Only difference is that this will go away, but I'm still out of options."

"Really? Because from where I'm sitting, you seem to have created some choices for yourself." Trisha said.

"What are you talking about?" Sandra asked.

"Let's examine it." Trisha suggested. "You haven't jumped already, which means you're entertaining those two options. Secondly, you could've done this anywhere. I don't think you believe what you're saying. I think the whole reason you came here instead of doing something drastic at home is because you know that there are people here who care. I think you want them to reach out."

"You got a hard time listening. Leave me alone. I've been here all night; that's why this is happening." Sandra disclosed.

Trisha saw Sandra's thoughts, afraid that her future would've been a prison. "Maybe you would've been fine, or maybe you would've been stuck in a life you didn't want to live because you didn't see any other way. You're right, it's my fault that you got put in that position. I provoked Amaya by trying to force you two on each other, and she wouldn't have had any issue with you if I had left you alone. But I tried to fix it. I dealt with her. She'll never come anywhere near you again."

"What does that do for me? Where am I going to go next year? Where am I going to live? I went home yesterday, and saw my dad's bags packed. Dear mom told me it was time for me to learn to live on my own. My parents' marriage is over, and they don't want anything to do with me. How am I going to make my money? I can't afford any of this shit! I can't do anything with my life. I'm not you, Trisha, with a bunch of talents and backup plans to fall back on. I had one opportunity, and you took it from me!"

"Then let me give you something back." Trisha begged. "The dean is going to pay for your tuition next semester. She's going to give you a job too, and you can always stay with me if you need to. I'll look out for you."

"Right, because that worked out so well the last time. Just get out of here, Trisha. I don't need your help."

"Okay; don't take my help. But let someone help you. Your life doesn't have to end here. We don't ever have to see each other again. You can take what the dean is going to give you and you can tell me to screw off all you want to. I just want to see you safe."

"You're obsessed, aren't you? You just gotta have your hands in everything. Doesn't matter if we see each other again, because you'll always know that I only have what I have because of you. You need people to need you, don't you? Well, I don't freaking need you anymore!" Sandra turned, and Trisha feared the worst. She read her mind again, and discovered a familiar feeling.

"I need you." Trisha said, and Sandra paused, and turned. "I need you most of all. I need to know that this is possible. I need to know that I can learn to love myself, the way that you're always working to do. I need to know that I am more than what society says I am, the way you keep trying to prove. I've had struggle, but I haven't learned more about enduring than getting to know you. You know how to take what life throws, and turn it into something. You're stronger than everything you've been faced with so far, and you're stronger than this, too. If you lose to this, then there's no hope for me. If you think that there is no one who is counting on you to be around, if you think that you don't make a difference, then get rid of that. You're looking at someone who's life you changed. You're a gem to this world, a gift, one that can't be replaced."

"You really believe that?" Sandra asked.

"More than anything right now. I look in the mirror and don't know what to think sometimes. I feel so inadequate sometimes, so in the way, and I hated people like you for so long. I didn't think you could understand what low self-esteem felt like. But then I met you, and I saw that you had to learn too, that you struggled as much as I did with your own body and your own purpose. I see hope when I look at you."

"No one has ever said anything like that to me. You've been a lot of firsts for me too. I'm so angry, and sad, and miserable, and I keep blaming you because I need someone to point the finger at, and I'm sick and tired of pointing it at myself. No one has ever told me that I inspired them, and I'm so sorry, but I can't carry that kind of weight. I can't live my life for you, just so you have validation. I would only end up letting you down. How could you ask me to take that kind of responsibility?"

What looked like success was once again devolving into failure. Trisha looked deeper into Sandra's mind, further than she had ever gone with

174

anyone else. She would take a reason, any reason she could find to use. Any part of Sandra that was hopeful might be enough to sway her, but Trisha couldn't find anything. The added pressure of Sandra wanting an answer for her question didn't help anything. Trisha began to believe that Sandra truly was hopeless, and that there was nothing she could say that would change anything. But then, a memory was uncovered. Buried deep within the subconscious of Sandra's mind, nearly forgotten, was the one time she had met Edward, the one time they had spoken.

It was Sandra's first day at the school, and he introduced himself when he caught her alone. They talked for twenty minutes, barely getting into details about one another, but Sandra got the idea that he was dealing with a lot. She had gotten so used to pretending everything was fine, that she learned how to pick up on others doing the same thing, and never had she felt so strong that sensation as the day she met Edward. They never spoke again, but she saw him around campus, using him as validation that everything would be okay. His death broke her spirit in many ways, confirming that it was only a matter of time before she succumbed as well. She knew that it was too much pressure to put on someone, because she had done it once before.

"Do you remember Edward?" Trisha asked sympathetically.

"Who?" Sandra asked.

"Edward. The one we lost." Trisha reminded.

"Of course I do." Sandra said.

"He was a sweetheart, one of the coolest guys I ever met. It was rough when it happened, and I still miss him sometimes. You ever think about him?"

"I try not to. I didn't know him, so I don't know why I always feel bad when I think about him." Sandra admitted.

"It's because you have empathy." Trisha explained. "The reason you think about the stuff you've said to people, the reason you apologized to Amaya for Justin, and the reason you feel bad about Edward is all about empathy. You don't like the idea of other people hurting. It hurts *you*." Trisha assessed.

"Guess we got that in common too. But Edward looked like the type of person who lived to make other people happy. That's what you're asking me to do. I can't do it."

"Then don't do it for me. Find a reason to live for you. I know that no matter what happens between us, you'll let me down at times. I've already let you down once. But that doesn't mean I'm going to lose all my faith in you, just like you standing here means you haven't completely lost all faith in me. Everyday, you can look for more reasons to keep yourself going, until you're strong enough to want to live again, to be hopeful again. We were all hurt when Edward did it, but he did it because he couldn't find a reason, and no one reached out to him in time. I'm right here in front of you, and Nita is down there waiting for both of us." By this time, Trisha's eyes were swelling from the tears.

"So, what? We're gonna walk down the steps hand in hand, and be best friends forever, always looking out for each other. You're living a fairytale. I'd rather just cut ties now than have to deal with more heartbreak and disappointment."

The words of her mother flowed from Trisha's mouth. "No matter what you do, or what happens, there are going to be setbacks in life. Things are going to happen that you wish didn't happen. I can't promise you that we'll always be together, or that your life will always work out. What I can, and do promise you right now, is that I'll always do as much as I can for you, just like I know you can for me. We'll keep each other strong, you me, and Nita. None of us have the answers, so let's look for some together."

"You want us to be strong for each other?" Sandra asked.

"No. I want you to be strong for you." Trisha answered.

Trisha stood up and walked slowly to Sandra. There was still an initial resistance, but a burning desire for peace overpowered it. Sandra stepped away from the edge and floated through the air, into Trisha's arms. Trisha wrapped her arms around tightly and capitulated to the ocean of tears that fell from her eyes as well as the eyes of Sandra. She heard apology after apology, but Trisha did not care for them. She was relieved that her friend was alright, and that they could both continue with their lives and learn together. There was warmth emanating from Sandra that Trisha bathed in, not of the body, but of the soul. And that's when Trisha recognized it. This was love, a real and specific kind of love that she had only ever experienced with one other person.

Plus Size

Chapter 14

Aesthetically Pleasing

Trisha's heart was heavy, not from sadness, but simply the sheer weight of everything that had happened over the last couple of days. Above that, she feared what she would have to do today. By the time she had gotten Sandra back down from the roof, and had the dean arrange her stay at a facility designed to help her with her grief, Trisha was worn out. However, she didn't stop there. The next few days were spent getting Sandra sorted. Trisha traveled to Sandra's home with her and began the moving process, grabbing as many essentials as would fit in Nita's car, and took them back to her home. It wasn't difficult to get her mother to agree to the terms either, once the entire story was explained. A second trip was made to pick up everything else, courtesy of Pastor Pauline and her truck. While tears of joy covered Sandra's face, Trisha experienced no such reaction. All her happiness was buried underneath a thick coat of relief. Her head was full of worrisome thoughts of what might have happened if she had ignored Sandra the day at her church. Part of Trisha believed that Sandra could have gone on to win her competition and do things exactly the way she claimed it would have gone. However, there was a bigger part that believed this collapse was inevitable, and she feared the worst outcome if Sandra had gone through it alone.

After Trisha moved all of Sandra's things into her basement, she traveled with her to 'Wondercare Health Institution.' Wondercare was a huge operation that controlled numerous facilities all over the country, from hospitals to orthodontics, and even a day care. This specific branch was dedicated to mental health. It was a long drive, three hours in total, and it felt like Trisha was dropping Sandra off the face of the Earth. Right now, that was the best thing. As with any thing of this magnitude, there was some skepticism and struggle. Part of it was caused by the idea itself, no matter what form it took. In this case, most of it came from the fact that Sandra was going to be taking part in the inhouse treatment. It was to last six weeks. Trisha had to do a lot of convincing, and ultimately escorted Sandra in. She met with some of the staff and served as Sandra's spokesperson, who in the wake of shedding the confident facade, found it difficult to converse with strangers. Trisha talked to her personally and discovered that Sandra felt like a freak, and didn't want to be classified with the type of people that frequented places like this. However, after Trisha explained that she came here for a few weeks after her father died, all remaining incredulity subsided. Trisha hugged her, promising that she would be back to pick her up with Nita when the day arrived, and then bid her farewell. Right before she left, Trisha felt Sandra place something in her pocket.

As Trisha left, she couldn't help but revel in the new form that Sandra had taken on. She was looking at the real Sandra, but not the overwhelmed version that was moments from plunging to her possible death. This was Sandra as she could exist in a thriving environment. There was no supermodel, or bully, best dressed designer, or even popular diva. Trisha saw only a young woman, a young woman in sweatpants, a beige sweater, and tied back brown hair. For so long Trisha had known Sandra as so many things, but most of all, she had known her as 'above the rest'. Today, Trisha experienced Sandra's humility; Sandra could be anyone, and in that, finally became herself.

This morning, Trisha was ready to attack the day. She rose from her bed victoriously and traveled to the bathroom to begin her morning routine. This time, she didn't leave any steps out. Once she had seen to her hygiene, she went back into her room and dove into the vast universe of cloth, silk, and polyester that filled her closet, searching for the perfect outfit. It took some time to find, but she settled on black pants with her usual knee-high boots. She found a blue shirt and a cardigan to match. She made sure that the shirt sat in a way that exposed her tattoo. Finally, she donned a black fedora. Consideration was made for her earrings and as she was leaving them behind, she had a change of heart and put them on. She also chose to wear Sandra's silver bracelet, the gift that had been placed in her pocket.

As was custom, there was another visit to the bathroom to examine herself in the mirror. While there were still voices in her head claiming that there were reasons she should be dissatisfied with how she looked, they were quieter, and less convincing. She was closer now to genuinely believing in her outer and inner beauty than she could ever remember, and it gave her a reason to smile. She even noticed the difference in the appearance of the real smile she held now, and the false one she had been practicing for so long. She turned the lights out in her room and the bathroom, and headed downstairs. She once again knocked boxes over, one of which was holding up her Phantasm DVD. She picked it up to find somewhere to put it, and that's when she saw something in the leading lady that she had never noticed before. The girl had a bump on her lip, cleverly disguised, but now impossible to miss.

Once in the kitchen, she was surprised that there wasn't an elaborate buffet of food waiting for her like before. There was no resentment, just simple shock. It was better that way. Like before, Trisha could not seem to find her appetite. Her mother was reading quietly, and they exchanged only a few words. When Trisha reached for a plum, her mother once again insisted that the bananas were going to spoil if she didn't eat them quickly. After some thought, Trisha asserted that she preferred the plum. When she said this, it caused her mother to look up.

"You look great." Annetta said with a friendly tone.

Trisha grabbed her things, walked outside, and was greeted by yet another warm and sunny day. Nita was just pulling up to collect her, and Trisha wasted no time getting in the car. Dominick was sitting in the back. This time, no music was played. No one said anything either. The awkward silence was nauseating, but Trisha knew that she needed to allow things to progress naturally. The sting of what had happened would permeate through all of them for a while, but even Dominick's close relationship with Amaya would not compare to what Nita must have been feeling. Guilt washed over Trisha as she realized that Nita had walked into her viciously beating Nita's sister, and still decided to make everything about Sandra. It was the kind of strength that Trisha believed made a hero, and now had another bar she aspired to reach. The worst part about the situation was that she didn't know if this was simply a result of no one knowing how to talk about what had happened, or if there was bitterness in the atmosphere. Time, and time alone would reveal that.

When the three of them arrived on their acquainted campus, they were met with a scene like the one they had seen right before classes started. However, this wasn't as sumptuous as the last school event had been. The amount of time devoted to putting together the beginning of the semester bash had not been allotted for this impromptu gathering, but no one had predicted the recent events. The school was simply making the best of a bad situation, and Trisha was on the same wavelength. As she rode past the other students, she couldn't help but wonder how many of them were going to attend the ceremony that the dean was having. She didn't anticipate a huge crowd, but it was engaging enough to attract a fair amount of people. The frustrating part about the entire engagement was that none of them knew the truth behind everything that happened, and it was likely that they never would. That was Trisha's burden to bear alone. Before she knew it, the car was parked, and only the walk remained.

She felt obligated to drag her feet, ignorantly or perhaps arrogantly, thinking that if she never arrived, the dreaded event would not come to pass. She was to take the center stage in mere moments, and spoon feed a group of unwitting students whatever twisted version of the truth her esteemed dean considered worthy of public recognition. Trisha's friend was becoming acclimated to a strange environment, surrounded by strange people by herself, without the wherewithal to wade through it, while she herself had to be here and be the puppet. It took some positive reinforcement, but she was able to ease the pain by convincing herself that her actions were worth it. Whether that was true was once again something that time would reveal.

The ceremony was held on the quad, right outside of the student lounge, a strategic location to ensure any uninformed passers would see and perhaps become interested. One could always count on the young adults' mutual inclination to gravitate towards the one place specifically made for them. This was the one time that Trisha didn't want to be there. Trisha examined all the white folding chairs that lined the freshly cut grass, in rows of five. A small stage had been built, and on the stage, a podium had been put in place where three chairs, boasting of marginally greater decor, sat waiting to be filled. Trisha and the others were the first three to arrive, and others began to join them after twenty minutes. She repeatedly displayed nervous tendencies, which Nita did her best to quell. Trisha clung to this as one of her many blessings helping her get through the ordeal.

The event had attracted a sizable gathering, well beyond what Trisha had expected, and it served as even added pressure. But there was no time to harp on it, as she saw her target arrive. The dean had come dressed more formally than Trisha had seen during their private encounter, choosing instead to play the part of respectable authority figure, rather than casual peer. Surprisingly, Trisha found her less threatening this way. She watched as the dean took her place on the stage, while her main security guard, Drexel Sharp, sat in one of the chairs behind her. Even though she was standing at the podium, the dean's presence with Drexel, accounted for two of the three seats. Trisha shuttered because she knew who the third seat was for.

The crowd quieted down at the sight of the dean, but they did not cease their many conversations entirely. Even when the speaking began, Trisha noticed that there was still a lot of soft commotion. She found herself listening in on what gossip she could pick up on, as opposed to the words coming out of the dean's mouth. The beginning was a summary of Sandra's actions, and what led to it. When the part of the story came up about Trisha specifically being requested to handle the problem, she found it difficult not to get up and leave. While it was true that she was asked to intervene, it was not by this vile, vindictive, poor excuse of a leader. She had been summoned by a concerned ally, but at this point she only had herself to blame. The dean was delivering the tale exactly as Trisha commanded.

Trisha felt many stares coming her way as the dean drew more and more attention to her, and she moved closer to Nita to keep her wits about her. Many reasons were attributed to Sandra's extreme reaction to what had happened. There were a few causes that Trisha would have named that the dean listed, including her recent rough handling at the hands of Amaya. However, there were also reasons that Trisha would never have gone into, like Sandra's poor academic performance. If anything, Trisha attributed the grades to what Sandra had been dealing with, not the other way around. When the topic of Amaya and her friends' beating of Sandra was revisited, the dean announced that they would be dismissed from the school permanently. There were small pockets of applause. Trisha noticed that one person was not clapping, in fact, he showed no signs of joy at all. Dominick stood up and walked away. Trisha felt the urge to chase after him, but she knew that she had a part to play in this farce as well, and she needed to be ready.

It was not long before the dean was able to segue into the topic of poor self-image. She explained that it was a condition that affected everyone, both positively and negatively. Trisha's skin crawled when she heard the dean suggest a negative response to self-image, as if an ebony body builder such as herself could ever come close to understanding what it was like to be dissatisfied with a reflection. Then again, she had been wrong about Sandra. Perhaps she was wrong about Isabelle as well. Then, the moment of truth was at hand. It was announced that after many long hours of debate, and late-night meetings, she was finally able to get her campaign passed for self-appreciation, and that Trisha would be her main consultant during the advancement of the campaign. She called it 'Confidence in Self' which Trisha found insulting, because she knew that a better name could have been thought up, if it had been left to the original hands of the idea. She saw the dean hold up a folder containing all her hard work and lamented that no one would ever know that. The hardest part of all, was listening to the dean tell everyone that Trisha had to be convinced to take part in the dean's undertaking. Everyone heard how Trisha was too nervous to be a part of it at first, and how she didn't think it mattered in the long run, however, now that someone so close to her had been radically affected, she understood the severity. That's when it was announced that she would address the people.

Knowing that there was no earthly way she would be able to refuse, Trisha stood up and walked to the stage. Once again, she entertained the idea that moving intentionally slow would aid in staving off this heinous moment. When she did finally take her place, the people in the crowd applauded her, and she was seen shaking hands with, and smiling in the face of, one of the most twisted people she had ever met in her life. While she was still engaged in this, a blinding light eclipsed her world for but a second, and she knew that she was going on the front page of the student newspaper, and the website.

Once finished with the dean, she stood alone behind the podium. As soon as she was standing by herself, everyone went silent. If nothing else, she would take this small victory as proof that she was more captivating than her enemy. Flashbacks of her audition reoccurred, and she knew that she would once again have to assume an identity not her own if she wanted to get through this successfully. That's when she turned back and looked at the dean, who winked at her. Perhaps it was insatiable curiosity, or maybe crippling paranoia, but Trisha instantly read the dean's mind and uncovered a dark thought there.

'Make them believe for your sake.'

Trisha cleared her throat, and prayed that the right words would come to her.

"It's not okay to be fat. That's what I used to think. That's what I thought the world was telling me. After all the fat shaming, cruel jokes, and stereotype media portrayals, it became easy for someone like me to believe that as the message the world is trying to convey. But, then I met Sandra, who was nothing like me. She was everything I thought beauty was supposed to be, everything you probably think beauty is. It always appears that she is what the world wants to promote, but it's not. I thought the world wanted you to think that being thin, or being light skinned, or dressing in expensive clothes was how you became, and remained happy. But, it isn't. I know this because I know the pain that I felt every day, the inadequacy. Behind Sandra's eyes, I saw the very same thing. Now, despite what our dean would have you believe, Sandra and I were not friends, not at first anyway. It was that mutual pain that brought us together, and that's how I figured it all out. The world says it's not okay to be fat, but the world also says it's not okay to be thin. The world says it's not okay to be light, or dark, black or white. The world doesn't deem anything as okay, because if people think something is not okay, they'll offer resistance, which breeds conflict. The world thrives on conflict. It gives us different messages, because it turns us on each other. The only thing that it is okay to be, is a puppet, playing your role until the world grows tired of you. What happens when media decides to fetishize bodies like me? Then the girls like Sandra become the black sheep, and it will go like this always, because it will always offer a fight. The world has made all of us prisoners, because none of us are made to feel comfortable in our own skin, and we never will be. We must decide ourselves that what we look like is okay, whatever that may be. See, I thought that poor self-image only effected heavy guys and girls, but even a priceless gem can be made to feel undesirable in a sea of garbage. Sandra struggled with many things, but none more than the expectation that she had to be the definition of beauty, or else she had no value, and it wasn't fair. We are, all of us, way more than what we look like. Sandra *is* the definition of beauty: her definition. Just like every single one of you listening can be your own definition of beauty. When you look in the mirror, see the value in yourself, in your soul, in your being, but also in your looks, because you can take pride in the skin you were put in. I'm five feet tall, fat as a beach ball, and black as coal. Despite that, I know that I'm a certified supermodel, and no one is taking that from me, and I challenge them to try. So, I will not be anyone's puppet. I won't let anyone twist and contort me into an instrument of their own cruel agenda. The world will always try to convince us to think on a surface level. If you must only go that deep, then see the beauty on the surface; be confident in self. Move through the world as if you're flawless, because you are!"

The applause was deafening, and a speech that started as the words of a character Trisha created, were transformed into a real philosophy for a moment. She finally came to a place where someone said something about her image that she could believe, and it had come from her. Even if the majority of what she had said fell away, even if this was just emotion in the moment, there would be a lasting effect somewhere. She had become such a convincing stage presence, that she had managed to convince the one person who needed it above all others. A huge smile captured her face in front of everyone, and before she knew it, she was fighting back tears. Then she was shaking hands with the dean again. She saw the wink, and while last time she looked because she wanted to know, this time it was a clear signal. So, Trisha dived into the mind of her dean.

'Is this to be the beginning of our game?' Isabelle thought.

As the grip between the two foes became tighter, Trisha nodded her head. The gauntlet had been thrown during a conversation that no one else would ever hear.

'Then I believe that makes it my move. Just remember, I gave you a chance.'

The handshake ended, and the two went their separate ways. Trisha knew that the ceremony was not over, and that the dean would have plenty more to say. However, she also knew that nothing else was going to directly concern her, and considering the last exchange between them, her time would be better spent preparing for the impending battle. It would take every resource at her disposal to combat Isabelle, let alone stop her. The scariest part of all, was that the next time they met, it would likely produce deadlier, and more permanent results. Trisha could only hope that she would cause more trouble than she took on. While she was walking, Nita caught up with her.

"That was the coolest thing I've ever seen from you. You made me feel like I could book any guy I wanted, if that was like a priority of mine. Seriously though, good job." Nita said as she swatted away a bumblebee.

"I hate those things." Trisha replied. "But, thanks, Nita."

"It just sucks though. After all the work you put into that idea, and the badass speech, you'll still be in the background. You'll do all of the work, and she'll get all of the credit."

Trisha chuckled. "I'm starting to think it's better that way. You work backstage on a play, no one sees your face, but they see your work. Isabelle is gonna see my work, ya dig? It's only a matter of time now. She has the power here, but she had to let me into her camp to get it. Best believe I'm not gonna let her get away with that for free."

"I'm totally punching her in the face when you guys face off. Anyway, I gotta get to class. I'll hit you up afterwards." Nita said.

"Wait." Trisha called out. When she saw that Nita had paused, she continued. "Are we good, you and me?"

Nita placed her hands on her hips and bit her lips. "I don't know, Trish. There's too much going on right now. I really don't know how I feel about any of it. The only thing I do know is that I'm not in a secure enough place to have this conversation with you. But I'm willing to bet that when it happens, it won't be pleasant. That's the best I can do for you."

"I understand." Trisha said in a defeated tone.

"But I still believe in you, always will." Nita reassured.

The two of them hugged and departed. Between her own motivation, Nita's encouragement, and the sudden burst of confidence needed to challenge the dean, Trisha was made to feel better about this situation. It was a chilling concept, stepping into the unknown, but it was what she had set out to do from the beginning, and she was going to see it through to the end. As she made her way to her first class of the day, she came across the first poster of Phantasm.

Her director had wasted no time in getting promotional material ready, and it would do him good in the long run, considering he was pushing an obscure musical. Most of the cast's names were not present, but the main stars had their names advertised. Trisha saw that the girl who was almost on her level in terms of acting and singing had gotten the part. Instead of the natural resentment that she had expected to feel, Trisha found that she had nothing but kind thoughts. She was sure that in the girl's hands, and the capable guidance of Theodore Henry, the show would be a success on opening day. Trisha continued her way to class, whistling her favorite tune of the musical, and leaving the thought of Theodore's production behind forever.

THE END

Epilogue

Outsource

Trisha received more attention than she had been expecting after her victorious speech at her school's ceremony. Word spread quickly about her bold stance on public opinion of beauty standards, and she endured compliments all day. Even Theodore Henry tracked her down to offer adoration. Of the things she had dealt with recently, it was a nice change of pace. It made it easier to float through the day, despite the numerous things on her mind. However, on her way back home, there were no more distractions.

She twiddled with the bracelet while she began to think of ways she would be able to engage the dean, now that confrontation was inevitable. She decided that she was going to focus her energies into figuring out how Isabelle knew about certain elements of her life. At first glance, it seemed easier to read the dean's mind to get whatever answers she needed, but Trisha supposed that the situation was more complicated than that. If the dean knew these things about her, then she wouldn't have pointed them out unless there were precautions in place. Leaving an enormous motivation to use her powers was an error so egregious that Trisha determined it had to be intentional. More frightening than how the dean knew about some things, was the fact that Trisha didn't know to what extent the knowledge reached. It had been heavily implied that more was known, and this bit of information was given as a tease. If that was the case, then Trisha knew that a lot of work had to be done before she could consider a battle with Isabelle again. Unfortunately, the dean made it clear that she was preparing her own retaliation, and it was not up to Trisha to decide when, where, or how it would take place.

When she reached her door, Trisha could sense that something wasn't right. Her first instinct was to panic. After all, she had formally declared war on the dean, with the only response being that there would be a reprisal. As for what that reprisal entailed, there was no telling, and Trisha had an awful feeling that she was about to find out. However, right before she whipped out her keys to burst through the door, she took a moment to herself.

Running into battle unprepared is exactly what got her into trouble the first time, and if she wanted to avoid getting herself caught in an entanglement that relied on the mercy of someone else to get her out of, then she would need to be ready. She breathed to calm her mind, and reminded herself to check the corners the second she opened the door. She inserted her key and heard the top lock turn. Then, she opened the door slowly.

As she had told herself, she checked the corners, but there was nothing. The feeling that she detected was directly in front of her. It was her mother, seemingly in high spirits, talking with another woman who was of Asian descent. Trisha was going to use her powers, but since the situation didn't look threatening, she figured she could adhere to her usual rule of allowing people their privacy. She did however, open her mouth to introduce herself. Her mother lit up as soon as she heard.

"Oh, I was hoping you would get home soon. This nice woman has been asking about you." Annetta said.

"Me? Why?" Then, Trisha turned to the mysterious guest. "Have we met before?"

"We hardly would have ever gotten the opportunity." The woman answered.

Trisha's mother weighed in to explain. "She's been here for a few hours now. She's told me a lot of where she comes from, even though she didn't really tell me who she is. She said she would wait for you. She's with…them."

"Come now, I'm not from a suspicious government organization. You don't have to speak of them or me as if I am." The woman said.

Trisha eyed her mother skeptically. "They're trying again, and you're letting them? I thought we dealt with this already, ma."

"Guess you're really popular. Just let her know what's up, and we can send her on her way. I'll be in my room, 'cause she wants to talk to you alone." Annetta left the two of them alone.

Trisha found herself to be more nervous than she thought she should be. The first time this happened, she was scared to death, because she didn't know how to engage a stranger. However, the more it happened, the more she got used to it, until it became another chore she had to do occasionally. This was the first time that she had felt anywhere near the way she had felt the first time, and there was no apparent cause. She just confronted the woman head on, hoping to end this exchange quickly.

"Look, if you're here on spiritual business, I already told everyone else I'm not interested. Let the others handle that." Trisha said.

"That's what I wanted to discuss, Miss Morgan. I pulled your file, and I've done as much extensive research as possible in the allotted time, and I've determined that it would be a waste of your time, and a blatant disregard for the city, to try and recruit you to a completely different prospect of life. I am curious, is this exactly where you want to be?"

"Without a doubt. I feel like God put me here, with the talents I was born with, because He knew that I was meant for what I was going to find here."

"Far beyond my station to question the will of the Almighty. You do have a particular skill set that could prove incredibly useful."

"So, you are trying to recruit me?" Trisha asked. "Who are you with? SOUL, Unit S? I've heard of them all, and I've been approached by a member of pretty much every single one of them.

"Fair point. I'm not with any of them now. I much rather prefer to scour the earth, searching for potential talent, than to be obligated to a group of people who likely get their wires crossed when it comes to this life anyway."

"Well then, why are you here? If you're trying to build a new crusade, I'm not with it. And even if I was, I don't know you. You haven't even told me who you are." Trisha accused.

"Let's not act like everything is a mystery." The woman said. "Use your gifts and figure it out."

After receiving an official invitation, Trisha dug through the mind of the woman. She came across one name, and it told her everything she needed to know.

"You're Kimora Itsuki. You're Wisdom Woman! Oh my God; you're Wisdom Woman! They tell me about you every time." Trisha yelled.

"I'm a lot of things to a lot of people. Right now, to you, I'm someone who needs help." Kimora said sternly.

"What could I possibly offer you that you couldn't do yourself?" Trisha asked.

"While it's true that there are a lot of accomplishments under my belt, I would never even begin to claim that it was all due to me. Part of what made me this way was knowing when I needed to involve someone else. This is one of those times." Kimora explained.

"I appreciate you thinking of me. I mean this is so freaking cool that Wisdom Woman came to my house! I just don't want to get in the middle of anything huge. My place is here."

"I won't argue that. I have no intentions of dragging you into anything long term. I need a single task handled, and you have the perfect ability to see it to completion, quickly as well as accurately."

Trisha pondered it for a moment. While she was serious that she would never become heavily involved with the spiritual side of the war, deciding instead to be the spokesman for the little guy, an isolated case of helping someone in need was her entire philosophy. She couldn't convince herself that it wouldn't be wrong to turn Wisdom away. Besides her moral upstanding, the inner fan girl inside of her would not let Wisdom Woman just walk away. After all the stories she had heard from potential recruiters, getting to meet the being herself was simply amazing.

"What kind of thing are we talking about here?" She asked.

"I left some colleagues of mine on their own to generate some new life in our ongoing war against the demons. . I would have been happy to let them walk their path alone, but it seems our objectives have aligned. A recent skirmish has afforded us an indispensable resource in our investigation. It's a young woman that we are holding as a prisoner. We've tried to accommodate her, get her to share her intel with us as we look for a solution to this looming threat, but she insists on remaining silent. I am no demon, that I would torture and manipulate her into giving me what I want, but we desperately need what she has to offer. I believe that you would be invaluable in this undertaking."

"I guess that would be the most painless way to do it." Trisha said. "Okay, I'll help you under one condition."

"See to it that it does not require the compromising of my morality, and to the best of my capacity, I shall see it done."

"You said you pulled my file. Are there records of other people?"

"Of course." Kimora began. " We have centers responsible for documenting every single person born, whether with powers, or not. In addition, we have a central hub containing all available information on all of them housed together."

"Is there anyway you could give me access to one on a particular person?" Trisha asked again.

"If the cause is deemed acceptable by the celestials that guard the archives, then absolutely. Who are you looking for?"

Trisha looked up to God, knowing that only he could have arranged such a gift. "Her name is Isabelle Dreyfus."

About the Author

Alex 'Hood' Fuller is author of *The Amen*, and multiple short stories that follow the adventures of the powerful angelic army known as the A-men. He has also written and directed two full-length plays and he serves as a musician at New Hope Baptist Church of Christ.

Made in the USA
Middletown, DE
24 December 2019